The Vulcan Examined
the Jeweled Dagger
Dispassionately . . .

It was beautiful, made by a fine craftsman on an unknown planet far away. Spock silently thanked the artisan for creating such an object of beauty for his purpose, then spoke to Julina, beside him on the stone pallet.

"I had no intention of asking you to assist me, but I feel I am too weak to use the knife effectively."

"I won't! I can't!" the Romulan sobbed, but she knew Spock's Vulcan logic would prove the request a necessary one.

"Julina, don't make me beg for your help . . ." Spock gripped her hand tightly.

He guided her hand, placing the dagger above his heart.

"Now," he commanded her.

Look for STAR TREK Fiction from Pocket Books

Star Trek: The Original Series

Star Trek: The Next Generation

BLACK FIRE

SONNI COOPER

A STAR TREK®
NOVEL

POCKET BOOKS

New York   London   Toronto   Sydney   Tokyo

An *Original* Publication of POCKET BOOKS

POCKET BOOKS, a division of Simon & Schuster Inc.
1230 Avenue of the Americas, New York, NY 10020

STAR TREK is a Registered Trademark of Paramount Pictures Corporation.

This book is published by Pocket Books, a division of Simon & Schuster Inc., under exclusive license from Paramount Pictures Corporation.

ISBN: 0-671-65747-X

First Pocket Books printing January 1983

17   16   15   14   13   12   11   10   9

POCKET and colophon are trademarks of Simon & Schuster Inc.

Printed in the U.S.A.

For Theodore Sturgeon,
my mentor and a loving friend

BLACK FIRE

Introduction

Once upon a time there was a tiny plump Jewish mama who knew how to make kreplach from scratch, and whose chicken soup so terrorized the local disease bacteria that you hardly had to eat it; you just mentioned it.

I knew a lady, the wife of a famous nuclear physicist, who, during a long tenure in New Mexico, turned with compassion and boundless energy to the plight of the Native Americans. It was more than study; she legally adopted a days-old Pueblo child, later became an honorary Blackfoot, and wrote a novel about Indians as they were and are.

There was a writer who decided for the first time in her life to write a novel. She did, and a publisher gave her a handsome advance and a sheaf of requests for editorial changes. Being new to the business, "Oh!," she said, and sat down and wrote *another* novel instead (and did it damned fast, too). A lot of strange things happen in publishing, but this was unprecedented. The only course the publisher could think of was to tell her to keep the money and forget the contract. Indignantly she refused to take money she felt she had not earned, and bashed away at her typewriter, rewriting the first book from beginning to end.

Hollywood has its share of glittering glamor-goddesses and magnetic sexpots; it came to me that none of these would ever be heard of were it not for the support of the dozens and sometimes hundreds of faces-in-the-crowd, spear-carriers, waitresses in the background. I realized this upon meeting an actress who had been in a great many movies in functions such as these. You have, if your eye is quick, seen her often.

We are all familiar with the phenomenon of fandom—baseball and football fans, crewel, dirt-bike, science fiction, Macedonian dirk-hilt fans. Did you know that the word "fan" in this context derives from "fanatic"? Well, there's one species of fan in whose light all others fade to the status of mild interest, and that's the Trekkie. It's the Trekkie who has kept *Star Trek* on the tube all over the world for (at this writing) thirteen years after network cancellation—something achieved by no other show in the history of television. I know a Trekkie so ardent that she has taped all 73 *Star Trek* episodes. She is so involved in Trekdom that she can pick up the phone just once and contact I don't know how many meticulously organized *Star Trek* fan clubs. Captain James T. Kirk's personal manager is a Trekkie. (He's otherwise known as William Shatner.)

I have a friend in the Bay area who owns a bathtub. You probably do too, but I doubt it's like this one. It stands on a pedestal like an altar; it's black; it's big enough for four people without crowding. It has two sets of gold faucets (his and hers, one presumes), and on command, water showers down from the living greenery hung overhead.

You must by this time be aware that all these paragraphs concern the same person, the author of this book. This small timid-seeming dynamo with her little-girl voice and her sofa-cushion aspect is in truth an irresistible force. There have been times in her life when she has had nothing to do, and she has gotten sick—very seriously so. The one therapy that works is for her to relax by doing eight or ten people's work and doing it all well.

This book begins with one hell of a bang, literally, and whizzes its way from there on through a surprisingly complex plot, in which it sets up an irresolvable situation and then, equally surprisingly, resolves it. The author treats certain of the laws of the universe cavalierly, but then so does *Star Trek* on the screen and Sonni Cooper in real life. When they're inconvenient she simply nods politely to them (she's not ignorant) and goes on. The really significant thing about the book is that it's real *Star Trek*.

Star Trek has had many imitators, and all have failed to reach the altitude of its original. Clearly there is a secret ingredient that has eluded the followers who are really a knowledgeable lot and know their trade and are especially adept in the techniques of following a trend. Yet none has been able to find that magic something that makes *Star Trek* capture the fans and endure.

The answer is (as somebody once said about Einstein's Theory) not at all difficult to understand; it's just impossible to believe. It is simply that the show comes straight from the basic convictions of its creator, Gene Roddenberry. These convictions are Mom and apple-pie convictions in the equality of the races and of the sexes; of faith in the dream of American democracy; of loyalty, the bondings of friendship and other kinds of love, like loyalty to personal commitment, and especially to duty. Most of the suspense in the episodes derives from the conflict between this last and all the others. And so it is with this story.

One other thing is very much worth mentioning: Sonni Cooper writes with her ears. Unlike so many authors of *Star Trek* novels, Sonni has captured the intonation of each of these familiar voices. Partly this comes out of the skill of an accomplished actress; mostly from the compulsions of the archetypical Trekkie.

So read, and enjoy.

Theodore Sturgeon
San Diego, 1981

Chapter 1

The Attack

1

"Oh, my God," Chief Engineer Montgomery Scott shouted as he was hurled against a bulkhead as the ship lurched, and his eardrums resonated painfully as the sound of a massive explosion echoed throughout. It was the sound of an internal blast, the shock waves pulling the *Enterprise* off her course into a spiral at warp speed. He watched his engineering crew spring into action, as he directed them to compensate for the erratic spin. He then raced to auxiliary control to get the ship back on course. All communications from the bridge were cut off; he was on his own.

Horrified, Scott realized that the bridge was the source of the explosion. The turbolift was useless, and the emergency repair crew was frantically working to clear the debris away from the stairway to the bridge. Scott joined the crew, torch in hand, working along with them—and praying.

He inched his way up the cluttered stairway and, with a strength he did not know he had, pushed against the unyielding hatch. He recruited two burly crewmen, and with their combined strength exerted against the resisting hatch, they managed to open it slowly. Scott raised himself onto the demolished bridge.

"My God," he whispered as he looked around. He observed that the blast had occurred in the center of the bridge. It was a vision of hell; the pattern of destruction radiated from the center of the blast to the outer walls. The inner sheathing of the hull was destroyed by the violence of the blast, and Scott soon detected a weak spot in the outer hull.

"Better get the injured out o' here quickly," he ordered. "That outer sheathin' will go any minute."

He checked the crewman nearest him—dead. Scrambling over the wreckage, he looked for the captain. What was left of the navigation console was scattered toward the darkened view-screen. He found Sulu first. The helmsman, pinned under the wreckage, was clawing at the floor trying to free himself.

Scott found the captain, his tunic covered with blood and as torn as the body within it. The entire area was spattered with blood and strewn with twisted metal. The body of the young navigation trainee was mangled almost beyond recognition. Beside him lay Chekov, whose condition was unknown; he was almost hidden under debris. A group of crewmen grimly started freeing him.

Spatters of green led Scott to the prone figure of Spock, lying face down near the smoking, blackened science console. A jagged piece of metal was protruding from his back. Lt. Uhura lay unconscious; Scott could see she had been slammed into the communications panel, which was now a sputtering, flaming mass of twisted wires.

All of his years of training and control, all of his years of experience, had not prepared Scott for this scene of mayhem. Unshed tears stung his eyes as he worked along with the crew, carrying the injured and dead from the completely demolished bridge.

"Concentrate on the living!" he shouted, watching the bulge in the outer hull enlarge.

McCoy stood in the corridor below the bridge, quickly evaluating the extent and nature of injuries as each bridge crew member was carried out and put on a stretcher to be taken to sick bay. A full disaster alert was sounding; the emergency medical team was assembling quickly.

"Everybody clear?" Scott asked as the last of the injured was being brought down the stairway. He sprang against the hatch, closing and securing it tightly. The rush of displaced air and the shattering of over-stressed metal combined into an awesome roar as the entire dome of the bridge broke off with a sudden tearing wrench, sending the ship into another series of erratic dips and spins.

McCoy, now in sick bay, was too intently absorbed for his usual complaining. The entire surgery was being utilized; each surgical team was working quickly and efficiently to repair the most life-threatening injuries.

Dr. M'Benga, more qualified than McCoy to cope with Vulcan anatomy and special problems, was applying his skills and experience to Spock's critical wounds.

Thank God we stocked some T-negative blood for Spock last time we took on supplies, McCoy thought. *At least we can meet any of his blood needs.*

But the doctor's main concern was on the severe condition of the captain; he hadn't yet assessed all of Kirk's injuries and McCoy entered surgery not knowing exactly what he would find. *At least he's alive—barely.*

It took all of McCoy's professional detachment to suppress his despair when he fully examined his patient and his friend. There were just so many organs one could transplant, just so much one could patch and mend in a human body. Kirk's wounds pressed that limit. He needed massive amounts of blood. The hard-pressed medical teams had exhausted the supply before Kirk's surgery started. A ship-wide plea for donors soon created a line in the corridor outside sick bay. Any crewman with the proper blood type was relieved of duty until the blood was drawn; yet since the ship needed her entire crew to deal with the emergency, as soon as the blood was taken they returned to their stations foregoing the normal period of recuperation.

Scott grimly and dispassionately assessed the damage to his beloved ship. The strain suffered when the bridge sheared off was too much for the *Enterprise,* and he knew the entire primary hull would have to be jettisoned or the resultant stresses would rip the ship apart. This would necessitate a complete evacuation of the primary hull—a systematic and thorough movement of personnel and supplies as rapidly as possible. But the emergency surgery could not be rushed. All but the medical team was shifted to the lower hull, and Scott was counting the minutes, then hours, anxiously hoping that the ship would hold together until all the vital surgery was completed and the patients could be safely moved.

McCoy grudgingly accepted the fact that his patients, no matter how critical their condition, would have to be moved immediately following surgery. He worked on relentlessly, hour upon hour, backed up by his proficient staff, losing all track of time as he worked to save the life of Jim Kirk.

The sophisticated medical technology of the day had made such extensive time in surgery unusual, but McCoy was essentially rebuilding a man. Another surgeon would possibly have given up, but McCoy continued diligently, repairing the body of the man he both admired and loved. Only when he had done as much as he believed he could, and his endurance would no longer sustain him, did he conclude the operation and retreat to the quarters assigned him in the cramped lower section of the ship. And then he quietly wept—for his friend, for his lack of skill—in his weariness, and with despair greater than any he had ever felt. Always before, when he thought Jim was dead, it was a quick realization that had to be accepted. The hours he had spent in rebuilding the man, the strain he had put upon himself, the acceptance of his limitations as a physician, the as-yet-unknown prognosis—all built up to this release of emotion and tension.

The buzzer to his quarters sounded and McCoy, regaining his composure, pushed the button that admitted his visitor. A young medic carrying his possessions entered. "Doctor Jonah Levine, sir." It was clear that the young man was as surprised as McCoy at being assigned bunk-mate to the head of the medical section.

"There must be an error. I haven't shared quarters in years," McCoy wearily protested.

"I wrote down the cabin assignment, sir. Seventeen B-O three."

The intercom signal interrupted them. McCoy answered promptly.

"Doctor, you're needed in sick bay—immediately." Nurse Christine Chapel sounded extremely agitated.

"Jim?" he asked.

"No, Doctor M'Benga has to see you right away."

"Spock," he said aloud, leaving young Dr. Levine to sort out the problem of room assignments.

"You look exhausted, McCoy. I know you're beat, but I've come across a problem with Spock I don't quite know how to handle," M'Benga said tiredly.

"You're the authority on Vulcan medicine aboard this ship, M'Benga. It must be really serious if you want my input."

"It is. Spock is not entirely Vulcan, remember? There seem to be some irregularities in his recovery patterns. He shouldn't be, but he is conscious. He seems to be fighting to keep from falling into the Vulcan healing mode. He is controlling the pain—but barely. I can't get him to relax. I knock him out with a hypo, and in the minimum time he's awake again. He keeps asking for Mister Scott."

The chief medical officer nodded grimly. "I'll check on him. Maybe I can get him to relax so that he can get on with that self-mending process. I don't entirely understand what it is, but it works and we've done all we can for him medically. You take a break, M'Benga. You need the rest. I'll stay with Spock."

Gratefully, M'Benga sank down into the lounge. It had been a marathon for the medical teams, both physically and mentally. He, like McCoy, was completely exhausted.

Spock was lying stiffly on his back, his face contorted by pain. McCoy heard the barely audible murmur of the Vulcan's litany of mental control: "I am Vulcan; there is no pain."

"But there is pain, Spock. Why are you fighting the natural healing process?"

Spock was startled into alertness by McCoy's voice. "No time, no time . . . ," Spock said hoarsely. "Mister Scott. I must see Mister Scott." He summoned all his discipline to suppress the pain in his back as he struggled to rise. McCoy gently pushed him back down.

"You must stay flat and immobile. That piece of metal came very close to your spinal cord. There's still a small sliver embedded in your back which we can remove only when you're more fully recovered from the initial surgery. Until then, you must let your natural healing process work."

"Get Mr. Scott . . . ," Spock insisted, the words weakly but precisely uttered.

Seeing he would get nowhere until Spock had relaxed, McCoy relented. "Okay, I'll get him. Now, rest."

"The captain . . . how is he?"

McCoy shook his head. "Not good," he answered quietly. "Now rest until Scott gets here. I'll stay with you until he arrives."

Spock closed his eyes. The Vulcan's brow was wet with the effort. McCoy ran a dampened cloth over Spock's forehead, taking note of the Vulcan's clenched fist, and shook his head in frustration as he watched the monitor above his patient's head register the inner battle Spock was waging.

In a very few minutes Scott arrived. He was running on sheer willpower, expending his last to keep the ship operating. As far as the engineer knew, this was the first time a starship had been forced to shed its upper hull. Decisions had to be made quickly and efficiently, and he had had no time to rest.

"Well, Doctor, make it fast. I've a ship ta hold together," he blurted out as he entered the room.

"Slow down, Scotty. You can't hold it together in that state. I'd recommend at least a few hours' sleep," McCoy advised.

"Is that why ye called me ta sick bay, Doctor? I don't ha' the time to rest now."

"No, Scotty. It's Spock. He wants to speak with you, and won't rest until he does. Try to calm him down."

Spock opened his eyes. Speaking deliberately, and with great effort, he addressed the engineer. "Mister Scott— sabotage—it had to be an act of sabotage—a bomb—nothing on the bridge could have caused an explosion of that magnitude—must be an intruder on board . . ."

"Aye, Mister Spock. That thought crossed my mind also. I've checked our personnel lists. There's no one on board who shouldna be. All are Starfleet cleared."

"An intruder could have slipped through Starfleet security —look further. Ship's status—tell me. . . ." An involuntary gasp escaped him. He closed his eyes tightly, struggling to regain his lapsed control.

Scott reported succinctly. "We came away in verra good

shape, considerin'. There were five deaths on the bridge, and five seriously injured. All personnel, except those on the bridge at the time, are accounted for and uninjured. The upper hull has been jettisoned. We're cramped down here, but all is functioning and under control. Ye can relax!"

"Good," Spock whispered. "Now help me up!" He weakly raised a hand for Scott's assistance. The engineer looked to McCoy, who motioned for Scott to leave.

"Nothing doing, Spock. You can't get up. I just explained why you can't move. Christine." McCoy motioned to the nurse, who was standing ready with a hypo-spray. She quickly administered the strong sedation.

"Make sure you keep him down," McCoy ordered, leaving the room to check on Kirk.

The medi-scanner showed all life functions at very low levels. McCoy examined Kirk's unconscious form and double-checked the instruments in the auxiliary sick bay. He was not entirely comfortable with the secondary facilities even though they were regularly checked and kept ready for such an emergency. It wasn't *his* sick bay. The three medics who had continually hovered near Kirk since McCoy had gone to his quarters waited for further orders.

"Get some rest. I'll stay with him—couldn't sleep anyway. Someone bring me some coffee." A young nurse he had never noticed before brought him a steaming hot cup.

"Where have you been hiding, young lady?" the doctor asked, more as a means of distraction from his growing fatigue than anything else.

"In the clinic, Doctor. I'm new on board. Cathy White. I'm one of the cadets from the Academy assigned for the training session."

"Ah, yes. I almost forgot about that. Not a very standard training session, is it? It's not always this bad."

"Will he be all right, sir?" She looked at the captain lying motionless on the bed.

"I don't know yet. His condition is marginal. I really can't tell at this point. All we can do now is wait." He sat down on a chair beside the bed, cupping the hot coffee in his hand, staring at his friend, and feeling completely helpless.

Christine Chapel's shouts interrupted the quiet of sick bay. "Mister Spock, you can't get up! Please lie down! Please!"

McCoy hastened to the other room, followed by the young trainee, to find Spock standing shakily, using the bed for support with one hand and using the other to brace his injured back. Either he wasn't trying to mask the pain or he wasn't succeeding in his attempt, McCoy wasn't sure which. Christine turned to him as he entered.

"I really tried to keep him flat, as you ordered, but he won't listen!"

"I'll handle this, Christine. Just leave us alone, please."

"Yes, sir," Christine responded, grabbing Cathy White and heading for the door.

Cathy was not prepared for such dire emergencies as were taking place one after the other aboard the *Enterprise*. "Is it always this difficult, Christine? I've had no experience with non-Terran patients at all."

"Mister Spock is a most unusual man. We all admire him very much. I'm sure that Doctor McCoy can settle him down. You might hear some shouting though—just ignore it."

As if cued by Christine's warning, McCoy's raised voice could be heard as he lashed out at Spock. "What are you trying to do? Kill yourself? Do you think we put you back together to have you destroy yourself? Get back on that bed! That's an order!"

"I have no intention of lying here while the ship is in jeopardy, Doctor. I will ask you to not interfere."

"Well, I am. And you don't have the strength to stop me."

"Just don't force me to. . . ." Spock raised his supporting hand from the bed and faltered a step.

"Look! You can't even stand up unsupported. Listen to reason, Spock. Now is no time for your Vulcan stubbornness."

Having sublimated the pain as much as he was able, Spock was feeling stronger. He slowly straightened up and took a tentative step. "I'm fine, Doctor. The discomfort is completely under control now." His voice reached its normal tenor. "You can set aside your bigotry."

"Bigotry? Why, you overgrown walking string bean, I have no time for . . . Wait a minute, Spock. I'm not about to start one of our verbal fencing matches." McCoy's anger subsided. "Listen to me, Spock, to McCoy, the physician. I know you respect that part of me even though you won't admit it. This is a medical judgment, not an arbitrary personal assessment. In this *I* am the authority. Now, please listen to me."

Spock leaned wearily against the bed, gathering the strength he knew he would need.

"I told you about your injury. Every movement you make jeopardizes your life. If that sliver moves, it could kill you, or leave you paralyzed. That's a fact. You can't just sublimate it or wish it away. You may be able to control the pain, but that fragment is inside of you. Pain is your friend now, Spock. Feel it! It indicates a real physical danger. You can suppress it, but you're fooling yourself. This time it's a signal, a signal warning you, trying to prevent you from further injury. If I can't convince you, let yourself feel that pain. Don't fight it. The severity of it will tell you that I'm right about this."

"I know what I am doing, Doctor," Spock answered with conviction. "I know what I must do." He then slowly walked out of the room, ignoring McCoy, almost achieving his usual dignified, erect bearing.

Spock turned toward the rest of the temporary sick bay ward. Sulu was gingerly testing his repaired limbs, facing away from the First Officer.

The Vulcan casually addressed the helmsman. "I see that you are recovering well, Lieutenant."

An astonished Sulu turned. "Mister Spock, you're all right! Rumor had it that you were seriously injured."

"Humans do have a propensity for rumor, Mister Sulu. As you can see, I am quite well. I have not come here to talk of my health, although it is an important consideration. How are the others?"

"It's a miracle we weren't all killed. It seems that the trainees from the Academy took the brunt of the blast. Except for you and the captain, we were all shielded from it by our students. We'll all be back on duty in no time." Sulu quieted. "I feel guilty about being alive at their expense."

"Yes," Spock said thoughtfully, "the trainees. Mister Sulu, do you remember anything unusual happening on the bridge before the explosion?"

"No."

"Are you sure? No one unfamiliar?"

"Who could have been there, Mister Spock? We're all Starfleet-cleared."

Characteristically, Spock did not respond. He sank deeper in thought. "Mister Sulu, I have an idea, but I require more information. Will you help me?"

"If it means finding out what happened on the bridge, I'll do anything you ask."

"Good. I suspect you saw more than you are able to recall. I believe the shock may have blocked your memory. If you will allow a limited mind probe, I might be able to draw out the fragments you are sublimating. Will you permit the probe?"

"Yes." Sulu realized the importance of this information; the Vulcan never made such a request lightly.

Spock put his fingertips to Sulu's temple, concentrating on reaching the helmsman's unconscious.

"I want you to think back to the period just before the explosion. I will ask you to describe the activity on the bridge in detail."

Spock was able to penetrate the upper levels of Sulu's memory with ease; but as he approached his experience of the accident, he met with increasing resistance. Gently, Spock eased the release of those memories of just preceding the explosion from the hold Sulu's subconscious exerted over them. Finally, the helmsman relaxed his vigilance over the disturbing scenes and they were made available to Spock. Sulu, now yielding his mind to Spock's, spoke slowly and clearly.

"I was teaching the cadet assigned to me how to switch from warp to sub-light speeds in emergency situations. The mechanism on board the *Enterprise* is more sophisticated than the Academy's simulations. His name was John Real. Behind me, Chekov was instructing his student. You were at the science console looking over a computer readout. Your back was turned to the center of the bridge. Lieutenant Uhura was having trouble with her cadet. I could hear her correcting her over and over again.

"Uhura was close to losing her patience. The captain was in the command chair. No. He got up. It's becoming clearer now. A yeoman, one of the cadets, entered the bridge. She had something for the captain to sign. She gave it to him. Then she left the bridge."

"She didn't wait for him to sign it?"

"No. She gave it to the captain and left."

"Then what happened?"

"The captain put the pad on his chair."

Spock prodded gently. "And then . . . ?"

"The explosion—I don't remember anything else."

Spock withdrew his hand from Sulu's brow. Sulu instantly snapped out of the trancelike state. "Was I of any help?"

"Yes, Lieutenant. You have given me a lead."

"Can I help you any further?"

"Not yet. It is too soon for me to reach a satisfactory conclusion. I will know what occurred more specifically when I have examined the facts you have just given me. I must be entirely sure before I act." Spock turned to leave but stopped. "One more thing. Can you describe the cadet who entered the bridge?"

With his memory jogged, Sulu, who had an acute eye for visual detail, remembered quickly. "She was very fair, short and stocky. She looked almost square. Know what I mean? Not fat, but strong for her size. Are you going to question her?"

"Perhaps," Spock answered absently as he walked out of the room. His concentration was already intently focused on his task.

After checking briefly with the other injured crewmen, Spock headed for the quiet, darkened room in which James Kirk lay. The captain was still unconscious. From what Spock could see of his condition, it was assuredly for the best.

Two unfamiliar nurses worked around the captain. Spock approached and sat down on the chair beside the bed. An agonizing pain pierced through his spine and he gasped; putting all his effort into regaining control, he re-established his Vulcan discipline of the mind. The gasp alerted one of the nurses who started to approach.

"I am all right. Please leave us alone," he ordered abruptly.

Spock's aura of unquestioned authority was overwhelming; the nurses reluctantly left. He then placed his hand on the captain's head, establishing a healing meld. Kirk groaned as he became aware of the Vulcan reaching into his mind. Spock strained his skills to the limit to suppress his friend's pain as well as his own.

Sometime later, when McCoy checked on his patient, he saw a marked difference.

"Spock's been here. Right?"

"Yes, Doctor. How did you know?"

"I've seen him do this before. There could be no other reason for so great an improvement so quickly. He may well have made the difference in Jim's recovery."

Kirk, regaining consciousness, struggled to speak.

"Don't try to talk, Jim. You've had a rough time." McCoy gestured to the nurse. She administered a shot which took immediate effect. As Kirk lapsed into a deep healing sleep, McCoy could read the word he formed with his lips.

"Spock."

The chief medical officer sighed with relief as he turned away from his sleeping captain. "The worst is over now," he said, as much to himself as to the nurse beside him.

2

Mister Scott finally allowed another engineer to supervise the remaining tasks. The lower section of the *Enterprise* had been prepared for towing back to Starbase 12, the nearest facility. When the ship had safely docked, Scott immediately retired to his assigned quarters there. He took a large shot of brandy, stepped into the sonic shower, and dropped into bed.

But he couldn't sleep. He tossed and turned with the events of the past two days flashing through his mind relentlessly. He rose, took another gulp of brandy straight from the bottle, and returned to bed. It seemed hours before he finally fell into a deep, exhausted sleep.

He was groggy when he acknowledged the buzzer to his quarters. Spock entered the darkened room. Scott eyed him blearily from his perch on the edge of the bed.

"What is it, Mister Spock? Ye look like ye've eaten somethin' verra sour," he said, yawning and lying back down, more asleep than awake.

"Mister Scott, I need your assistance. I suspect the explosion on board the *Enterprise* was sabotage. I believe I've already shared this theory with you."

"Aye, but ye were in no condition ta discuss the possibilities then."

"True. But now I must investigate further. I must have concrete proof. I will require a ship large enough to return to the jettisoned hull quickly, and will need the assistance of an engineer. I propose that we return to the jettisoned section and search thoroughly until we find the evidence to corroborate my suspicions."

"I examined all o' the record tapes myself, Mister Spock. The relays ta the auxiliary bridge worked verra well. I couldna find anythin' ta indicate the explosion was anything but an accident."

"Mister Scott, you of all people must be aware that there is no mechanism on the bridge which could have caused a blast of that magnitude. It had to be a foreign object."

"Aye, that crossed my mind, too. But I couldna find anythin' ta substantiate that theory."

"That is why we must return to the abandoned hull. We must investigate before anyone disturbs the remains of the bridge. Once they send out a tow, the evidence may be obliterated."

"Have ye requested a ship, Mister Spock?"

"That is one of the difficulties. Doctor McCoy will not give me medical clearance. I cannot obtain permission to leave the starbase. *You* must request the ship. It is logical for you to request to return to the jettisoned hull to ready her for the towing procedure. I will accompany you."

"Aye, but ye still will na have clearance ta leave, Mister Spock."

"That is my responsibility. Will you assist me?"

"I will," Scott answered without hesitation. "If my ship was sabotaged, I want ta be the first ta find the one who did it."

"I believed that would be your probable response," Spock admitted.

As Spock predicted, Scott was readily provided with an appropriate vessel, and the two officers arrived at the site of the hull separation in less than a day. With their life-support suits and packs firmly attached, Spock and Scott floated toward the abandoned upper section of the *Enterprise*. Small beacon lights outlined her circular rim. All else was dark. All systems had been shut down; she lay dead, drifting slightly in space.

They worked their way toward the upper section, where the explosion had pierced the sheathing. A mass of twisted metal was all that remained of the bridge. From one end to the other and from top to bottom, they examined every inch of the shattered bridge, concentrating on the central area where the explosion had originated. Not one shred of evidence could be found in the debris. They returned to their scout ship, removed the bulky suits, and held a brief conference.

"The outward rush of atmosphere when the sheathing blew ejected whatever there was for us to find, Mister Scott. We will find nothing on what remains of the bridge to substantiate our suspicions. I do have another idea. It is not logical . . . it is more intuitive. But it is our only alternative. I rarely permit myself to follow what you would call 'a hunch' but I feel I have no choice.

"If you will remember, we had some sixty-three cadets on the *Enterprise* at the time of the explosion. They were all Starfleet-cleared, but if somehow only one were an imposter, we might have a lead. I have established that one of the cadets, a young woman, was on the bridge just prior to the explosion. If I could determine her identity, I think I may be able to find our saboteur. The computer has that information. With that data and with what I have learned from the crew, I should be able to trace her. Can you give me enough power to tap the computer banks?"

"Aye, I can run a line from the scout ship to the computer. It'll be jury-rigged, but it'll work for a time."

"Excellent. Please do so."

Scott, now absorbed in his task, did not notice Spock flinch as he tried to assume a comfortable position over an instrument panel. The Vulcan gritted his teeth, took a deep breath, and released the air rather explosively. Scott turned at the sound only to find Spock busily adjusting some circuitry.

With the computer link completed, Spock was again in touch with his alter ego, the main computer on board the *Enterprise*. He searched the records of the female cadets assigned to the ship for the training session. When he had completed the first data-retrieval run, five candidates remained. All were blond, average or short in stature, and all had access to the bridge. He then set about the process of elimination. All were Terran; all their records indicated superior skill in their chosen fields. They were all about the same age.

"Mister Spock, my temporary connection is about ta come apart. I hope ye've finished," Scott announced as the wire began to sputter near the terminal. It finally gave way with a dramatic spark.

"I have narrowed it down to five, Mister Scott. But any of them could be guilty—or none of them. We must examine their quarters—check everything, no matter how insignificant it may seem."

Both donned their space suits again and returned to the abandoned section. They searched through four of the cabins, finding nothing. Spock was examining the contents of a lower drawer in the fifth, finding it hard to concentrate on the search because of the growing discomfort in his back. He grasped the drawer for support when he felt his back give way and pulled it free as he floated momentarily out of control.

"Are ye all right?" Scott drifted toward the Vulcan as fast as he could manage in his weightless state.

"Yes," Spock managed to reply, suppressing his pain again. He floated back to his original position. The drawer had been pulled completely away and its contents had drifted out into the room. He retrieved an oddly flattened bottle and a crumpled piece of paper. Neither he nor Scott found anything else of interest.

Back on board the scout ship, Spock examined the two pieces of evidence he had found. The bottle contained a chemical he would have to analyze when he returned to the base. On the paper was a series of dots in what appeared to be a random pattern. As Scott turned the ship about to return to Starbase 12, Spock was already deep into his analysis of the series of dots.

When they returned, Spock stationed himself at the computer terminal nearest his quarters without any further indication as to what he was looking for. Scott returned to the salvaging plans, and no more was said of their investigation.

The towing operation had begun, and still Spock remained at the computer terminal, taking no time to eat or sleep. McCoy clucked and fretted and did the physician's equivalent of a gavotte around the obsessed Vulcan, but he was ignored completely.

During one of his infrequent breaks, Spock finally acknowledged the doctor's presence. McCoy was hovering like an anxious mother, waiting for Spock to collapse. "All right, Spock. What do you think you're going to find? You've been at it for hours."

"That is correct, Doctor. It might be days before I find that for which I am searching. I estimate at least ten million possibilities."

"What are you looking for, Spock? That's a question from Jim. You remember him? Captain James T. Kirk?"

"To put it precisely, Doctor, I am looking for a planet."

"A planet! There are billions of them!"

"Exactly, Doctor. That is why I cannot waste my time acknowledging your tantrums. Now, kindly leave me undisturbed." He turned to the computer, flashing star system upon star system on the screen as fast as his eyes could scan.

3

At Spock's request, the inquiry into the explosion on board the *Enterprise* was set at 1500 hours, shortly after he had finally concluded his relentless study of star configurations. He donned his formal jacket with difficulty, careful of his injured back. He reviewed the facts and theories he would set forth at the hearing while he walked down the corridor to the hearing room. To the casual observer, Spock's bearing seemed his normal stalwart one. To McCoy, who was observing Spock's every move, it was an indication that all was far from well with his recalcitrant patient.

With the exception of the captain, who was still far too weak to attend the hearing, the entire complement of the

Enterprise's officers was present. Uhura, Sulu, and Chekov were having a very quiet conversation in a corner of the room. Scott sat in the chair assigned him, chafing to get back to his primary concern—recovering and repairing the *Enterprise*. Lt. Lowry, who had been on-duty as security officer that day, sat behind Scott, clearly uncomfortable. Spock took the seat beside McCoy.

The medical officer whispered to Spock, "You realize, of course, that you went off without my medical clearance."

"I am quite aware of that, Doctor," Spock returned impassively. As he spoke, the Board of Inquiry was brought to order. The three officers at the table, all above the rank of captain, asked for quiet. All took their seats, and the hearing began.

Commodore Kingston Clark, a well-respected elder statesman of the fleet, officiated. In the old days of sailing ships, he might have been referred to as an "old salt." Clark now addressed the assembled officers.

"This is a formal hearing, gentlemen, but I think we will accomplish more if we relax a bit. We are all here to try to ascertain what happened on the *Enterprise*. All of us assembled here have the same goal. With that in mind, we will begin this inquiry." Spotting McCoy, he added, "We will deal with Commander Spock's defiance of medical orders at another time. Call the first witness, please."

The clerk called Lt. Uhura to the stand. Commodore Clark smiled at her after she was seated. Uhura gave her identification tape to the clerk and fidgeted nervously while her service record was being recorded.

Clark questioned, "Lt. Uhura, you are communications officer on board the *Enterprise*. Did you see or hear anything prior to the explosion that was in any way unusual?"

"No, sir. I was entirely absorbed in training the cadet assigned to me. She was having trouble with the subspace channels. Nothing unusual showed up on the communications panel. She was leaning over my shoulder at the time of the explosion; she took the force of the blast and was killed." She hesitated. "I owe her my life, sir."

Ensign Chekov followed Uhura. His description of the events on the bridge just previous to the explosion was much like Uhura's. Sulu followed Chekov, with very much the same portrayal of events on the bridge at that time. But he added one thing.

"Mister Spock visited me in sick bay. He said that I had provided a clue which he was going to investigate. I believe it concerned a cadet who left the bridge just before the blast occurred."

Lt. Lowry testified next. He could offer no additional information, but accepted full responsibility since he was on duty that day. Scott was called next. He related events as they occurred in engineering. Since he had not been on the bridge at the time of the explosion, he could offer nothing in the way of direct evidence. When he mentioned Spock, all eyes turned to the Vulcan, who sat unperturbed, looking straight ahead.

Glaring at Spock, McCoy gave his medical report. "I wish to state for the record that I have not given Commander Spock medical clearance to attend this hearing. He must rest so that we can complete his surgery—in his present condition we can do nothing. His injuries were extremely serious."

Spock faced Clark squarely, ignoring McCoy's outburst. "As you can see, Commodore, I am quite well. Doctor McCoy is exaggerating. I find that he is frequently overzealous in fulfilling his duties. Please go on with the investigation."

Clark looked carefully at Spock. "We generally would not hear your statement if you are considered unfit for duty. I have to admit, though, you do seem fit enough."

McCoy chafed. "It's a Vulcan skill. He's masking symptoms. Believe me, he's in pain. He's just not letting it show."

"Is that true, Commander Spock?" Clark asked.

Spock emphasized. "At this moment, I am fully fit for duty."

McCoy's medical scanner whirred; he knew better. He started to speak.

"Well, then," Clark said, cutting McCoy off, "we will get on with this investigation."

McCoy glowered at Spock, mumbling oaths under his breath, while the remainder of the *Enterprise* officers observed the exchange, understanding completely what Spock was doing.

"Commander Spock," the Commodore continued, "it was at your request that this hearing was convened at this time. I see no evidence at this point that the explosion on board the *Enterprise* was anything but an unfortunate accident."

"Commodore," Spock answered respectfully, "if you will permit me to continue, I will try to convince you with physical evidence."

"Continue, Mister Spock. But I warn you, it will take very persuasive evidence to convince this panel to the contrary."

In his very deliberate way, Spock began his presentation of the facts concerning Sulu's memory of the cadet, and his and Scott's resulting examination of the jettisoned hull. From time to time, Scott nodded in agreement. Otherwise, the room remained very still.

"As you know, my race is known for its reliance on logic as the mode of conduct in any difficulty. What evidence I do present, therefore, is most carefully considered. After the explosion, I analyzed the force factor it would have taken to cause such complete devastation. I am as well-informed as any in Starfleet as to a starship's tolerance. Mister Scott concurs with my conclusions. We took it upon ourselves to return to the blasted hull to investigate the explosion. There was no physical evidence in what remained of the bridge.

"It was then we followed Lt. Sulu's lead. The only person who was not a regular member of the crew who had entered the bridge and departed just before the explosion was one of the cadets assigned for the training session we were conducting at that time. I searched the computer records and, by a process of elimination, narrowed the search to five potential female candidates. Mister Scott and I then searched their quarters on the jettisoned hull of the *Enterprise* for anything unusual. All but one had the standard gear for a short tour of duty. The exception, Yeoman Isabel Tomari, had hidden in a drawer in her quarters two unusual objects. One, a flattened bottle which contained a chemical substance, identified after analysis as lauric-mono ethanolamide stearic diethanolamine sorbatin triolate; the other item was a crumpled piece of paper with a series of dots drawn on it, which I believe to be a star chart. It has taken me a great deal of time to find the equivalent star placement in Starfleet's records. Admittedly, the map detail I am now going to show you and the chart I found on the *Enterprise* show differences. I interpret them as omissions rather than significant variations."

Spock relayed the appropriate directions to the computer which then displayed the visuals on the screen. "The chart on the left is the one I found on the *Enterprise*, the other, a computer readout from Starfleet's library. As you can see, they match well enough to be considered the same, since one is obviously hand-rendered and the other is a projection from our telescopic probes. This section has never been thoroughly mapped. It is far to the other end of our galaxy. We have never physically ventured into it at all. I suggest our suspect is from one of the star systems projected here."

Commodore Clark grimaced disapprovingly. "Are you suggesting we were sabotaged by someone from a planet as remote as *that?*"

"Correct." Spock answered without hesitation.

Clark shook his head negatively. "What was that chemical you found again?"

"Lauric-mono ethanolamide . . ."

"In simple terms, what is it?"

"A depilatory, sir. A substance to remove excess hair."

"Mister Spock, I don't know about Vulcan women, but human women use such things regularly. I see nothing strange about that particular substance being present in a woman's quarters."

"Sir," Spock responded. "The potency indicates a quantity of chemical present that would serve the needs of a Terran woman for a period of ten years three months and an odd number of days if she chose to remain completely hairless during that period."

As usual, Spock had not intended to be amusing, but the hearing room hummed with stifled mirth when he presented his last statement. Spock's only response was the slight raising of an eyebrow in consternation.

"This hearing will come to order," Clark boomed. "I will not have this investigation turned into a circus." He turned to the two officers sitting beside him. They whispered for a short time, then Clark turned to Spock.

"Mr. Spock, we know how upset you must be after the explosion on your ship and the deaths and injuries that occurred, but we can see no reason to believe it was anything but an unfortunate mechanical accident. The depilatory certainly doesn't prove anything, and even you admit the star map and the dots you found on the piece of paper do not match exactly."

"Sir, I wish to add one more thing. Yeoman Isabel Tomari seems to have vanished completely. There is no record of her at the Academy or in any Starfleet file—only the computer on board the *Enterprise* acknowledges her existence. It is significant that she vanished so completely."

Clark looked exasperated. "Then, Commander Spock, the computer on board the *Enterprise* must be in error."

"*I* am responsible for that computer, sir. There was no malfunction indicated."

"Commander Spock, we have reached our decision. Your evidence is insufficient to support your case. It is the decision of this board that the explosion on the *Enterprise* is still of undetermined origin, and probably accidental. This hearing is closed."

"But, Commodore Clark, I am convinced there is sufficient evidence to warrant further investigation," Spock insisted. "You must hear my reasons. I believe we are in extreme jeopardy, and if we prove ourselves vulnerable, we may be leaving ourselves open for further, more serious attack."

"I see no reason to believe we are threatened, Commander Spock. You have presented your evidence; I order you to return to the hospital with Commander McCoy and remain there until he declares you physically fit to return to duty." The Commodore rose, as did the others on the board of inquiry, and left the room.

Spock rose painfully from his seat and motioned for Scott to join him. McCoy was standing close beside Spock and failed to suppress a look of triumph.

"Okay, Spock, you've delayed long enough. Now you're in my hands. Back to sick bay on the double!"

"I have no intention of returning to sick bay with you, Doctor. I have some business to discuss with Mister Scott. If you will leave us now, I will . . ."

"Nothing doing, Spock," McCoy interrupted. "You have a direct order from the commodore. You're in enough trouble already, what with going off without orders or clearance."

Ignoring the angry McCoy, Spock took Scott by the arm and walked out of the room without further comment.

There was a loud murmuring throughout the hearing room. A feeling of dissatisfaction was prevalent.

"Why did Clark ignore the testimony?" Sulu asked McCoy as they left the room.

"Damned if I know, Mr. Sulu. I'm just an old country doctor who can't hold onto a patient long enough to treat him—but something does seem not quite right about all this. . . ."

Chapter II

The Search

1

U.S.S. RAVEN: CLASS AA CRUISER. WARP POTEN-
TIAL: 5 MAX. CAPTAIN ROSS FONTAINE. CREW: 17, 8
HUMAN - 8 ANDORIAN - 1 VULCAN. PRESENT
CREW STATUS: REST LEAVE—STARBASE 12. SHIP'S
STATUS: PROVISIONING COMPLETED. LAUNCH SYS-
TEMS CHECK IN PROGRESS—ENGINEER FESTUS
PARKER AUTHORIZED ON BOARD. LOCATION:
STARBASE 12, LOCK 6. STANDARD SECURITY.

Spock read the computer readout with satisfaction. The
Raven, docked two days before, would serve his purpose
well. Scott, peering over Spock's shoulder, nodded in agreement. They had found their ship. But the Scotsman was
uneasy.

"Are ye sure this is the only way, Mr. Spock? Starfleet
doesna' take kindly ta unauthorized borrowing of its ships, ye
know."

"If you have reservations, Mister Scott, you are under no
obligation to accompany me," Spock replied calmly. "I am
determined to prove my suspicions are correct regarding the
explosion. Your company, however, would be most helpful
and welcome."

34

"It'll be a bit tricky handlin' a ship o' that size with only two aboard, but I think we can do it," Scott answered. "When do we borrow her?"

"Tonight. Only personal items are necessary; the ship is fully provisioned."

The lone guard in front of the docking bay checked his chronometer every few minutes. Guard duty on a starbase was more a matter of form than necessity and a good night's sleep was being sacrificed for a nonessential task.

Yawning, he leaned against the wall, peering down its length, wishing for his long watch to end. He didn't sense Spock's presence until the Vulcan was directly behind him. He turned, recognized Spock, and smiled. That was the last he remembered. The precise pressure on his shoulder brought instant unconsciousness. Spock gently lowered him and beckoned to Scott. Carrying their gear, they quietly entered the ship.

Heading straight for the computer, Spock snapped a tape into its console. The communications board came to life, signaling the starbase flight-control center. Spock activated the tape's audio mechanism and addressed the control-center personnel.

"U.S.S. *Raven:* Standard launch check. Limited flight. Clearance requested."

"State authorization," droned the response.

"Commander Festus Parker, chief engineer. Safety-systems check. Authorization: standard procedure."

"Permission granted—limited-duration flight. Please inform base of ship's status upon return."

"Orders received and understood. Parker out."

Spock nodded and Scott punched in the launch sequence. Once cleared, Spock modified access to the navigational computer bank so that they couldn't be tracked. They were in deep space before anyone at the base realized there was anything irregular.

Scott had his hands full running the ship alone during the long voyage, while on the *Raven*'s limited computer Spock tediously searched for the most likely of the solar systems in the sector indicated on the rough star map Spock had found in Yeoman Tomari's quarters.

As they neared the area, he focused on those with planets

which could sustain life. Of the ten stars in the sector, only one had a planet which was at all habitable, so they set a course for the fourth planet of a small, bright sun.

They touched down on a flat plain below a ridge of hills in a desert area of the small planet they designated as "Quest." With the marginal equipment on board the *Raven*, Spock was unable to determine whether any sapient life forms existed on the planet. It was just barely habitable, with the oxygen level merely adequate. The only region that could properly sustain life appeared to be at the northern pole, where they had landed, since the remainder of the small world was extremely hot. Spock assumed that since Yeoman Isabel Tomari appeared human, the life form they were searching for was of humanoid appearance, or had the ability to appear human.

After utilizing the sensors and other scanning equipment on board to check for any menace that was detectable, they cautiously disembarked.

They scrambled up the rock face of a small hill, Spock following Scott with difficulty, masking his pain with ever-increasing effort. Scott extended a hand to Spock to help him up to the crest of the hill, and Spock gratefully accepted. The engineer had silently agreed not to press Spock about his physical condition, but was continually aware of his companion's problem and assisted Spock whenever he could without making it seem too apparent.

As far as they could see, the barren landscape stretched interminably without a sign of life. Its rolling hills were tinted by an orange sun, giving the landscape the look of perpetual sunset. Vegetation was scarce, with predominantly yellow bushlike growth scattered on the lower slopes of the hills. There was no safe cover should any be needed, and the two officers were uncomfortably aware of their vulnerability without a security escort or portable tricorders.

They returned to the ship discouraged. The planet seemed completely without evidence of intelligent life. Behind them, another group of low hills obscured the remaining landscape. Both men were approaching these hills, hoping to find more promising terrain on the other side, when a phaser blast shot past Spock.

"You will remain very still, with your hands in sight and away from your weapons," came the woman's voice from behind the rocks. "Don't turn around. Just stay as you are," the voice continued. Spock could hear three distinct sets of footsteps approach; a hand from behind reached for his phaser. Scott was also relieved of his weapon.

"Turn around now."

Both turned to face their captors and stood in mute surprise as three Romulan officers smiled with satisfaction at their prisoners.

It was the woman who caught Spock's attention. Taller than the average Romulan, she stood straight and confident. Her dark hair was tied back efficiently, giving her chiseled features prominence. While Spock was rarely susceptible to female beauty, Commander Julina's radiance elicited aesthetic appreciation.

"I should have known the Federation would be involved," she announced angrily.

Scott started to protest, but she would hear no explanation. "Two Federation captives will be a worthy prize to display when we return. Prisoners are not ordinarily taken by Romulans, but you are an exception." The Romulan commander moved off to confer with her officers.

The Federation prisoners were taken to the Romulan scout ship which was secreted in a nearby gully and detained in a small storage area. The quarters were cramped and uncomfortable. Scott explored every inch of their prison, but could find no way of escaping. "Looks like we're in for a long ride in close quarters, Mister Spock."

But Spock was not listening to his companion; he was concentrating on the voices of their Romulan captors and obtaining much illuminating information. Spock leaned against the bulkhead, putting his hands to his throbbing back and trying to stretch. He caught his breath as a burst of sharp pain shot from his back down his right leg.

"Are ye all right?" Scott asked, becoming increasingly concerned.

In his usual manner, the first officer denied his discomfort, and when the pain lessened, Spock quietly addressed Scott.

"It seems that the Romulans also suffered an act of sabotage much like our own on board the *Enterprise*. Now they believe, since they have found us here, that we are the culprits. They were led here by a map similar to the one I discovered. It seems our adversary did not attack the Federation exclusively. That widens the scope of our problem greatly."

"We'll have ta tell them we're searchin' for a common enemy."

"We are in no position to tell them anything at this moment, Mister Scott. I doubt if they would accept our word, even if we do explain what we are doing on this planet. Obviously we were led here, but why, and by whom? The Romulans think we were responsible for the sabotage of one of their installations and that they were led here for some foul purpose. If they take us to Romulus, we will be in a very grave position."

"Aye, Mister Spock, and we've no way o' gettin' any help."

Spock lapsed into silence and Scott leaned back helplessly. They sat in silence for some time before the sound of an explosion near the ship snapped them both to attention. Another explosion, much closer this time, rocked the Romulan ship violently. Spock could hear the commander shouting orders to her crew as they prepared to defend themselves. The sound of a disrupter from the Romulan ship was cut short as they were jolted with a blast close to the storage section.

"You are surrounded!" shouted a deep voice from outside the ship. "Surrender. It is hopeless for you to continue to resist."

Spock could hear the commander in tense conference with her officers.

"We have no self-destruct mechanism on this ship. We have no alternative. We cannot destroy ourselves and the ship. . . ."

Then a deafening explosion ripped the ship's hatch completely off, cutting off the commander's words.

Scott and Spock, imprisoned and completely helpless, realized that all they could do was await their discovery by the newcomers.

"Will we be rescued, or prisoners of another bunch?"

Spock answered with typical rational calm. "We will soon find out."

Scott helped Spock to his feet as the door to their chamber banged open. The officers exchanged glances, Spock with raised eyebrow and Scott with alarm.

Facing them were two Klingons.

"Out!" ordered the now-familiar deep voice. "What is this? Federation representatives? Hiding? Did you think the Klingon Empire could be attacked? Did you think the combined force of the Romulan Empire and the Federation could destroy us? We are not so easily defeated!"

The Romulan commander protested. "We didn't attack your empire. There is no alliance with the Federation. These men are our prisoners, not our allies."

"A good attempt, Commander. But we will not be duped. An obvious ploy to catch us unaware." The Klingon motioned for all to leave the ship. "We will have a great deal of time to get the truth from you when we return to my ship."

"Mister Spock," Scott whispered. "Tell them we're not involved in any attack upon anyone. They'll believe you."

Overhearing Scott, the Klingon turned to Spock, eyes narrowing. "So you are the famous Commander Spock from the *Enterprise*. Your reputation precedes you. You are a particularly rich prize."

Spock spoke calmly. "If my reputation precedes me, then you must know of my integrity. On my Vulcan honor, the Federation had nothing to do with the attacks on either of your empires. We, in fact, were attacked much as you were. I would assume you also have a map much like the one I carry."

Spock reached into his utility belt; the Klingons raised their disrupters.

"I assure you, I have no weapon. I am retrieving a piece of paper which will help us settle our differences. I believe the commander," Spock indicated the Romulan woman standing beside him, "also has a map which led her here. It would be most interesting to compare all of the maps. I believe we have a common foe. Why we were led here and for what purpose still remains a mystery. But that we were definitely enticed here by a very clever adversary seems certain."

The Klingon took the map from Spock and the Romulan commander produced another one. The Klingon compared his map, passing all three to Spock and the Romulan.

"You might be correct, Vulcan. We might very well have been tricked into coming here. I don't like this. Who . . . ?"

"That is still to be determined," Spock answered. "But, since it appears we have a common enemy, it would be in our best interest, under the circumstances, to put aside our differences."

The Klingons grumbled at the suggestion. The Romulans, more inclined to logic, accepted the situation more easily.

"A truce, then," the Klingon commander barked.

"Agreed," Spock answered quickly.

They held a conference in the clearing beside the Klingon ship. Both the Klingon and Romulan contingents had come to this planet in small scout ships, in the same class as the one Spock and Scott had appropriated. Neither ship was equipped with a transporter or sophisticated sensors. It seemed the other groups had no more felt the venture worthy of a serious well-equipped probe than the Federation had.

The three Romulans, the trio of Klingons, and the Vulcan and Terran, who represented the Federation, sat around a table erected on the desert floor. Spock's logic and ability to maintain dispassionate objectivity made him the natural choice as leader.

"It would be much easier to work together if we formally introduce ourselves. If we think of one another as individuals with a common problem, we may more effectively transcend our past differences."

Scott was impressed by Spock's understanding of the psychological and sociological aspects of an alliance of such long-term adversaries. The Vulcan was not known for his sensitivity to the intricacies of interpersonal relationships.

"I am Commander Spock, first officer of the U.S.S. *Enterprise,* from the planet Vulcan. My companion is Lieutenant Commander Scott, chief engineer, a Terran."

To Spock's right, the Romulan commander took her turn. "Commander Julina of the Romulan flagship *Bird of Prey;* my planet of origin, Relus, in the system of Romulus."

Her officers followed. "Sub-commander Placus, *Bird of Prey,* from Romulus." "Delus, weapons officer, *Bird of Prey,* from Romulus."

The Klingon commander introduced himself in a characteristic snarl. "Commander Klee, the Klingon vessel, *Force.*" He introduced his crew. "To my right, my first officer, Lieutenant Commander Melek. My other officer, Lieutenant Kasus. All originate from the planet Klingon. Now that we have identified ourselves, I suggest we try to find out what we are doing here."

"May I propose a possibility?" Spock asked. All nodded assent.

"I suggest we are dealing with an adversary who is testing our strength and possibly our ingenuity. What is alarming is that we were *all* attacked. I cannot imagine a force large or strong enough to handle all of our three combined military strengths simultaneously—unless they had intended to let us think their acts of sabotage were perpetrated by our known enemies to set us at each other's throats."

"If we hadn't met here, the Klingon Empire might very well have blamed the Federation," Klee agreed.

"The Romulan Empire would also have blamed the Federation," Julina added.

"But," Spock interrupted, "we did meet, on this planet, where we were all led. I do not think . . ."

From behind the hills surrounding the new allies, a voice boomed from some sort of amplifier.

"Drop your weapons to the ground! You will all remain perfectly still. Do not attempt to escape. We have no desire to kill you."

A Klingon, Lt. Kasus, reached for his disrupter and spun quickly around, shooting as he turned. A phaserlike blast hit him squarely as he fired and he disappeared in a flash of light and color.

"It is useless to resist. Follow my orders exactly!"

The Federation representatives had been previously disarmed by the Romulans, so both Spock and Scott stood by helplessly while the Romulans and Klingons threw their weapons onto the desert floor with angry resignation.

"Now, place your hands behind your backs," ordered the disembodied voice from behind the hill. Spock suddenly found his hands bound behind him with a force he was unable to resist. He saw no visible restraints on the others when they, too, appeared to have their hands held behind them with an invisible bond.

"If this is a sample of their technology and power, I may have underestimated our enemy," Spock observed.

"Aye," Scott agreed. "We're in a sorry predicament now!"

From all sides, small, stocky men approached their captives. Spock raised an eyebrow of interest when he got a clear look at his captors. They were fair skinned and covered by a thick coat of very fair hair which became heavier around their faces, giving the appearance of a full beard. They were wearing animal skins, draped in primitive fashion over one shoulder and over their hips. They were armed with clubs and spears.

"I see why the depilatory was necessary," Spock commented.

The aliens' leader cuffed Spock. "Quiet!" he barked, treating the Vulcan like an inferior form of life. Spock remained still: *no need to aggravate an already grave situation.*

The prisoners were lined up in single file and marched over the surrounding hills. As soon as they reached the top of a slope and began their descent, they were able to see what the hills had obscured: a large chemical fuel rocket on a launching pad, ready for lift-off. Spock's eyebrow raised again when he saw the primitive propulsion system.

Scott was tantalized by this apparition from the past. "Look at that!" he exclaimed. "A working sample of early spaceflight. Better than a museum exhibit!" He was quieted by the jab of a spear in his back.

They were led to an elevator which took them up the gantry and inside the ship, where they were put into a chamber in the lower section. The door was closed, and the prisoners found themselves in a dark, cylindrical, smooth-walled cell. They also discovered their hands were now free of the invisible restraints. In the dimness of the chamber, the Klingon contingent—now reduced to two—sat in sullen silence. Spock entered into conversation with Commander Julina and her two officers, while Scott concentrated on the sounds of the ship, absorbed in the opportunity to study primitive propulsion methods firsthand.

The launch was bumpy but effective, and the flight seemed very smooth. The ship, once launched, seemed to function on different principles of physics: artificial gravity was established. The engineer was intrigued.

After a time each prisoner sank into his own thoughts. Their quarters were cold and uncomfortable. Spock's inner clock ticked away, giving him more of a sense of time elapsed than the others, but after a while even he lost track in the absence of instruments, due to the tight security of their prison. Food was supplied at regular intervals, always meat, which Spock refused. He was existing on water and air.

Scott grew increasingly concerned. He couldn't see Spock clearly in the gloom, but he knew his friend was suffering. Yet, typically, Spock denied any problem. "Vulcans can go on indefinitely without sustenance, if necessary," he claimed.

After what seemed an interminable journey, the ship plummeted out of space into the atmosphere of its home planet. It landed with a jolt, throwing the prisoners to the floor. When most had recovered their balance, Spock was still prone and Scott and Julina went to help him.

"I will be all right in a moment. Please, I need no assistance."

He forced himself to stand, straightening up very slowly, trying not to reveal his deteriorating condition. The door to the cell was finally opened. The haggard prisoners gratefully left the confines of the chamber, and they were taken out of the ship.

They found themselves on a bleak and desolate world, whose red sun barely provided enough warmth for survival. Most of the landscape was barren rock, covered with a dusting of frost. The bitter cold seemed to knife through the prisoners' uniforms, designed for the artificial environment of a ship. They were marched into a stone building, separated according to race, and then placed in cells. For the first time since they had begun their search for the saboteur, Scott and Spock were separated as Spock was placed in a cell with the Romulans, whom he closely resembled.

Food and water were provided. Again, Spock refused the animal flesh offered to him. His jailer took note of his refusal.

"You do not eat. It is required that you retain your strength." He pushed the food at Spock, who turned away. With a wrenching force, Spock felt his hands bound behind him by the invisible force. He was roughly pushed out of the cell, through a corridor, and into a small room in which sat a female of the species.

The woman had considerably less hair than the others. She nodded her head toward the door and two guards stationed themselves outside.

"Well, Mister Spock, the guards say you have refused to eat. Is that true?"

"Yes" was all Spock said.

"You have been offered meat. It is true, then: you are an eater of plants exclusively?"

Again Spock answered, "Yes."

"This is a harsh world, Spock. Our climate does not permit the growth of edible plants. You will have to subsist on meat until we can bring in vegetable food for you. We have very little in the way of any other food so you will eat what we provide!"

Spock remained silent.

"I was told of your Vulcan stubbornness. It seems the ship's rumors were correct. . . ."

It was then Spock realized that she must be the mysterious yeoman on the bridge. She was short, stocky, almost square, as Sulu had described her. Her face was broad, and seemed even fuller with the growth of hair beginning to sprout abundantly about it. "Yeoman Isabel Tomari," he said aloud.

"Partially correct, Spock. A name I derived when I took my place aboard the *Enterprise*. A combination of my true name, IIsa, and that of this planet, Tomarii. You are very observant to recognize me with my hair partially regrown. Now, back to our problem. You will eat, even if we have to force you. We need you at your full strength."

"For what purpose?" Spock shifted his weight from his numbing right leg, trying to conceal his increasing discomfort. She didn't answer his question and called a guard into the room.

"Where have you placed him?"

"With the others of his kind, Begum IIsa."

"He is not like the others. I have a special interest in him. Put him in a cell by himself."

This time he was led to and placed inside a small cell alone. Again, his hands were released as the door closed with a loud clank. It was bitterly cold. The Vulcan was finding it difficult to maintain his tolerance to the frigid temperatures, and the lack of nourishment was beginning to take its toll as well. He concentrated on stabilizing his physical condition, blocking the discomfort as much as possible, and on analyzing the information he had observed about his captors to this point.

Sometime later, Spock could hear guards approaching his cell; he forced himself to his feet. The heavy door opened and he was ushered into the corridor. The invisible force snapped his hands together, this time in front of him. One by one, the cell doors were opened and the prisoners brought forth. The

Klingons were tense and sullen, not adjusting to their capture or imprisonment with ease. But, much like Spock, the Romulans were more analytical about their predicament.

Scott came out of his cell and headed directly for Spock before being detained by one of the guards. The engineer looked at his companion with genuine concern. He could see that Spock's condition was not good; his pallor alone was alarming to one familiar with the Vulcan.

They were lined up in a large room adjoining the cell block. The walls were covered with moisture, making the room dank and clammy; it was close to freezing temperature. The Tomariians were entirely comfortable in the cold; the prisoners were suffering greatly.

IIsa entered the room, followed by a large group of high-ranking Tomariians. Placing herself directly in front of Spock, IIsa was first to speak.

"This one, the Vulcan, is of great interest. His race is known for great physical strength and logic. I am told they are peaceful. We will see. I will have him as my standard-bearer. The Romulan woman will serve me as well. The others are for you to select. The battles will commence in one solar cycle."

A male Tomariian, wearing a spotted skin, spun Scott around, examining the Scotsman with interest. "He will serve as my standard-bearer. He is the engineer, I understand. Useful. What are you called?" he asked Scott.

Scott didn't answer. He turned to Spock, who gave a small affirmative nod. Scott then responded, "Commander Montgomery Scott."

"Good, Montgomery. We shall be a winning team. I am IIob."

Another of the Tomariians, broader and stronger than the others, stood in front of the Klingons. "I will have these two. They seem to be more likely warriors than the others. My band needs strong men."

"No. I will have one of them," another Tomariian shouted, grabbing Commander Klee's arm and pulling him to his side. The Klingon resisted fiercely. "He will make a fine addition to my ranks."

The argument between the Tomariians over possession of the two Klingons came close to blows. IIsa finally stepped between them.

"They should be separated. Each of you will take one. I will not tolerate any argument. We will proceed."

Another Tomariian chose Delas, the tallest of the Romulans. Sub-commander Placus, the remaining Romulan, was claimed by a smaller Tomariian, who looked his captive over with disapproval.

"He seems too slight to be of much use. I think I have drawn the weakest of the lot. But I will do my best." He turned to IIsa. "I do not understand your choice, Begum. You seem to have chosen the least likely of the group."

"It is my choice, IIram. We shall see. Come, Spock. We have much to do. Follow me." She touched Julina. "You will come with me as well."

They walked, surrounded by an armed escort, through the bleak Tomariian landscape. Spock's scientific eye perceived the lack of mineral potential of the rock as he walked.

"This is one of the most resource-poor planets I have ever seen support life of a higher order," Spock murmured to his fellow prisoner. "There are too many inconsistencies. The technology of spaceflight should be accompanied by a more complex material culture than we see here. Their ability to control a force such as the one holding our hands and their use of knives and spears as weapons is incongruous. There are further discrepancies. Finally, I don't understand what they want of us."

"Neither do I," Julina agreed. "We must be patient."

"I must have more facts before I can make a proper analysis," he said, thinking aloud.

The prod of a spear in his back brought Spock back to attention. He had been lagging behind the others and was forced to quicken his pace to catch up. Each step caused a jabbing pain in his back; he was breathless when he reached IIsa's side. She looked at Spock with a puzzled expression. All she had heard on the *Enterprise* about the Vulcan seemed wrong—he didn't seem able to keep the pace of a normal march.

They soon reached a quadrangle of stone buildings and entered the compound through a narrow, guarded passage. The courtyard was large and bare. All the structures were built of gray stone, as was the courtyard floor. It was by far the most colorless of living compounds Spock had ever seen.

He watched IIsa's every move. She lightly touched a ring on her third finger, releasing the bond on his hands. Julina, once freed, was flexing her arms, encouraging the circulation which had been inhibited; Spock stamped his feet, trying to get some sensation back into his right leg. The numbness was becoming more pronounced. He wasn't sure how long it would be before his weakness would be discovered and his usefulness ended. He was convinced by all he had seen, and by his conversation with IIsa, that physical strength was of prime importance in this culture. He concentrated on appearing vigorous.

A curious group of Tomariians had surrounded them when they entered the courtyard. A female, obviously a retainer of some kind, handed IIsa a bulky packet of skins. She handed a rich, spotted one to Spock, and a tawny gold one to Julina.

"Put these on," she ordered, presenting the scanty clothing to her prisoners. Spock and Julina both hesitated but IIsa was insistent. "Put them on now!"

"Now?" Spock asked, looking around at the staring crowd.

"Here and now, as I demand. Or do you want me to have you stripped and dressed forcibly?"

Resigned to the fact that he had no choice, Spock yielded. "Force will not be necessary; we will comply with your order."

He started removing his tunic, and Julina, following his lead, did the same. As Spock stripped, a young male Tomariian approached and ran his hand up the Vulcan's bare arm and chest. Spock maintained his exterior calm thanks to years of Vulcan disciplinary training. Other Tomariians followed the boy's example, murmuring startled comments when they touched the bare skin of the strange man and woman. But it was Julina whom Spock studied. The barbaric skins hid nothing of her beauty. She looked like a primitive goddess, challenging all comers. *She could be an ancient Vulcan warmaiden*, he thought, staring pensively at her.

Julina returned Spock's gaze. The spotted skin he was wearing was made for a stockier form. It hung loosely on his thin frame, exposing his recent weight loss.

IIsa examined him carefully. "We must put some meat on those bones, Spock. Maybe that will quicken your step." She ran her hand over the deep scar on Spock's back, touching the area in which the sliver still lay embedded near his spine. "This looks like a recent wound," she observed.

Spock did not respond.

"You were on the bridge when I set the explosion. I remember seeing you there. You were injured in the blast?"

"Yes."

"Seriously?"

"The injury has not deterred my ability to function."

She ran her hand over the scar again. "I'm glad it was not more serious. You are the most interesting of our prisoners."

Without another word, IIsa walked toward the central building, indicating with a flourish of her hand for Spock and Julina to follow. They were grateful to move, both to get away from the staring crowd and to keep from freezing in the Tomariian cold.

2

The engineer in Scott was in a constant state of excitement over the opportunity to explore the unique technology of Tomarii. He went through the military maneuvers each day as he was expected to, but returned each afternoon to the rocket base with his captor, IIob, the general of the Tomariian fleet.

These primitive computers would be a marvel to Spock if he could see them. I must find a way to get to Spock. But then his attention would focus on another archaic technical wonder and he would find himself studying the new discovery with avid interest.

The launch system was simple; it required a great deal of manpower, but basically it was a simple chemical rocket launch from a standard gantry. Scott had the opportunity to examine the inside of one of the vessels and discovered another level of technological achievement. Once in orbit, the vehicle had warp potential, a matter/antimatter drive, and a life-support system as sophisticated as any he had ever seen. He could discover no transporterlike device. It seemed they simply dropped to the planet's surface in much the same archaic manner as they were launched, accounting for the jolt upon landing.

IIob was a relatively reasonable being. Once he understood just how much Scott's knowledge of engineering surpassed his own, he gave the engineer a free hand, studying his procedures and absorbing them quickly. IIsa had indicated how advanced the Federation's technology was. It was IIob's responsibility to incorporate the new knowledge into the Tomariian systems; he expected to have a more advanced launch technique soon. His contributions to the upcoming maneuvers would be vital.

Wearing the skins he was given, and with the thick beard and longer hair he was growing, Scott looked like a Celtic warrior of old. In the morning's military practice, he carried IIob's banner at the head of the march, appearing as primitive as his hairy companions.

While he taught IIob a few technological tricks, IIob in turn had told him almost all he needed to know about Tomariian technology. It was information crucial in formulating an escape plan. His apparent cooperation allowed Scott to move freely and study the Tomariian weaknesses. He hadn't seen Spock, nor had he heard anything of the others who had been captured with him. With no other option, he was biding his time, awaiting the opportunity to communicate his discoveries to one of the others.

The Klingons fared very well since the Tomariian warrior society was not unlike their own. Yet they, too, were studying the weaknesses of their enemy with the intention to escape. With typical pragmatism, Commander Klee was contemplating, with vengeful anticipation, the possibilities of a Klingon takeover in this virgin territory.

Placus and Delus, the Romulan captives, took more of an intellectual approach to their confinement. They surprised their captors with their physical strength and endurance. The Romulans were capable of ferocity equal to the Klingons'—if adequately provoked. Julina was a born warrior; trained in the Romulan tradition, she was an expert in rapid strategic decision-making, the use of complex weaponry, and hand-to-hand combat. She outdid IIsa in the training sessions each

morning, particularly in those exercises which required agility
and speed. IIsa watched the Romulan commander with great
interest, and some jealousy.

Spock's prowess with the primitive weapons was almost
equal to IIsa's; had he been in top physical condition, he
would have astounded his captors with his abilities. As it was,
he held his own by forcing himself to perform each task while
masking his growing disability. But from what IIsa had
learned on the *Enterprise,* Spock should have been performing even better. She decided to confront him with her
disappointment in his training-session performance. In the
cavernous room which served for her audiences, IIsa questioned her prisoner.

"Spock, you are not performing well enough in the preparations for battle. I find your prowess is not equal to what I
expected. Is there some difficulty?"

"Begum," he addressed her respectfully, "it must be the
lack of food. There is insufficient plant life to sustain me."

"Then you must eat the meat we provide for you."

"I cannot eat animal flesh."

"You mean you *will not,* Spock. You choose not to
cooperate. I will not have you weakened further because of
some Vulcan ideal. It is wasteful and would spoil my plan.
Must I force the food into you?"

Spock placed his hands behind his back and took a
determined stance. "That would be an unfortunate choice on
your part, Begum. I would be forced to resist, which could
cause me injury. I know you do not wish me injured. I do not
entirely understand why you have taken me and the other
prisoners, but I can see it is definitely to your advantage that
we remain strong and healthy. I am correct, am I not?"

"Yes, Spock," IIsa conceded. "I do need you at your full
strength. I have sent for the food you require. In turn, you
must promise to try to perform better."

"I will do my best, Begum." Spock replied docilely, aware
that he would have a much more difficult time masking his
physical deterioration from IIsa in the future.

The nights were nearly unbearable. Both Spock and Julina
suffered intensely from the cold. They were quartered together as IIsa's captives. For Spock, the lack of privacy was just
one more annoyance; for Julina, accustomed to bivouacking
with her men, it was a satisfactory arrangement. They slept

on a pile of furs on the stone floor, which barely provided enough warmth. It was the practical Romulan commander who finally arrived at a partial solution to remedy the discomfort.

"Spock, we are both freezing. If we sleep together and share our body warmth, we'd both benefit."

"I prefer to sleep alone" was the stiff response.

"Consider the arrangement as a practical necessity. It is a logical solution to the problem."

He had to concede she was right.

It didn't take Julina long to notice her companion's discomfort when she made even the slightest move beside him in the night. She also noticed his difficulty in rising in the morning. Finally, after a particularly grueling day, when Spock lay down beside her in the dark, Julina could hear his uneven breathing as he fought to control the pain. She drew close to him for warmth; he winced when she touched him.

The darkness and the intimacy of their sleeping arrangements made Julina breach the unspoken agreement between them to keep their rapport on the level of a pragmatic alliance. Julina was aware of Spock's emotional restraint concerning her; she understood and accepted it. She had made no advances toward Spock, but that did not reflect any lack of desire on her part to do so. Her concern now was more immediate—Spock was in pain. She spoke with the darkness as an ally, hiding her deep concern.

"Spock, I must speak with you."

He was silent, struggling to cover his discomfort.

"I know you are in pain. I have been aware of it for some time. It is time you told me what is wrong. I want to help you."

"I prefer not to discuss my physical condition. I am quite all right."

"You might be able to hide your problem from Ilsa, but not from me. The slightest move on my part causes you severe discomfort. I can tell it's getting worse. Please, permit me to share your burden. I might be able to ease your condition."

"There is no way you can help me," Spock said wearily.

"I'm sure you are aware of Romulan abilities, Spock; we are of the same genetic strain. We have a limited ability to link with the mind."

"Yes, I am aware of Romulan telepathic abilities. You are

not the first Romulan I have met, Julina. My experience with another Romulan commander was quite . . . illuminating."

For an instant, a flash of jealousy struck Julina. Her competitive nature took precedence over her normal calm stoicism. "You have known another Romulan woman?"

Spock didn't answer; he remained silent in the darkness.

Julina controlled her jealous outburst. "It doesn't matter, Spock. We are here now, and you need help. Permit me to relieve you of some of your pain. Tell me why you suffer so."

Her persistence could not be ignored. Spock realized he would have no peace until he told her what she wanted to know. He spoke quietly.

"I told IIsa a half-truth. The explosion on board the *Enterprise* was devastating. I carry a sliver of metal near my spine which could not be removed immediately. It is causing me great pain. I am able to control it, marginally. I am beginning to lose feeling in my right leg. I can hardly keep from limping now. Soon I will be unable to hide the weakness. You cannot keep the metal from moving, or the physical deterioration from taking place. I was warned of this possibility, but I chose to ignore it."

Julina turned toward Spock, placing her hands lightly on his temple. She pressed the area much as a Vulcan would, sharing his pain for a brief moment before she pulled away, unable to tolerate any more.

"Spock, I hadn't realized how intensely you were suffering. I am afraid I can only partially help you."

He held her hands to prevent another meld, but she freed them, again placing her probing fingers on his head, drawing some of his pain into herself.

3

The solar cycle was nearly over. The red sun that dominated the Tomariian day faded even more and the planet became unbearably cold. It was time for the war campaigns to begin.

The prisoners had been trained and now preparations were

being made for battle. The rockets were ready for firing; their on-ground support crews were ready to retreat to warmer, underground chambers throughout the long cycle of Tomariian cold. The purpose of the warfare and where it would occur were still mysteries to the prisoners, who, with their Tomariian captors, boarded the ships to leave the planet. Spock and Julina were placed in the lead ship with Ilsa. The others went with their Tomariian custodians into the other ships, ready for takeoff.

Spock's curiosity could not be suppressed; he was too reliant on information to formulate some strategy to deal with the situation, to be kept completely uninformed for much longer. He chafed to be on the bridge where the Begum was directing her forces. Forced to sit in the confines of a small compartment in the bowels of the ship, the Vulcan reflected on the facts he did possess, sharing his observations with Julina.

"These Tomariians remain an enigma. Their architecture and other material culture is as bleak as any I have ever encountered. Ilsa's household, however, contains some objects of astonishing beauty. That gold cup she is so proud of is so finely wrought that it has the intricacy of a spider's web, and the plate on the wall is cast with a delicacy of workmanship beyond anything I have ever seen in the craft. A sculpture which she has half-obscured in a corner has lines so carefully balanced they would overwhelm even a Vulcan's sense of aesthetics.

"There are other things which do not fit in with the Tomariian utilitarian existence. These artifacts seem to be from different planets, with different concepts of design and material, collected in what seems to be a random sampling. And not all of what has been accumulated is of value. Some is absolutely worthless. The Tomariians seem to make no distinction between the truly artistic masterpiece and the tourist items sold on pleasure planets."

"It makes no sense to me at all, Spock. I have never confronted any race or culture like this in all of my space experience."

"Neither have I," Spock said, continuing his analysis. "The animal skins Tomariians choose to wear are primitive—I can think of no better word to describe them. Their jewelry, except for that which is obviously a device, such as Ilsa's ring, varies in quality as much as the other artifacts I have examined. I am convinced they are the spoils of war, a collection of samples taken from many different worlds by the Tomariians."

"I tend to agree with you. But if what you say is true, they have a much greater sphere of influence than I would have imagined."

"Yes, and in this context, the inconsistencies in technology are explained," he commented. "The Tomariians use the technology they acquire from their conquered enemies, taking what they find useful. They discard things they regard as superfluous, so their technology, like their collection of artifacts, is piecemeal. They are not innovators, simply scavengers, developing only enough of their own technology to have started them in their ventures of conquest. How broad their influence is remains to be determined. But from what I can deduce, it is impressively extensive."

The Tomariians were on a new mission now, though whether one of conquest or otherwise, the Vulcan did not know. He thought back to their preparations: They had taken a sportsman's pleasure in the prospective war, wagering on the results. Spock was sure they had wagered on their prisoners' performances as well. As he thought the entire Tomariian rationale became clear.

"I now understand what our role must be. We are a test sample. Our performance in battle will be an indication of our respective forces' potential strength."

"So that is why we were attacked," Julina said. "It was not an overt act designed to start a confrontation. It was a successful breach of the Empire's security, proof of a weakness in our defenses. It was a test to draw victims into the Tomariian web and we took the bait. The attacks on the Federation and the Klingon Empire were the same."

"Now the final test is about to take place. It will be a trial of survival, testing our tenacity, ingenuity, and prowess under battle conditions, Julina. It is imperative to prove to the Tomariians our determination to protect our peoples. Ironic," Spock pondered wryly, "that I represent the Federation in this test. A citizen of the one planet most dedicated to nonviolence."

He looked over to Julina, who'd been unusually quiet during the journey. She had hoped to take advantage of the coming battle to reunite her party and escape, but that opportunity would never present itself. The others' ships were deployed elsewhere; evidently, the forces would not join for a single battle. Three attack groups were sent forth, each to a different planet, each with a different mission.

Last-minute preparations were in progress; a final session was called. "We are assigned a noble task," Ilsa proclaimed to the gathered forces. "Our duty calls for stopping the insurrection of Tomariian forces on this planet. It is the ultimate of missions. Tomariian fighting Tomariian, a battle between forces who equally enjoy the skills and risks of battle." Spock could see the Tomariians literally lick their lips in anticipation.

With battle strategy being planned, Spock and Julina had been brought to the briefing room and given their instructions. Spock was handed a long spear on which a flag was attached. He noticed that the Tomariians carried spears and knives, but as a backup, in holsters around their waists, they also wore phaserlike weapons. Obviously, they carried advanced weapons should their more traditional ones prove inadequate. Evidently, the Tomariians were not bound by integrity; they were quite capable of stacking the deck, if necessary.

"Is this my only weapon?" Spock inquired of the officer in charge.

"Afraid?" the burly Tomariian commander asked, sneering at what he interpreted as fear on Spock's part.

Spock raised an eyebrow of consternation, while testing the sharpness of the point with the edge of his finger. He felt no need to respond.

Ilsa entered the room followed by an entourage of armed soldiers. She went directly to Spock, running a hand up his right arm, fondling the gold armband she had given him earlier. Then she drew her hand down his back, feeling the lack of flesh near his ribs. He bit his lip, restraining the pain caused by her probing.

"I do wish you would have put on more heft, Spock. You will need all of your strength in the coming battle. You will not disappoint me, will you?"

The Vulcan turned toward Ilsa, gripping the spear tightly. His expression of barely restrained rage—and dignity—was enough to prevent her from bothering him further.

They dropped out of orbit with an abrupt jolt, as before. It was a small force, yet certainly one of the most savage Spock had ever seen. He looked as primitive as his comrades-in-arms; the sleek fur of the skin he wore glistened in the sun. The jewelry he had been made to wear was carefully chosen, even to the earring in his right ear. He recalled the placement of the earring by IIsa; it was then that he first experienced the full force of the restraining beam, which had held him immobile as she pierced his ear with a large awl and set the shining stone in place. He recalled her avid interest when she examined the unfamiliar green blood. She had become even more intrigued with him after that.

A touch on the arm brought Spock out of his thoughts. "It's time for us to leave the ship," Julina alerted him. "Spock, before we go into battle, I must say something to you. I must tell you how I feel. You have the ability to mask your feelings with logic. My people are of your strain. I know you have emotions, masked, but they *are* definitely present. I have not been as restrained as you have been. I care deeply for you. You must realize how I feel—the bond between us has gone beyond my sharing your pain."

"True," Spock replied, "the mental link has gone further. There was no need for words, Julina."

"There is one more thing, Spock. If you should survive me, I want to be sure the Romulan Empire is warned of the Tomariian threat. Will you contact the Empire for me if our escape attempt fails and I should die? I know I am asking you to help an enemy of the Federation . . ."

"We have formed an alliance for these special circumstances, Julina. You have my word. If I am able, I will inform your empire of the danger. I feel obligated to inform the Klingons as well. We did pledge to ally ourselves during this period of mutual danger."

After a long glance between them, cementing what had just been expressed verbally, Spock took up his spear and they prepared to go into battle.

IIob and Scott achieved a relationship which was much closer to friendship than could be imagined between a prisoner and his captor. The Tomariian general in charge of the launch complex found a kindred spirit in the engineer.

Under other circumstances, Scott might have called him friend. Even so, their relationship was amicable and Scott's life was not entirely unpleasant.

For Scott, the main inconvenience, once he became accustomed to the discomfort of the Tomariian cold, was the lack of alcoholic beverages. Liquor, a plant product, was unknown. The enterprising Scotsman salvaged a number of metal parts from the launch complex and in record time had distilled a dandelionlike brew with a formidable kick. He made a flask for his concoction out of an animal bladder which he attached to his waist on a leather thong. Ilob thought his prisoner's diversion interesting, but not dangerous, and continued to permit Scott the opportunity to collect plants and run his still.

It wasn't long before the Tomariian, with his race's penchant for imitation, was sharing Scott's moonshine. Since he had become Scott's drinking companion, it was increasingly difficult for Ilob to think of Scott as his prisoner.

Scott had even assisted in the launch of the attack force before he was required to board the last craft. Unlike Spock, Scott was not only allowed in the control room but he helped in directing operations as well. Once again he marveled at the lack of advanced technology used in the takeoff but was impressed with the sophistication of the ship's mechanics once airborne.

He had independently come to the same conclusion as Spock: The technology was borrowed. It was clear that the Tomariians didn't completely understand the principles which ran their ships. He concluded they must have more knowledgeable support crews elsewhere, and he was in part correct. When the ships needed repair, the resourceful Tomariians would bring the true inventors of their machines to maintain them. It wasn't efficient, but that seemed not to concern them. As long as things worked, they weren't concerned with procedural detail.

Ilob, in addition to his duties as head of the launch complex, was assigned a battle mission. He was to capture the small planet of Paxas on the border of the quadrant nearest the Klingon domain. The planet was strategically important but held no other interest to the Tomariians. With the command ship *Illan,* named for the Tomariian sun, Ilob had a fleet of two other large ships. One Romulan captive was placed on each of the ships in Ilob's convoy with the Tomariians who had been responsible for his training.

They dropped to the surface of the planet in an isolated region and disembarked. Scott was handed a spear with a flag attached; in addition Ilob placed a belt around Scott containing a sheathed knife and a weapon resembling a phaser.

"Montgomery," the general boomed, "I like you. These weapons were not to be given to you, but I will give you a fighting chance. I do not wish you killed. We are very much alike, you and I."

"Aye," Scott acknowledged, "verra much. We dinna have ta be enemies, Ilob. The Federation would be willin' ta discuss a treaty wi' Tomarii."

"That may be true, Montgomery," the general conceded. "I understand that, but I know my people. There is no chance of a treaty. We are dedicated to conquer and fight. It is our way."

"Even though there may be another way?" The Scotsman leaned on the spear, not really expecting a reply from Ilob. But as a Starfleet officer, he was honor-bound to try to reach the Tomariian, in spite of the evident futility of bridging the gap in cultural values.

Scott observed the approach of the advance parties from the other ships. Each was preceded by a Romulan, dressed in skins as he was and carrying a spear with a battle flag attached. A brief last-minute war council was held and the troops were deployed.

The first surge of battle caught the people of Paxas by surprise. The small settlement directly in the path of the oncoming Tomariian force was completely devastated. To Scott, the enemy seemed unprepared for the attack. The residents of the planet seemed to be simple farmers with crude weapon potential. It was all too easy a victory for the violence-loving Tomariian warriors. With success easily in their grasp, Ilob's soldiers enjoyed the pillage immensely. The next day they planned to attack a major city on the continent on which they had landed. They caroused all night in Tomariian fashion, eating and gambling.

Carrying the battle flag put Scott in the forefront of the next day's battle. He was disgusted by the blood-lust displayed by the Tomariian soldiers. More unnerving still was the realization that the wounded Tomariians were not being treated, nor did they seem to have any medical personnel in their company. The badly wounded were dispatched much like their enemies, with hardly a second glance.

Suddenly, the tide of the battle turned. The Paxans advanced in great numbers with weapons much like phasers. The Tomariian force was stopped, then turned back in full retreat.

Scott dropped the spear he was carrying and prepared to defend himself with the phaserlike weapon at his belt. The two Romulans were behind him, preparing to do battle with their spears. Sub-Commander Placus was nearest Scott when the Paxan defense force caught up with the retreating invaders. The Tomariians dropped their useless spears and knives and began using the more sophisticated backup weapons.

Scott pushed Placus, who was inadequately armed, behind him. Both watched helplessly as Delus fell. Hob led the final surge to the gantry, leading his men back to the safety of the ship. Scott felt a stab of pain in his right shoulder just as he went through the hatch. He regained consciousness in the ship with a concerned Placus at his side.

"Wha' happened?" the dazed Scotsman asked, trying to rise.

"You were hit by one of the Paxan's darts."

"Wha' did they use? I feel groggy." He gave up trying to sit as a wave of nausea took hold.

Placus shook his head. "I can't see anything but a small wound in your shoulder. The dart is still embedded."

"Aye," Scott moaned, "an' makin' me feel like the mornin' after a binge. We've got ta get it out. Can ye manage it?"

The Romulan looked incredulous. "Surely the Tomariians have a physician who can remove the object."

"I doubt it," Scott replied. "Haven't ye noticed? They dinna treat their own wounded. Those who can, make it on their own. They permit the others ta die, or kill 'em . . ." Then he lost consciousness again.

The Romulan had never had to treat a fallen comrade. He stared down at the wounded human, the unfamiliar splotch of red on Scott's shoulder unnerving him. When Scott regained consciousness, he encouraged Placus to take the risk of removing the dart.

"Well, laddie, I'm in as much trouble if ye dinna get the

thing out as if ye do. It's makin' me feel verra odd. I dinna know how long I can keep alert enough ta assist ye."

Finally convinced of the necessity, Placus drew the knife he carried on his belt. "It seems our captors feel we can do them no harm. They permitted me to keep this knife."

"Aye, that restrainin' beam is verra effective, but . . ." Scott paused, his stomach churning. "Ye better get ta that dart, laddie."

"I have never had to do this before, Scott. Not even on a Romulan. I have no idea how a human may react. We have no antiseptic or anything to deaden the pain. I'm a good soldier, but I'm not a butcher."

"I've a remedy for both, Placus. In the canteen on ma belt. 'Tis a waste o' good liquor ta pour it on the outside, but it's necessary. Gi' me a swig o' it before ye use the rest. That's a good lad."

Placus took the flask from Scott's belt and lifted it to him; the Scotsman took a large swallow. The alcohol in combination with the dart's effect made him reel.

"All right, laddie, now the shoulder," Scott slurred bravely, bracing himself for the removal of the dart.

Placus cut into Scott's shoulder, wincing as he pierced the sensitive area. Scott caught his breath, trying to keep from moving. The Romulan probed the area, searching for the foreign object with no initial success. He gritted his teeth as he probed deeper; mercifully, Scott blacked out.

The small dart was embedded deep in the flesh below the shoulder blade. As Placus removed it, he noticed its peculiar crystalline structure. It seemed to have a life of its own, vibrating in his hand, giving him the same sensation Scott had experienced when it was embedded in his flesh. Placus wrapped the unusual crystal in a piece of cloth and tucked it into his belt. He then set about bandaging the gaping wound caused by his unskillful incision, using a piece of hide he had cut from his garment and soaked in alcohol.

It was hours before Scott regained consciousness. He smiled wearily at the Romulan, who had not moved from his side, and whispered a simple thanks. Placus, satisfied that Scott would recover, lay down beside the now-sleeping Scotsman to share his warmth in the cold of the Tomariian ship.

4

Spock and Julina were quickly drawn into the fight between the Tomariians. The conflict was, by far, the bloodiest Spock had ever witnessed. The Tomariians felt no need for backup devices between evenly matched forces. Their lust for blood manifested itself vividly as they hacked away at each other, much too gleefully for Spock's taste.

Carrying IIsa's battle flag put him in the forefront of the fray, and he found himself, in mere self-defense, attacking the enemy force with as much savagery as his captors. Occasionally he caught a glimpse of Julina, wielding her spear and knife as expertly as anyone on the field. She remained within his sight, sometimes close enough to touch.

Julina had purposely placed herself near Spock. She was acting as a buffer for him, subtly protecting him as much as possible. She marveled at how well he was performing, knowing how excruciating the pain in his back was. She mowed her way through two Tomariians bent on killing the strange warrior, and arrived just in time to catch Spock as he fell, doubled over with pain.

"Are you hurt?" Julina murmured.

"No, it's my back. It just gave out—I'll be on my feet quickly."

"Stay down, Spock. You can't keep up this pace. It'll kill you."

"So will the Tomariians if I don't." He raised his hand to her and she helped him to his feet.

IIsa shouted over her shoulder to Spock. "Are you injured?"

"No," Spock called back. "I am all right." Unsteadily, he had just regained his balance when another Tomariian charged. He took the brunt of the blow in his midsection, he went down again, this time losing consciousness.

He awoke in the confines of IIsa's ship. Julina was lying beside him, asleep.

Why did they rescue me? The Tomariians destroy their wounded. What further use can IIsa have for me?

Julina awoke with a start when she sensed Spock's movement beside her. "Are you all right?" she asked, passing him a cup of water. "I could find no wounds."

"I seem to be in one piece," he reassured her, "except for my old injury. How did I get here?"

"IIsa ordered you carried to the ship. Her comrades wanted to leave you with the other wounded, but she wouldn't give in. You've been unconscious for a long time. I think there is a guard outside the door just waiting to finish you off."

"I wonder what IIsa's motive was in preserving my life?"

"You must be blind, Spock. She's obviously in love with you."

"Don't be absurd, Julina. She's of an entirely different species. It wouldn't be possible . . . it's not logical . . ."

Julina laughed. "Since when did logic have anything to do with our situation? I'd say that's the last thing a Tomariian could be accused of."

"Indeed," Spock said seriously, "but if you are correct, we are in grave difficulty. There is no way I can return any interest in her."

"And," Julina added, "she is jealous of me."

"Is that so?" Spock raised an eyebrow. "I hadn't noticed."

"You wouldn't," Julina replied matter-of-factly.

The door to their chamber opened and IIsa came toward Spock. She examined him from head to foot with clinical thoroughness; finding no obvious wound, she looked relieved. Spock, trying to maintain some dignity throughout the examination, retreated far into himself until she had completed her probing. Satisfied that Spock was not seriously injured, IIsa swept past Julina, giving her a warning glare, and then she left them without saying a word. Shortly after her departure, a guard entered and moved Julina to another part of the ship.

She was correct, Spock thought. *We will have to be very careful from now on.*

Back on Tomarii, the returning armies went to their different camps while the officers of the three attack groups met in council. The large audience chamber was full of strutting warriors talking in loud voices, boasting of their exploits in the recent battles. The brief Tomariian cycle of severe cold had ended; the dull, red sun was closer, making the planet's temperature at least tolerable for the returned captives. Spock speculated on the change in the weather, trying to calculate the orbit of the planet around its sun. It was good mental exercise, keeping his mind off his discomfort and IIsa's more pronounced advances toward him. He hadn't conferred with Julina since his return to Tomarii.

On a view-screen set into the stone wall of the large room was a projected image of the Tomariian Empire. Spock and Julina, never far from IIsa, were in the rear of the room studying the chart intently.

"If what we see indicated on the map is true, and I have no reason to doubt it, the Tomariians' sphere of influence is spread over extensive territory," Spock observed to Julina. "It is more than one-eighth of the known galaxy."

"The Klingon Empire is closest to that of the Tomariians," Julina said. "It would be interesting to observe the conflict when they overlap."

"From what I have observed, that will merely be a matter of time," Spock commented.

IIob reported his defeat in great detail, promising a much better showing in the next invasion attempt. The other generals, smug with their victories, gave lavish accounts of their exploits. After the formal reports, IIsa ordered silence.

"It is time for us to discuss our prisoners' performance."

Spock's attention became sharply focused, but he and Julina were hustled out of the room before the discussion got started. Spock had difficulty hearing the reports from the adjoining room, where they were put, in spite of his highly developed auditory sense.

IIob spoke first. "Montgomery is a fine engineer and an adequate soldier. I found no complaint with him. He was brave in battle. The Romulans also proved good soldiers. Unfortunately, one of them was killed by the Paxans. Scott and Placus behaved strangely. The human placed himself before the Romulan in an attempt to protect him. When the human took a Paxan dart, the Romulan removed it, saving his life. I have never witnessed this kind of behavior before."

The room buzzed with comment. Tomariian custom had

been seriously breached. Ilob then interjected, "They knew no better; perhaps it is customary with them and they were ignorant of our ways."

"Are you defending the prisoners, Ilob?" Ilsa asked in disbelief.

"No, no," Ilob stammered. "I was just making an observation."

"The Klingons, how did they perform?" Ilsa asked.

"Magnificently,Begum. They are much like us in many ways. They will prove worthy adversaries," a general boomed.

"They are closest to us," Ilsa considered. "It would be convenient to deal with them first. It is a challenge we want," she proclaimed. "We will begin with the Klingons." A roar of approval greeted her announcement.

The decision made, attention turned to the disposition of the prisoners.

"We have no use for them any longer, Begum. They have served their purpose. I say kill them now and go on to planning the invasion."

"Kill them!" came the unanimous chant. "Kill them now!"

"No!" Ilsa shouted. "Not yet. There may yet be a use for them. I will determine the time."

A hush of surprise followed her decree. "Keep them under guard," she ordered.

She swept out of the council chamber, trying not to show her emotional turmoil at the prospect of Spock's death.

Together for the first time since their capture, the prisoners found little comfort in each other. The Klingons were determined to escape at any cost in order to report to their Empire the danger they had discovered. Placus and Julina compared notes of their experiences and the implications for the Romulan Empire, and Spock and Scott shared conclusions on the technological inconsistencies of the Tomariian culture. If not for Spock's logical presentation of the facts, it would have been chaotic.

"We are in no better a position than we were when we first decided to cooperate. I suggest we try to formulate a plan of escape. It can't be long before we will have served our purpose and the Tomariians decide to eliminate us. Let us pool our knowledge before we are rendered completely helpless, or separated again. Scott, what have you discovered that can be of help?"

"The most important thing, I think, is their constant readiness for launch. If we can get ta the gantry, we have a verra good chance o' blastin' off."

Julina, less hopeful, questioned him. "But how do we get through their holding beam? I haven't seen a way to neutralize it."

"The beam has a limited range," Klee interjected.

Spock turned to the Klingon. "How did you come to that conclusion, Commander Klee?"

"Melek tested it. At three hundred meters the beam loses its effect."

"That's quite a distance," Scott exclaimed.

"Yes," Spock agreed, "but not impossible to achieve as long as we know the limits."

"Their armory isn't well guarded," Placus added. "If we could distract the guard at the proper time, we could steal some of their phasers. It seems they don't consider us too great a threat."

"Don't underestimate them, Placus," Spock warned. "We must be careful. We must be resigned to catching them off guard."

"No Klingon would behave so!" Klee proclaimed scornfully.

"Then make an exception in this case, Commander Klee. We all have the same goal—escape," Spock explained.

Growling, the Klingon agreed.

"I dislike rushing the attempt, but I don't think the Tomariians will give us much more time. Our elimination is imminent," Spock said grimly. "We must maneuver ourselves close enough to the launch site to take advantage of their contempt. Scott has told me only a light guard is kept at the gantry between flights. If we make it that far, some of us will be able to escape."

"Placus," Julina ordered. "If I fail in this attempt, keep going. One of us must return to warn the Empire of the danger." The Romulan sub-commander grudgingly acknowledged the order.

The next day dawned with the dull red sun of Tomarii; it was beginning to get colder again. Spock had been computing the orbit of the planet, trying to understand the erratic seasonal changes, but he had not determined the full details— his sketchy computations would have to suffice. They were critical in computing the trajectory of their ship's escape path. He briefed Scott, who in turn told Placus. All information was shared in the event that not all would make it to the rocket in escape.

Under guard, the prisoners were allowed to exercise outside of the compound. Ilsa's infatuation with Spock was crucial. In order to preserve his life, she had to permit the others to live; so as not to appear she was favoring Spock, she allowed the others the same privileges. Her weakness would provide the conditions they needed today.

The Tomariian guards, perceiving no threat, allowed their charges to walk toward the launch site. The guards were dispatched quietly and efficiently, as soon as they were out of sight of the compound. The captives inched toward the gantry with the Klingons in the lead. Placus followed close behind them with Julina; Scott came next, followed by the limping Spock.

The elevator to the top of the gantry was deactivated. Klee took the lead, climbing the vertical ladder, with Melek, Placus, and Julina following closely. Scott was far ahead of Spock when the Vulcan reached for the first rung and began to pull himself painfully up. He got halfway up when an excruciating pain ripped through his back and he felt his legs go numb. Holding fast to the ladder, Spock attempted to pull himself up with his arms, but it was useless. He fell to the ground with a thud, losing consciousness.

Scott turned just in time to see Spock fall. He reversed his direction, climbing down the ladder to assist his friend. He reached Spock as the Vulcan regained consciousness.

"Go back," Spock insisted. "I cannot move. Save yourself . . ." With an ironic half-smile, he added, "It's an unfortunate time for Doctor McCoy to be proven correct. Now go. That's an order!"

Julina looked to the ground at the motionless Spock and climbed back down the ladder.

"Come, try to lift him. We can carry him up," Scott shouted as she approached. They raised the helpless Vulcan, and, half carrying, half dragging his limp form, Scott and Julina tried to pull him up the ladder to the ship. But without warning the invisible vise gripped them all. They dropped Spock as they fell helplessly to the ground.

During the aborted rescue of Spock, the others had had a chance to get to the ship on top of the gantry. The hatch locked, and Klee, highest ranking of the escapees, gave the command to blast off in spite of the heated objections of Placus.

The Tomariian guards released their prisoners from the restraining force and directed them to drag Spock along. They retreated quickly from the launch area to escape the blast effect. The rocket fired and rose in a lurching lift-off.

"They will bring help," Julina assured Scott.

"Aye, Placus will do everythin' he can ta get back ta us, but I dinna trust the Klingons."

They were put into a barren cell and left alone. Julina hovered over Spock. Scott had lain him on a stone bench to the rear of the cell; it was hard and cold, but it was better than the floor. When Spock opened his eyes, Scott came over to him.

"You should have left me," Spock said grimly.

"Too late for us to look back now. We're here and will have ta make the best o' it. Julina's sure her man will come back to rescue her, and us, too." Scott spoke with a conviction he didn't feel.

The cell door opened. Ilsa, in a rage, stood in the doorway. Julina and Scott were roughly pushed out of the cell, leaving Spock alone with the angry Begum.

"You were their leader, Spock. You will regret planning that escape. Get up!" She gripped his arm tightly, trying to wrench him off the bench. "Get up, I said!" she demanded, kicking him hard in the back.

Unprepared for the blow to his injured spine, Spock cried out in agony. He fainted into welcome oblivion.

Scott, hearing Spock's cry, turned to help his friend. He fought to free himself from the guards, but it was hopeless. He and Julina were pushed into the courtyard to await their fate.

The guards lifted Spock back onto the bench. Ilsa pointed to the water bowl on the floor. One of the guards picked it up, splashing the ice-cold water over Spock. He came to abruptly.

"Now you will obey me, Spock. Get up!" Ilsa again demanded.

"I am unable to comply, Begum," Spock replied weakly. "The injury I sustained when the *Enterprise* was bombed has paralyzed me. I am unable to move from mid-back down."

"You showed no indication of weakness before. I do not trust you, Spock," she snapped. "Get him to his feet!"

The guards lifted Spock, supporting him.

"Let go. I believe he is lying."

They released him and he dropped heavily to the floor. She had the guards place him back on the stone bench. Ilsa watched Spock's fingers clutch the edge of the stone shelf in an effort not to show his pain.

A bowl of meat was placed just within Spock's reach—the water bowl was filled and placed just beyond it. Enraged by Spock's role in the escape, and at her inability to elicit the desired response from the object of her interest, Ilsa was set on revenge.

"You will have to get the water yourself, or beg for it." She smiled, leaving the door open behind her. "I shall leave it open," she teased. "You will not escape."

Spock was left alone. He looked about the gray colorless cell. A dim light in the corridor was the only illumination. *This room could become my tomb,* he realized. He made a tentative attempt to reach the water. It was indeed just out of his reach. Giving up, he tried to relax. It was hopeless to resist his captors any longer; logic dictated another course. He closed his eyes and tried, unsuccessfully, to sleep.

There was no sign of a guard. Spock, suffering with thirst, tried again to reach the water. He stretched his arm, straining at the last bit of space with his outstretched fingers. The pain was gone, replaced by complete numbness. His lips were dry and parched. The combination of the cold, pain, and thirst had weakened him greatly. He drew his arm back with the realization that he could possibly die of thirst before his injury would kill him. He chose to face death rather than beg, and he finally fell into a fitful sleep.

Spock awoke to the sound of footsteps approaching his cell. He strained to see in the darkness, aware of his total vulnerability. Slipping quietly around the door was Julina. She ran toward him, triumphant in her success at reaching him until she saw how weak he had become. She got the bowl of water and, cradling his head in her lap, moistened his lips with the cool liquid. She gave him a small sip, and then a little more. He rested his head in her lap, grateful for her arrival.

"I can't stay long. I slipped away from the guards." She saw the still-full bowl of meat, which was beginning to go rancid. "You haven't eaten anything since we were caught, have you?"

He shook his head.

"I will try to find something you can eat before I return."

"How is Mister Scott?" he asked, wanting to turn the conversation away from himself.

"I haven't seen him since we were separated. I imagine he's having a difficult time as well."

"How did you manage to get away from the guards?"

"It was relatively simple. They have set patterns. All I had to do was wait until they were at their lowest manpower and take advantage of the situation. But I must leave before I am missed. I'm sure I'll be able to get away again. Ilsa is keeping me and Scott alive to cover her interest in you. I will leave the water where you can reach it." She touched his face gently, hinting at the bond which had been established between them.

Shortly after she left, a guard came into the cell and moved the bowl of water beyond his reach again.

At every opportunity, Julina searched for Scott. She was allowed brief periods of exercise, which she took in the vicinity of the hills outside the compound. The guards thought her preoccupation with plants strange, but harmless, and permitted her to collect the sparse dandelionlike growth as she wished. She stored the pathetic plants, planning to give them to Spock at the earliest opportunity. A full day passed before she got away again.

She found him much weaker than before: He was barely conscious. Gently reviving him, she forced the wilted greens into Spock to give him strength.

"You must try to hold on, Spock. Placus will return with a rescue group. Please try. You must live. Tell me you will try."

"I will," he promised faintly, watching her leave.

5

Scott's engineering skills made him valuable. He was assigned to the launch complex under IIob's supervision, but under closer guard. He was waiting for the opportunity to slip by the guards to find Julina and Spock. During his exercise period, he worked his way closer and closer to the compound, until he got a glimpse of Julina collecting plants. He made a dash for her, pursued by his guards.

"Have ye seen Spock?" he asked, as they dragged him away.

"Yes," she shouted. "He needs help very soon or we will lose him."

"Try ta meet me here again!" he shouted.

She was determined to try. Once more, Julina slipped to Spock's side—it even seemed easier for her to get away this time. *The guards are getting lax,* she hoped. She was finding a way to get to Spock regularly, providing him with food and water. Even so, he was barely getting enough to survive, and was getting progressively weaker. It was only because of her persistent care that he was still alive at all. He asked about Scott. She vowed to meet with the engineer before her next visit.

The next day she foraged further, reaching the edge of the launch site. Scott spotted her and took his exercise toward the field where she was collecting her plants. He worked his way toward her casually and this time got close enough to speak to her. Their apparent placid behavior fooled the guards, so they were permitted to converse uninterrupted.

"How is Spock?" was Scott's greeting.

"He's very weak. Help must come soon. He wants us to try to escape without him. If we choose to do so, he will surely die."

". . . And if we don't, we all may," Scott said grimly. "But I willna leave without him. Would you?"

"No," Julina said firmly. Scott saw how deeply she had come to care for Spock.

"Julina," he tried to reassure her, "Placus will return soon."

"He will—if he is able."

"The Klingons won't. I don't think a rescue party would ha' come for them even if they could be found."

"True, Scott. Klee told me as much. Our Empire considered our mission a minor one as well. No one will be sent to rescue us either. If Placus does not return, we have no hope of rescue. What about the Federation?"

"Our mission was . . ." He paused. "Ye might say it was, ah, unofficial. No one knows where we are."

"Oh . . ." Julina was about to say something else when the guards, having permitted their charges as much time as they thought sufficient, prodded Scott to return to work. Julina, with an armful of wilted greens and flowers, walked back to the compound.

Spock felt himself getting weaker. He knew his Vulcan strength would keep him alive for a long period of time after he lost consciousness and that he could remain comatose for days before he finally died. He awaited Julina's next visit with a firm resolve to make a vital request of her.

When she returned, Julina found Spock sleeping. She took his hand, which seemed very thin, in hers, and sat quietly beside him as he slept. She studied his gaunt features and wondered if Spock would survive. Suddenly, Spock's hand tightened on hers with surprising strength. She raised the water bowl to his lips as she always did, but this time he refused to drink.

His voice was hoarse and he spoke with effort. "We must talk, Julina."

Gently, she brought the water to his lips. "First you eat and drink—then we talk."

"No, Julina. I must speak now." He tightened his grasp on her hand. "Would you escape now if you could?"

"Yes, but I would not leave you here, helpless."

"If I were able to leave, would you consider escape?"

"I would. But you are helpless. Without my visits you would die. I won't leave you!"

"And Scott—he feels as you do?"

"Yes."

"I thought so," Spock said firmly. "Julina, you must do something for me. I have considered this very carefully. What I ask will not be easy for you, but it is the logical and necessary thing to do."

"What would you have me do? I will not attempt to escape without you."

"It does not concern an escape attempt."

"I will help you in any way. You know that."

"Then bring me a way of ending my life. A weapon, poison, whatever you can obtain for that purpose."

"No!" She tried to draw her hand from his. "I will not help you destroy yourself!"

"You must. I will explain my reasoning. Your Romulan teaching has equipped you to understand the necessity of my request. I am completely helpless, a deterrent to both your and Scott's survival. As long as I live, you will not try to escape. Therefore, the deterring factor must be eliminated. I am that factor. In my position, you, also, would choose death with dignity. I am slowly dying. Soon I will be unable to destroy myself. Each time you come you find me weaker. I believe you are permitted to come here to help prolong my suffering so that IIsa will obtain more perverse satisfaction from my situation. You would release your Romulan companions from such a fate. Would you condemn me to a lingering death to entertain an enemy—or will you permit me to die quickly, with dignity?"

She broke down. "You are right. I would choose a quick death rather than allow an enemy to enjoy my suffering. I can do no less for you. I will bring you what you wish." She calmed.

"Thank you," Spock said, releasing her hand.

Julina returned with a small dagger IIsa customarily wore on her arm for ceremonies. It was more decorative than useful. The blade was very short, which made it easy for Julina to secrete the dagger and bring it to Spock. It wouldn't be missed until the next day, if IIsa chose to wear it.

The Vulcan examined the jeweled dagger dispassionately. It was beautiful, made by a fine craftsman on an unknown planet far away. Spock made silent tribute to the artisan who created such an object of beauty for his purpose. Then he spoke to Julina, who sat beside him on the stone pallet, studying him.

"I had no intention of asking you to assist me, but I feel I am too weak to use the knife effectively. I will guide the dagger; you must help provide the thrust."

"I won't! I can't!" she protested fiercely, but she knew his Vulcan logic would prove his request an undeniable one.

"Julina, don't make me beg for your help. . . ." He gripped her hand tightly.

"No, Spock, don't say any more. You're right. I will do whatever you say."

He guided her hand, placing the dagger above his heart. "Now," he commanded her. She added thrust to his, plunging the knife fiercely into his side.

She drew back, releasing the knife, and Spock's hand slid limply from beneath hers. She ran her fingertips over his features, lingering a moment over his mouth, and whispered, "I love you," into his deaf ear. She quietly left.

The guard, who was under orders to check Spock after each of Julina's visits, casually entered the cell. A pool of green had already formed on the gray stone floor. At the sight of the blood, the guard rushed to Spock's side, finding the dagger protruding from him. He sounded the alarm and the other guards responded efficiently. They apprehended Julina immediately.

The commotion could be heard all the way to the launch site. Hob and Scott ran to the compound with the others to see what had happened. Scott could see Julina held by two strong guards. Ilsa, carrying a spear, came toward her. He raced toward Julina, watching in horror as Ilsa raised the spear and plunged it into the Romulan woman, killing her instantly.

"What's happened?" Scott shouted. "Why did you kill her?" He ran toward the body of the beautiful Romulan he had come to trust and admire, cradling her limp form in his arms, ignoring the streams of blood seeping from her wound.

"Why?" was all he could ask, looking up at Ilsa, who stood looking down at him and her victim.

Ilsa turned to the guard. "Is the Vulcan dead? If he is, you will pay. You were ordered to watch the woman when she visited him."

"I don't know, Begum," he said fearfully. "I didn't have the time to check carefully."

"Bring him along," she ordered the guard, gesturing to Scott. He pushed Scott ahead of him into Spock's cell.

Scott was stunned at the sight of Spock's seemingly lifeless form lying with the jeweled knife still embedded in his side. He tried to find a trace of life. He couldn't find a heartbeat or pulse, but that wasn't unusual with Vulcans. Ilsa had a brightly polished buckle on her belt; Scott ripped it from her before he could be stopped.

"I need it to see if he's still alive," he explained.

"Go to him," Ilsa said quietly.

With evidence of the Vulcan's faint breathing on the mirrored surface, Scott kneeled beside Spock, examining the wound in the Vulcan's side. The seepage of blood was an ominous sign. Scott could hardly understand how Spock could have survived this long in his weakened condition. *Why did Julina try ta kill him? It doesn't make sense. What could have possessed her?* The thoughts poured through his head while he tried to think of what to do next.

"Can you save him?" Ilsa asked worriedly.

"You're the one responsible for his condition," he retorted. "But I'll do ma best. I'm nae physician—I may kill him. He's Vulcan, and even for a human I'm nae equipped ta handle this. First we've got ta get him out o' this hole into a clean, warm place. I dinna think we can move him with that knife still in him. I'm goin' ta remove it an' try ta keep him from bleedin' ta death before I do anythin' else. Then we can move him."

"Do as he says," Ilsa ordered the guards.

Scott clenched his jaw and reached for the knife, pulling it out. A stream of fresh blood welled out of the wound. He quickly placed a piece of hide cut from Spock's garment onto the wound and applied pressure.

"Now, carry him carefully while I keep pressure on this," Scott ordered.

The guards obeyed him, gently lifting the limp form of the Vulcan and carrying him into the Begum's quarters.

"He must be kept warm," Scott directed, and a fire was started. "Blankets, I'll need lots o' blankets," the Scotsman demanded. A thick pile of furs was brought to his side.

He covered Spock with the hides, fur side toward him for

extra warmth. Spock was in deep shock. Scott shook his head hopelessly.

"I dinna know if I can really help him," he said sadly. He withdrew his hand from the wound, causing a river of green to flow onto the shining furs.

"I think it missed his heart an' hit a rib—maybe pierced a lung—I canna tell."

With a rough bone needle and gut soaked in his ever-present pouch of home brew, Scott sewed the layers of flesh as best he could. When he had finished, he sank back, exhausted and drained.

"It's out of ma hands now," he muttered. He rested his head on his arms, prepared for a long night's vigil. Throughout the entire operation, Ilsa stood behind Scott, fascinated by what he was doing; she had never witnessed an attempt to save a wounded man before.

Reason for her actions would be hard to justify to her subjects. It wasn't a rational decision; it was purely an emotional one. Even she couldn't completely understand her attraction to this alien captive. She placed herself on a couch covered with rich furs and waited with Scott.

The engineer wrapped himself in a fur robe and sank down on the floor beside Spock. He dozed occasionally in the quiet and warmth of the room. It seemed forever since he had been comfortable.

A small movement of Spock's hand brought him to attention. Spock was beginning to regain consciousness. His eyelids fluttered, then he opened his eyes. He looked up at a broadly smiling Scott. Then he closed his eyes and slept.

In the following days, broth was forced into Spock, who was too weak to resist. Ilsa supervised his care personally, making sure he was regularly fed and kept warm. When it was apparent he would live, Spock yielded to the inevitable and stopped fighting his recovery. But he was completely silent and withdrawn.

Scott was alarmed. He tried to find a way to interest Spock in life again. He stayed up all night carving a crude chess set from bone, but Spock failed to respond. He had to find a way to bring the detached and remote Vulcan back to full alertness. Removing a small piece of hide from his belt, Scott took out the crystalline dart from Paxas, placing it into Spock's unresisting hand. The odd sensation emanating from the crystal resonated through the Vulcan's arm. As the strange sensation grew, so did his interest.

"Where did you get this?" were the first words he spoke since his suicide attempt. He now had a mental challenge, and the scientist in him was functioning again.

"Ye sure had me worried, Mister Spock. I'm glad ta see ye more like yeself. Are ye in pain?" Spock was lying completely flat, just as he had been placed.

"No, Scott. There is no more pain. I have no sensation from the area of the wound down. Help me to sit. This crystal is *fascinating*."

Chapter III

The Enterprise

1

"Captain Kirk to Transporter Room. One to beam up."

James T. Kirk said the familiar words with deep satisfaction. Finally, after the prolonged forced rest, he was returning to his true home. It was a day earlier than his orders indicated—a day to reacquaint himself with the repaired and rebuilt *Enterprise*, a day to get the feel of the ship and to relish being back before his duties absorbed his attention.

"I'm sorry, sir. My orders are to beam up all personnel only when their orders indicate. You're a day early," came the reply from the ship.

"This is the captain. The commanding officer. One to beam up."

"Sorry, sir. It's against my orders," the unfamiliar voice repeated.

"Transporter Room, this is an order! I will take full responsibility. Beam me up immediately!" His pleasant feeling gave way to exasperation.

"Yes, sir, if you insist." The transporter was engaged.

Kirk was fuming when he stepped out of the transporter. "Lieutenant, when I give an order, you obey it. Do you understand me?"

"Yes, sir. But I . . ."

"No buts, Lieutenant. You are relieved. Report to your superior—and brush up on protocol. . . ."

Now, why was I so hard on him? Kirk asked himself as he strode from the room. *He was only following previous orders. Why did I jump so hard on him? Something's wrong. I can feel it. But that's irrational,* he assured himself, *first-day-back jitters.*

In his quarters he checked the safe, tucking his new orders into their proper spot. He hadn't received his new uniforms yet. The accident, the long recovery process, and the forced rest had given him time to exercise and get back into top shape and he had lost weight. His old uniforms hung on him so he had ordered new ones, which would arrive tomorrow. No crew was on board yet so he decided his regulation uniform wasn't necessary. He put on a T-shirt and pants, eased into a well-worn pair of boots which felt like old friends, and hustled out of his quarters.

He stepped into the turbolift. "Bridge." The familiar word sounded good.

The bridge was empty. The temporary skeleton crew was controlling the ship from the auxiliary bridge. He was glad to be alone in the nerve center of the ship—he knew it would be impossible after today. But this was *his* day, a day to enjoy *his* ship. He toured the upper level of the bridge, running his hand over the newly replaced instruments. Peering into the sensor, he flipped a lever and watched the instrument register the life forms on the station below. The engineering console screen was showing an energy-flow diagram. He stepped down into the lower section and checked the navigation station. He swiveled the chair in the helmsman's position and watched it spin with ease.

Smiling, he sat down in the familiar command position. The chair cushion gave way to his weight. It was more fully padded, feeling subtly different. A twinge of anxiety went through him. It *felt* different, this *Enterprise*. He had studied the design modifications: All of the plans and specifications were firmly embedded in his mind. They were planning even more drastic changes in the future. It made him feel vaguely uncomfortable.

He stretched his feet in front of him, trying to relax. Automatically reaching for the switch to record his log, his finger missed the button: different. He readjusted, and flipped the switch.

"Captain's log, Stardate 6205.7, James T. Kirk, Captain. I have returned to my ship."

But it was different!

He threw the switch to engage the darkened view-screen. A view of Starbase 12 flashed on. Kirk swiveled his chair and glanced at the communications and science stations. The instrument panels were now gray. He rose from his chair, heading for the turbolift, but stopped short at the doors; they were no longer red—gray had replaced the familiar color. He felt somewhat unnerved.

Back in his quarters again, he stripped off the T-shirt and lay back on the bed. He switched on the library console, selected the specifications for the bridge, and studied the changes, trying to reconcile himself to the differences. He never thought of himself as rigid. In fact, it was necessary for a starship captain to be open to new situations and flexible in his approach to rapid, unexpected change. Kirk was annoyed with himself. *Why am I so ill at ease? A new paint job shouldn't make me jittery. Something's wrong— I can feel it.* He stripped, programmed the computer to awaken him early, began reading, and fell into a restless sleep.

"O-six-hundred, Captain James T. Kirk, wake-up call," the computer's voice droned over and over again.

"I hear you!" Kirk grumbled at the machine. Then he paused, frowning. "Computer, what time is it?"

"O-six-hundred hours and thirty seconds," the computer answered immediately in a pleasant male voice.

Kirk shook the cobwebs out of his head. *I'll be damned! They even changed the voice on the computer! Wonder what Spock will think of that?* The thought of his first officer and friend reassured Kirk and caused him to smile. He was anticipating the reunion with all of his officers, but particularly Spock. If nothing else, Spock's presence would render all the disturbing changes insignificant.

The buzzer sounded. "Sir, Yeoman Helman with your uniforms."

"Just a minute, Yeoman." He slipped on a robe and pressed the door release. The new yeoman entered tentatively. "Come on in. I won't bite you."

"Yes, sir," she responded, unconvinced. "This is my first assignment, sir."

"Imagine that!" he said, amused by her bewilderment. "Don't you think you should hang those things up, Yeoman, ah . . . ?"

"Helman, sir. Yes, sir . . ."

The new uniform was gray; the new issue had occurred while he was recovering. He frowned, put it on, and looked in the mirror. It was surprisingly flattering. "Not bad!" he commented, "another new thing to get used to."

Now officially uniformed, the captain of the *Enterprise* walked through the corridor to the turbolift. He was tempted to go to the transporter room to greet his returning officers but resisted the urge, deciding instead to monitor the crew's return from the bridge. "There'll be lots of time to catch up," he told himself. He hadn't seen most of his officers at all during his recovery and rest period. He assumed that, like him, they had decided to make the interval after the explosion as completely restorative as possible, trying to avoid episodes of needless rehashing of the ghastly experience they had all suffered.

Entering the bridge, he was greeted by a rush of perfume and an uninhibited hug from Uhura. She had decided to forgo all military decorum for now. Kirk, as happy as she was to see a familiar face, returned her embrace with gusto, much to the surprise of the helmsman who was new on board and had never encountered a captain who greeted his officers so effusively.

The captain took his seat, enjoying the feel of being back in action again. Next to enter was Sulu, who tapped the helmsman on the shoulder. "I relieve you, Lieutenant." He turned to Kirk. "It's great to be back on board, sir."

Kirk smiled broadly.

Chekov arrived next. He was sporting a new stripe on his uniform. "*Lieutenant* Chekov, reporting for duty, sir."

"Congratulations on the stripe, Lieutenant." Kirk shook his hand. "And Chekov, it's good to have you back on board."

Chekov and Sulu greeted each other warmly. It was beginning to feel like his ship again. Kirk eased back into his chair. He listened to the sounds of the mechanisms: each beep and buzz, each light that blinked, welcomed him back. *It's good to be alive—and to be back.*

"Transporter Room, sir. All personnel aboard."

"Acknowledged," Kirk answered routinely.

At the science console an unfamiliar man leaned over the instruments. Kirk noted Spock's absence. *He must be checking the computers.*

The voice from the transporter room had not been Scott's. *Must be in engineering, somewhere,* the captain supposed.

Kirk pressed the intercom button. "Mister Scott, we warp out in ten minutes." A long silence followed. "Mister Scott, do you hear me? Acknowledge, please."

"Lieutenant Commander Douglas, sir, Engineering. There is no one down here by that name, sir."

"Who's in charge down there?"

"I am, sir."

"Come up to the bridge, Douglas."

"Now, sir?"

"I didn't mean tomorrow. Get up here on the double!"

Sulu and Chekov glanced furtively over their shoulders at Kirk. Uhura turned to watch him, caught his eye, and quickly turned away. When he looked back, he caught Sulu staring at him.

"Mister Sulu, is there something I should know?"

Sulu squirmed uncomfortably and turned back to the helm; he punched the console buttons rapidly, attempting to look too absorbed to respond right away.

Kirk turned his chair and looked to the science station, now unmanned. He pushed the intercom button again.

"Mister Spock, report to the bridge immediately."

Uhura, in direct sight of the captain, tried to look inconspicuous.

Pushing the button again, Kirk spoke. "McCoy, report to the bridge."

"Yes, sir," came the quick reply from the chief surgeon. "On my way, Jim."

At last! A familiar voice.

The small, dark man entering the bridge smiled engagingly. "Commander Leonidas, reporting for duty, sir." His tousled hair gave him an air of rakish abandon.

Kirk swiveled his chair to get a look at the unfamiliar

officer. "I'm at a disadvantage, Commander. What is your position?"

"First officer, sir."

"First officer? I thought I already had a first officer—Spock. Where's Spock?"

Sulu turned, furtively glanced at Kirk, and looked back to his instruments.

"Lieutenant Commander Douglas, sir," the engineering officer reported smartly when he entered the bridge.

"You say you were assigned as chief engineer?" Kirk asked, obviously puzzled.

"Yes, sir."

"I need a computer readout. Where's Spock?" the captain demanded again.

A tall, large-boned blond entered the bridge. "Lieutenant Commander Martin, sir. Reporting for duty."

"What is *your* assignment?" a baffled Kirk asked the newcomer.

"Science officer, sir."

Kirk caught Sulu staring at him again. "Mister Sulu, do you know what's going on here? Why am I the last to know what's going on on *my* ship?" He turned to the science officer. "I want a readout of the duty roster. Right now!"

Martin stepped up to the computer terminal and pushed the appropriate buttons. Sitting tensely, Kirk waited. The others stood rigidly, not knowing what to expect from the evidently angered captain.

McCoy entered the bridge and immediately felt the tension. *Oh, boy! He's found out about Spock and Scott. All hell's gonna break loose! I should've told him before he got back onto the ship.*

"Bones!" Kirk just about shouted as he got up to greet his chief medical officer. "At least you're on board!"

Martin handed the duty roster to Kirk. He studied it, and looked up at his unfamiliar senior officers.

"We will meet in the briefing room in a half hour," he ordered in a low voice.

McCoy started to leave.

"You stay here, Bones!" Scowling, Kirk snapped at McCoy. "What's going on? You knew that Scotty and Spock weren't on board, didn't you?"

Sulu, Chekov, and Uhura stiffened as if ready for a blow.

"Not here, Jim. Let's go somewhere private."

"I won't be put off, Bones. Ship's business can be conducted on the bridge. Now, answer me!"

"Not here, Jim." McCoy walked to the turbolift with a reluctant Kirk following him.

They entered the doctor's office in sick bay and McCoy reached for his bottle of brandy. He handed Kirk a glass and took a large gulp of his own. The captain put his glass down untouched.

"I'm waiting, Bones."

"Jim, it was in your best interest."

"What was in my best interest?"

"Not telling you."

"Not telling me what? Stop beating around the bush, McCoy. Just tell me what's going on. I didn't even get a duty roster before I came on board. I assumed I would have my entire crew back intact. You know why my two best officers are not on board. Stop delaying and tell me why!"

McCoy handed two computer tapes to Kirk, who turned them nervously in his hand. "This is your answer? Record tapes?"

"It's the official explanation, Jim."

"Explanation? Explanation of what?"

"You were too badly injured to be informed, Jim. It was my medical judgment to keep you in the dark. If you had gotten wind of the situation, you would have taken off, no matter how sick you were. There was nothing you could do, then or now."

Kirk inserted a tape into the playback.

Stardate 6101.1: Preliminary hearing, court-martial proceedings, Commander Spock and Lieutenant Commander Montgomery Scott. Charges: Desertion—theft of a Starfleet vehicle. Present location of defendants unknown. Case pending.

The second tape was a transcript of the hearing.

"Is this it?" Kirk took the tape out of the computer terminal and placed it on the table. He sat, waiting for McCoy to explain further. "Well, Bones?"

"What can I tell you, Jim? They disappeared. Not a clue as to where. No one really looked."

"Are you telling me no one has the slightest idea of where they went?"

McCoy shook his head. "Jim, if there was anything I could have done—they just took off and vanished. I suppose they headed for that series of dots Spock thought was so important. He was clearly dissatisfied with Starfleet's response—or lack of one—regarding what he believed to be sufficient evidence of sabotage behind the bridge explosion."

"It's not like Spock not to give his whereabouts or intentions. He must have left some clue." Kirk mulled over Spock's most likely move.

McCoy had another drink, waiting for Kirk to accept the situation. "Jim, they're gone. If he could have, Spock would have let us know where they are. It's been a long time. You'll have to accept the fact that they're gone."

Kirk looked up at McCoy with an anger he rarely outwardly displayed. He was angry at McCoy for not telling him what was going on, and he was angrier at himself for assuming too readily that all would be back to normal when he returned to his ship. He lashed out at the doctor in resentment and frustration.

"You're partially responsible! If you had let me know, I could have found them. I could have stopped them! Now it's been too long." He stood up and stalked out of sick bay, leaving a thoroughly depressed McCoy.

Kirk had no desire to convene a meeting until he fully absorbed the devastating news and formulated a strategy. He went to his cabin and switched on the intercom. "Cancel that meeting I had scheduled, Uhura. Schedule it for o-seven-hundred hours tomorrow."

Uhura's steady voice acknowledged the change and she notified the officers involved.

Kirk's thoughts were dark ones. *I sensed something wrong —and now that I know what it is . . . what now?*

2

What would Spock do? He wouldn't go off without leaving a message for me. Where would he have left a clue? Kirk was obsessed with finding answers. He headed down the corridor, letting himself into Spock's quarters. It was late—the ship's lights were dimmed for the night cycle. He reached for the light panel and was immediately sorry.

All was changed. Gone were the strange Vulcan artifacts: the small flame which had always given these quarters a different quality, the rich red tapestries which added mystery to Spock's surroundings; all was gone.

With the light's brightening, Alexander Leonidas blinked and sat up abruptly, awakening with a jolt.

"Is there something wrong, sir?" he asked sleepily, when he saw the captain standing in the doorway.

"Nothing is wrong," Kirk responded. "I was looking for something. Were these quarters empty when you were assigned them?"

"Empty, sir?"

"Had they been vacated? Was there anything besides the regulation furnishings?"

Kirk noticed a few of Leonidas's personal touches: a photo of a girl and an Academy class picture.

"There was nothing here, sir. Should there have been?"

"No, Commander. I hope you don't think I make a habit of walking into my officers' quarters uninvited, but . . ."

"Can I help you find whatever it is you're looking for, sir?"

"When I figure out what it is, I'll let you know. Sorry I awakened you. And, Commander, please don't mention this visit to anyone."

"No, sir," the puzzled first officer answered, not entirely convinced that he shouldn't be telling someone about the captain's odd behavior.

Kirk went back to his quarters, took off his tunic and boots, and lay down on the bed. He lay in the dark, trying to reconstruct Spock's logic. He was very tired. It had been a long, full day, full of new people, a new ship, painful disappointment, anger, and frustration. *Damn!* He clenched his fists and hit the bed. He lay there for hours, staring at the overhead until exhaustion finally overcame him and he slept.

When he entered the briefing room the next morning, Captain James T. Kirk had controlled his anxiety. He looked at the gathering of command personnel on the *Enterprise* with an almost detached interest. The familiar face of Sulu, smiling as usual, lifted his spirits somewhat.

McCoy was talking to Uhura. First Officer Alexander Leonidas was sipping a cup of coffee while he absently flipped through a series of star charts. Lieutenant Thorin Martin, wearing the orange insignia of the science section, was having an animated conversation with the engineer, Heath Douglas.

Kirk took his seat. Yeoman Yolanda Helman handed him a fresh cup of coffee. The group settled down. The captain waited for a few beats; then he spoke.

"Gentlemen, some of you know me well; others of you will come to know me. No captain can run a starship alone. You are all essential to the well-being of the ship and her crew. Our success depends upon being able to work as a team. I rely upon your expertise and your loyalty, to me and to the ship. There are times when we encounter problems beyond any prior experience, and we must be capable of dealing with the new, the unusual, and sometimes the terrifying. Some of you have served on the *Enterprise* before. I welcome you back. Those of you who are new on board, I welcome you to the finest ship in the fleet.

"Now we will get to business. Our mission is a simple one: A shakedown cruise to test the ship. Then we are ordered to map a section of the Omega Six system. Any questions or comments?"

McCoy watched Kirk carefully. *His calm is a sham. I know him too well. What is Jim really up to?*

The questions were technical—no pressing business was presented; the meeting ended.

"Martin, Leonidas," Kirk called as they were leaving, "would you stay behind a moment?"

McCoy turned to come back into the room. "You're not needed at this meeting, Doctor."

Kirk turned his attention to his new officers. Perched on the edge of his chair, he spoke. "Mister Leonidas, I want a full computer search. I want to know what Mister Spock was using the computers for before he disappeared—and where he went. Mister Martin, what is your computer rating?"

"A six, sir. Only one below Commander Spock. He has the only seven in Starfleet."

"Good. I need someone as good as Spock to find what I'm after. Look for anything unusual. Any clue. This is a priority-*one* situation. Those computers are Spock's other self. He must have programmed something into them. It might be very subtle. Go to it!" He got up and left.

Leonidas ran his hand through his curly hair in confusion. "What was that all about?"

Martin was just as confused. He shrugged. "I guess we'll figure it out sooner or later." They left the briefing room together, heading for the main computer terminal on the bridge.

The *Enterprise* performed beautifully. Kirk should have felt great joy in the rebirth of the *Enterprise*, but he felt none. He fulfilled his duties automatically, requiring those around him to perform at peak efficiency, giving no clue as to the satisfaction he felt with his ship or crew in spite of his frustration regarding his missing friends.

The lone figure sitting in the command position was completely unapproachable. McCoy didn't come up to the bridge, deciding that any intervention would only aggravate the situation. *Let him work it out. He always does.*

Leonidas had a habit which Kirk found grating. The Greek first officer owned a set of worry beads which he held in his hand and clicked when he was concentrating. Above all of the bleeps and static which was considered normal in the routine of the *Enterprise*, the sound of the click, click, click of Leonidas's beads beating a nervous rhythm was like itching powder crawling up the captain's back, bringing him close to losing control.

Leonidas, unaware of the effect he was having on Kirk, stood beside him, beads rattling. With a quick motion, Kirk grabbed his wrist, forcing him to drop the beads. "Don't bring them back on the bridge again, Mister!"

Kirk rushed off the bridge. Sulu and Chekov turned to

watch the captain leave. They were relieved to have the
clicking stop, but had never seen the captain behave that way
before. Leonidas picked up the beads, put them into his belt,
and sat down in the command chair.

He saw Sulu and Chekov staring at him. "Don't you have
anything better to do?" he asked, signing a report handed to
him by Yeoman Helman.

Retreating to his quarters on his break, Kirk realized that
his stern and grim attitude was distressing his officers, but all
he could think about was Spock and Scott. There had to be a
clue; he was certain. He opened his safe and took out his
personal log.

He used the log as a record but also as a sounding board for
particularly complex, frustrating problems. As he pulled the
log from its niche, a computer tape dropped to the floor. He
picked it up and examined it. There was no standard ID
number. In the lower-right-hand corner of the red square was
a small recognizable symbol.

The IDIC—Spock's message! He had missed it before. Kirk
put the tape into his private console. Spock's image appeared
on the screen.

"Captain—Jim—if you are listening to this tape, I
will assume I am either missing or dead, and you are
planning to search for me. If I have not succeeded in
my quest, it will be hopeless for you to take up the
search. If you have heard the tape of the hearing
examining the explosion on the *Enterprise,* you will
know I have gone to find our unknown adversary. I do
not undertake this lightly. I believe the Federation is in
great danger, but I do not have enough physical
evidence to prove my position. Mister Scott has agreed
to accompany me, to lend assistance in engineering and
navigation. Jim, do not search for us. I will endeavor to
get a message to you if we find something. Do not
follow us! Live long and prosper, my friend. . . ."

The tape ended.
Kirk removed it and turned it in his hand. It was as close as
he had been to Spock since that nightmare on the bridge. He

ran his finger over the IDIC symbol. *Peculiar, I don't remember Spock using a tag like that before. Come to think of it, Spock never used a visual identification code, not on any of the computer tapes he handled. If he marked this one, maybe he tagged others. Spock is always consistent.*

I must get myself together. Bones was doing what he thought was his medical duty—trying to protect me—I can't blame him for that. Got to snap myself back to efficiency—no time for self-indulgence.

"Mister Martin, report to Captain's Quarters," he summoned via the intercom.

When Martin arrived, Kirk handed him the message tape with the small IDIC in the corner. "I want you to search the computer banks for *any* tape marked like this."

The science officer examined the dot. "What's the symbol, sir?"

"It's a Vulcan IDIC, Commander. I'll explain it some other time."

"But, sir, there are thousands of computer tapes. It could take a great deal of time."

"Then get some help, but find those tapes."

"Yes, Captain." Martin left the captain's quarters as confused as ever.

Hours later, Martin was still searching. He was beginning to dream of computer tapes, red ones, blue ones, all neatly stacked—all with little IDIC symbols in the lower-right corner. No one had ever told him that serving on a starship could be so tedious. He had developed a rhythm: A quick flip of the thumb brought all of the corners into view. For what seemed like the millionth time, he searched through another section of tapes. He almost missed the small symbol as it went by. He flipped through the deck again. There it was! He called Kirk.

The three executive officers huddled over the chart on the screen. "Can you make out what that is?" Kirk asked.

Martin shrugged. Leonidas examined the image more closely. "Captain!" he said excitedly, "It's a star chart! My hobby is collecting maps of obscure star systems and I'd bet my career on it! I'm not familiar with the area, but that's definitely what it is."

The image on the screen changed. A full-scale galactic map appeared, superimposed on the smaller chart. "What do you make of it, Leonidas?"

"It's our galaxy, sir. The section detailed on the chart is at the far end—the other end. We've never fully mapped that area. It's too far away." Leonidas was bouncing with enthusiasm. "I've never seen this galactic map before, Captain. It's about the most advanced one of our system. Where did Spock get it?"

"Vulcan, I'd bet," Kirk surmised aloud. "He always had a scientific ace in the hole. Is there a habitable planet in that detailed area?"

"I can't tell. It's just a star chart; no planets are indicated."

Spock's got to be there. He must have found a planet. There's no other lead, Kirk thought. "How long will it take us to get to that quadrant?" he asked.

Leonidas pondered the question, then answered. "About three days at maximum warp. But, sir, it will be awkward to explain to Starfleet why we are going in the opposite direction from our designated course."

"I'm going to exercise my captain's prerogative and gamble on Spock's map. He never does anything without a definite purpose. We're going to follow his lead. If he thinks sabotage was involved, I want to know who blew up the *Enterprise!*"

He vowed silently, *To hell with orders! I'm going to find Spock! I'll need a legitimate reason to go into that region.*

"Is there anything of special interest in that area, Mister Leonidas?"

"I'll need some time to analyze the data, sir," Leonidas answered, eager to study the chart.

An hour later, Leonidas looked up from the computer's navigational terminal and reported excitedly, "Captain, I think I've found something!"

"What?" Kirk rose from his seat and joined Leonidas at the console.

"A red giant, sir. I mean *really* large, Captain. Bigger than any I have ever seen before. It's not exactly in the quadrant we're interested in, but it's close."

"Is it of sufficient interest to study?"

"It's of great interest, sir. One of a kind!"

"Leonidas, you've earned your pay! Helmsman, set a course on the coordinates given to you by Mister Leonidas."

"But, Captain, that red giant isn't in the quadrant Spock indicated."

Kirk answered in a soothing voice. "Close enough, Mister. Close enough. Uhura, send a message to Starfleet, space normal. Investigating unusual red giant of great interest—and give the coordinates."

Uhura turned to Kirk. "Space normal, Captain? It'll take a week to get there."

Kirk grinned knowingly. "So what's the hurry?"

3

Entering the recreation room, Alexander Leonidas smiled warmly. His daily visit was something the crew was beginning to count on. This was his first assignment as first officer, a promotion he deserved and had long anticipated. He was a small man, only five feet six inches, just making it into Starfleet. He was dwarfed by the complement of tall men on board.

He loved women, and they loved him. His smile could charm the most sober of them. Leonidas was a startling contrast to their former first officer, Spock, whose serious manner and alien ways set him apart.

Each evening, when he completed his duties, Leonidas went to the recreation room. The first officer's dancing lessons had become legend in record time. In a few days, he had a bevy of dancing enthusiasts, men and women. The hilarity in the rec room echoed through the corridors as the fun-loving Greek taught the crew of the *Enterprise* how to exult in movement.

He taught the ancient Greek folk dances, and he played a stringed musical instrument whose poignant strains seemed to have a soul. He was the picture of warmth, whirling and singing, his black hair, longer than regulation, curling around

his face—a true embodiment of the joy of life. His presence
was a welcome bright spot in the tedium of spaceflight.

This night Leonidas was in great form. Kirk, hearing the
laughter as he passed by, peeked in to see what was going on.
A flash of color went by the door, and a hand reached out to
grab him. He was pulled into the center of the circle of
dancing crew members. Whirling and singing, they drew him
inexorably into the spirit of the dance, until they all stopped in
sheer exhaustion.

Laughing, Kirk dropped to the floor with the others. He
realized he felt good; for the first time since the explosion, he
felt one with the ship and her crew—the way he remembered
feeling before that terrible event. Leaving the rec room, he
continued on to his quarters, reluctantly admitting that he
had developed a fondness for his new first officer. In his own
way, Leonidas was a valuable asset to the ship. He was vastly
different from Spock: so relaxed, so affable. Kirk liked him.

McCoy had just finished the routine physicals required of
the entire crew. He sat back in his office and poured a glass of
brandy. The buzzer sounded.

"Come."

The tall blond figure of the new science officer, Thorin
Martin, stood in the doorway.

"Come on in and have a drink, Mister Martin. You look
like you can use one," McCoy commented.

"Is it that obvious, Doctor?"

McCoy nodded. "What's your problem? Women?"

"I wish it was that simple, sir. It's the captain . . ."

"Oh?"

"Sir, I seem to have a problem communicating with him.
Maybe you can tell me what I'm doing wrong."

McCoy instantly understood. "Martin, it's not *your* problem. It's the *captain's*. You just can't help being you."

"Would you explain that, sir?"

"Simply, you are not Spock. And you can't be Spock,
either. I've watched you on the bridge. You're human, not a
walking Vulcan computer. Spock could think twice, maybe
three times, faster than any of us. He has answers before
there were questions. It's impossible for any one man to
replace him. Jim—the captain—keeps expecting you to perform like Spock. It's impossible!"

"Then what do I do?"

"Relax. Do the best you can. It's all any of us can do."

"But the captain's unhappy with my performance. I can tell."

"No, Martin. He's a fair man. He's just asking you to fill in for his lost science officer. Spock was also his best friend. I guess just seeing you there makes him feel the loss all the more. Just give him some time. Do you want me to talk to him?"

"Oh, no, sir," Martin answered quickly. "I don't want to cause any more friction!"

"Have another drink, Mister Martin."

"Please call me Thorin."

"Okay, Thorin, take another swig. It's good for you."

In Douglas's opinion, the extended period of maximum warp drive needed to bring the *Enterprise* to her destination was straining the ship too far.

"But, Captain," the conservative engineer protested, "I can't see any reason to tax the ship at this point. There's no press for time. We're asking for an engineering disaster."

"My decision stands, Douglas," Kirk insisted. "I believe time is a factor. I can sense it."

The engineer logged his objections and grumbled, but the ship remained at maximum warp. Content in reading his journals Douglas retreated to his quarters. He removed the rumpled suit he was wearing, brushed the wave of his red hair back and settled his bulky six-foot frame into bed.

He had no real friend on board the *Enterprise* yet. The first officer was too flamboyant, the science officer too busy. The only person of interest he noticed was Yolanda Helman. *Wonder what it's like to be the moody captain's yeoman,* he thought. *How close to him is she?* He found himself a little jealous. *Her job doesn't automatically imply a deeper relationship, but she is pretty, and young, and desirable. If I were the captain . . .*

4

The feeling of uneasiness began to creep over James Kirk again. The nearer they came to the star cluster Spock had marked in blue, the more necessary he felt was the need for speed. It was almost as if he were being magnetically drawn. He didn't understand it, but his whole being pulsed with the urgency. He was jumpy—every sound on the ship seemed magnified.

"Captain, we're approaching the Xi star cluster. Sensors pick up one habitable planet orbiting the fourth star. Its oxygen level is adequate, but I wouldn't recommend any athletics. There seems to be a cool spot on the northern pole; the rest of it seems too hot for life as we know it." Martin continued to peer into the sensor, calling out the data as he read it.

Kirk turned to the science officer, listening with great interest. Leonidas was studying another sensor, tapping his foot in excitement.

"Navigator, set a course for that planet. High orbit. We don't want to be spotted."

"Aye, sir."

"Mister Sulu, as soon as you receive the coordinates, I want you to make the course change."

"Aye, sir. Course plotted and laid in."

They all watched the view-screen as the course change was executed, eagerly anticipating a clearer view of the planet. Leonidas was standing beside the captain, primed for an adventure. He had served on other ships, but had never before had the authority of the first officer to utilize the potential of a starship for his exploratory urges.

Kirk looked around at the crew, mentally selecting the men for a landing party. He was feeling uneasy about taking his new officers with him; they were going into unknown and probably hostile territory. *I must be able to trust them! No better time than now*, he thought with determination.

"Mister Leonidas, equip a landing party. You, Martin, Sulu, Chekov, and Doctor McCoy will accompany me." He chose a balance of his old reliable crew and new officers, hoping the mix would work smoothly.

Obviously disapproving, Douglas balanced the transporter, testing it before beam-down. "Captain," he said hesitantly, "You are beaming down into an unknown situation. Shouldn't you have security check it out first?"

"Douglas, I can't ask any man to risk more than I would. It's my responsibility and my choice. Just do your job and be prepared to beam us up in a hurry."

Douglas frowned. "Yes, sir."

Entering the transporter room with arms full, Chekov handed phasers to all members of the landing party.

Martin, taking a last-minute scan of the planet, announced his findings.

"Captain, sensors pick up life forms, about three dozen, at the center of the cool spot. They have a high metabolism and a great deal of body heat. There seems to be an energy source indicated in the area as well." Martin looked perplexed. "It's peculiar, sir. Something's wrong. It doesn't seem likely that on a planet that's so hot, a life form with that high a body temperature would evolve. I'll bet the life forms down there don't originate on this planet."

"Well, we seem to have a puzzle already," Kirk observed. "Gentlemen, let's solve it!" He stepped into the transporter. The five others joined him on the platform.

"Douglas, keep us out of sight of those beings. Energize!"

They materialized behind a hill some distance from the inhabited area. No one was in sight. "Standard search pattern," Kirk said. "Move out."

Leonidas and Sulu moved toward the range of low hills. Martin and Chekov headed warily toward the settlement. McCoy was left alone with the captain.

"I have a strange feeling in my bones, Jim," he said. "It's hot, but I've got a cold chill. Let's get out of here."

"You feel uneasy every time we beam down. Keep busy. Get at that medical scanner. See if there's anything of interest in the flora or something."

Kirk's communicator signaled. It was Leonidas, extremely agitated but controlled.

"Captain! We found the *Raven*. It's abandoned—no one around—not even footprints."

"Did you go into the ship?"

"No, Captain," Leonidas answered, "we thought you'd like to see it first." He was gradually learning about James Kirk and his command style.

Chekov's voice broke in over the communicator. "Keptin, ve found a Klingon ship! It's abandoned." His thick Russian accent clipped the words.

"Are you sure, Chekov?"

"Keptin, I know a Klingon ship vhen I see vun."

"Yes, you do, Lieutenant," Kirk agreed. "We will rendezvous at Leonidas's coordinates immediately. Kirk out."

They all approached the abandoned Federation ship. Kirk mulled over the puzzle. *The* Raven *and a Klingon ship. What is the connection?*

All was as Spock had left it. The chart which had led them here, identical to that which Kirk used, was displayed on the navigation panel. A fresh change of clothes was spread out in the rear section. Martin ran the tricorder over everything. There was nothing unusual.

"Looks like they planned on returning," Kirk observed.

McCoy examined the medical supplies. "Jim, the painkillers are all gone. Spock must really have been hurting. Damn fool! I told him . . ."

"Not now, Bones," Kirk warned.

"No signs of a struggle, Captain," Martin commented.

Sulu looked for their weapons. "Their phasers are gone, sir."

They all left the ship.

"What we have is an empty *Raven*, no struggle, no weapons, and a Klingon ship. Let's check that ship out."

The Klingon ship offered no more information than had the *Raven*. They could tell she had carried three crewmen. The main point of interest was the map—the same coordinates Spock and the *Enterprise* had followed. It was clear the Klingons were given the same lead. Why?

Chekov and Leonidas, too curious to stay in one place, climbed the next hill to investigate further. They found the Romulan ship and stared at each other in amazement. Attempts to signal Kirk and the rest of the party proved futile. Running was quite strenuous in the thin atmosphere of the small planet, but they made it back to the remainder of the landing party in record time.

"Ve found a Romulan ship!" Chekov gasped. "Our communicators didn't vork. Must be something in de atmosphere here vhich inhibits certain transmissions . . ."

Leonidas pointed in the direction of the scout ship. "Yes, sir, it's just over that hill . . ."

"Abandoned?" Kirk anticipated their answer.

They answered in unison. "Yes, sir."

At the Romulan ship, they found weapons lying on the ground: Romulan stunguns and Klingon disrupters. In the ship they found the Federation phasers locked in the arsenal. The wind had blown away any sign of footprints. There was no evidence at all as to what had happened to any of them.

The captain synthesized the findings as he tried to formulate some hypothesis.

"We've found a chart on the Romulan ship similar to the ones on the Klingon ship and the *Raven*. Could we all have been led here?" He looked over his shoulder. "It must be a trap. If Spock was in jeopardy, then we may be in similar trouble. How far away are those life-readings?"

"About a half mile north, sir."

"We haven't been spotted yet. Odd. They don't seem to have sensors. Leonidas, Sulu, you two take the lead—and be quiet."

They crept up the hill toward the life-readings and came into view of the launch gantry. On top of the structure was a rocket ready for takeoff.

Leonidas whistled low. "Wow, look at that!"

Sulu, for once in his life, was speechless.

Kirk was wide-eyed with the discovery.

The Tomariian crew was preparing to launch the rocket. The men from the *Enterprise* watched from behind the hill. The rocket took off with a flare of light, heat, and noise.

Chekov was very impressed. "Vhat is it?"

"An old-type chemical rocket, Lieutenant," Martin explained. "An old dinosaur. I never thought I'd ever see that primitive a device in action!"

Their voices had begun to rise. Kirk quieted them. "We don't want to be spotted. Keep it quiet," he ordered.

McCoy was very still. He had observed the Tomariian launch, but was more interested in the men of the ground crew. "Jim, look, they're hairy! I'll bet that explains Spock's depilatory. We must be on the right track."

"You're right, Bones. I read the transcript. He did mention a depilatory!" He spoke into his communicator. "Douglas, beam us up!"

Upon their return to the *Enterprise,* Kirk addressed his landing party.

"This planet can't be the right place. There were only about three dozen men down there; this has to be some sort of an outpost. We have to find out where they came from and we haven't got a clue." He turned to Martin. "Any other sapient life-reading other than our furry friends?"

"No, sir."

"Then Spock isn't here and neither are the Romulans or Klingons. But I'll bet those life forms down there know where they are. It's not a dead end yet."

"Keptin," Chekov called out from the security sensor, "they haf launched another rocket."

"That's it!" Kirk ordered, "Chekov, trace the course of that launch. We're going to follow it. Sulu, I want us to match its speed. Stay at a discreet distance. I don't want to be spotted now."

"I don't believe it!" Douglas said in astonishment as he studied the sensor readings. "That ship has warp potential and a matter/antimatter drive! It's smaller and more maneuverable than the *Enterprise.* Its drive isn't consistent with the method of launch they used."

"Stay with them, Mister Sulu," Kirk said calmly. "We'll have our answers soon."

Leonidas was exultant. The first officer observed and charted and enjoyed every bit. His excitement grew as they neared the huge red giant he had mentioned before. It completely dominated the region around it. Its glow could be seen from an incredible distance.

"Captain," the first officer announced, "we're getting awfully close to that red giant."

The view-screen showed the dull, red object overwhelming everything around it. Martin was at the science station, eyes on the sensors. "Sir, we're headed directly toward it. It could have a tremendous magnetic field. We can't get too close until we know for certain."

"What about the ship we're following?"

"Heading right for the sun, Captain. No, it's veered; it's skirting the red giant."

"Keep following it, Helmsman. Adjust course," Kirk ordered quietly.

The sun was so large it took a full day at warp three to circumvent it. When they arrived at the far side, Leonidas was riveted to the view-screen.

"Look, Captain, a small, very hot sun, a baby, probably formed when the other exploded. That must have been something! I'll bet it engulfed everything in this area when it went red. There can't be a planet here, sir. Not with all of that energy spewing out. It must have destroyed all of its planets, if it had any."

"No possible way there could be a planet in this sector?"

"I can't see how."

"Then where are our furry friends going?"

"I'm at a loss, Captain. Their course is taking them between the two suns. The gravitational forces will pull them into one sun or the other."

"I don't think they're suicidal, Leonidas. They must know were they're going. Follow them, Helmsman."

Sulu acknowledged, and continued concentrating on their course. It was Martin who hesitated. "Captain, we're getting too close. We're becoming affected by the pull of the large sun, and if the helm compensates, we'll be pulled toward the small one. We can't safely go any further."

"Are you sure, Martin?"

"He's correct, Captain," Leonidas reported. "We'll burn up if we attempt to go any further."

"Hold it right here, Sulu. Any solutions, gentlemen? Their ship seemed to go into a corridor between the two suns. Why can't we?"

"We're too big, Captain. A small ship could manage it, if it were careful to stay in between the pulls of both suns and travel at an awesome speed. It's a real tightrope in there!"

"A shuttle, then," Kirk suggested.

"No, Captain," Leonidas interjected. "The distances are immense. A shuttle wouldn't have the range or the speed necessary."

Kirk retreated to his quarters to be alone with the problem. He wasn't going to give up now that he had come this far. He was determined to follow that rocket ship. After an hour of deep concentration, he called his staff together.

"Gentlemen, I have made a decision. We are going to follow that ship into the corridor."

"But, sir." Douglas nearly jumped out of his chair; standing abruptly, he voiced his objections loudly.

Kirk's eyes narrowed. "I appreciate your opinion, but my mind is made up." Looking squarely at Douglas, he continued, "This is an order. We will take the *Enterprise* through the corridor despite the difficulty and the danger. I don't promise it will be easy, but we have no choice. I believe we were too conservative in our earlier estimation of the size of the corridor. We have the best crew in Starfleet. If anyone can get through, we can—and we are going to! It is up to you, gentlemen, to do it with the largest safety factor possible. We must hurry.

"Sulu, you will take the helm during the entire maneuver. It'll be tricky and you're the best we have. Martin, you will navigate."

Martin interrupted. "Captain, I suggest we go through the corridor at maximum speed. The magnetic fields will not affect us if we are traveling at multi-warp speeds. However, I think the entire mission too dangerous. I must log my objection."

"Then do so, Martin. But do your duty." Kirk instructed, "Douglas, I want all ship's systems at peak efficiency. We might have to draw upon our reserves quickly. Uhura, send a message to Starfleet headquarters, announcing our rescue attempt and location."

Douglas was livid. "Captain, it's impossible," he shouted.

Kirk replied in a steely voice. "To find out if something is impossible—try it!"

The *Enterprise* followed the rocket, balancing her way through the corridor with the precision of a man on a tightrope. With Kirk at her helm, she made her perilous way through the magnetic fields, balancing carefully so as not to be drawn to either star and a fiery end.

Kirk looked around at the tense faces of the crew on the

bridge. They all reflected intense strain. Each was silently guiding the ship, as if by individual will, through the dangerous passage. Only when Martin announced the sensor readings of the planet ahead did anyone relax, and with a common deep breath they eased their tension. Once more, the *Enterprise,* whose captain would not be defeated by what seemed impossible odds, had successfully ventured where no man had gone before.

The crew had mixed feelings about the captain's obsession. Those who knew him trusted his judgment; they knew he would risk death to save his ship. Those who were new on board wondered about his sanity. Kirk wasn't worried about any of their opinions. The decision, and the responsibility, was his.

Kirk's meeting with McCoy was private. "Just what condition are we likely to find Spock in, if we're lucky enough to find him at all?" he asked.

"I thought you'd get around to that question soon." McCoy gestured to a chair and the captain sat down. "I'll be blunt. There are three possibilities: one, he's fine."

"Odds?"

"I'm not Spock, Jim, but I'd say eighty or ninety to one—against."

"That bad?"

The doctor nodded. "Two: The sliver's moved and he's paralyzed. Odds: I'd say an eighty percent probability. Three: He's dead; probability of the injury killing him, twenty percent. All this is conjecture, Jim. He could have been killed by those furry creatures, you know. I'm a doctor, not an actuary!"

"I know," Kirk said softly. "I know, but I've got to believe we'll find them—alive. If only I had been there when Spock decided to take off . . ."

"It's not your fault, Jim. You were barely alive. And I don't like the strain you've been under lately. You aren't made of iron, you know."

"I was declared fit for duty, Bones. I can handle it, if you'll just help me. Don't put false barriers in the way. Equip yourself as well as you can. I don't know what we'll find."

"I've already put together a medical kit," McCoy said, anticipating Kirk's request. "I've got everything imaginable in there, including the kitchen sink."

The ship had to come first on his list of priorities, but Kirk found his priorities becoming confused. He had already chosen between his first officer—no, his friend—and his ship, surprising himself with the ease he had in risking the *Enterprise* and her crew on a possible wild-goose chase. He had always recognized the complexity of his feelings for Spock. They had always had the military, professional aspects, yet he knew Spock's friendship was one of the most important personal relationships he had had in his adult life.

Losing Spock was like losing a part of himself. Together, they were in balance: the emotional human sometimes feeling too much, and the logical Vulcan who masked his human side needed the humanity of his friend to be whole. Each complemented the other. He wondered if Spock realized how close they had become.

Lying in the dark of his cabin, Kirk realized it would be difficult to fully accept Spock's loss. *Maybe that's what drove me to this far sector of the galaxy. If I can't find him, or find him dead, I know I'll be able to adjust. I'll function. I'll carry on with my duty. I'll even be able to enjoy life eventually, but I'll miss him deeply.*

Premature gloom, he chastised himself. *First we seek, then we adjust to whatever we find—and I will find Spock—I can feel it!*

5

"It's very tricky, Captain," Leonidas briefed Kirk. "We have managed to keep within a narrow passage between the gravitational pull of both suns. Those life forms are more advanced than we first thought. They managed to find the precise corridor between the magnetic fields."

Kirk watched the view-screen as Leonidas spoke. "I don't

underestimate them, Leonidas. They blew up the *Enterprise* and lured Spock into their trap. If that's a sample, we're dealing with very dangerous opponents."

"I can draw a map of this system now, sir. I believe we are coming up on a planet hidden between the two suns. It has to have a strange orbit, trapped as it is." He programmed the ship's computer to render a graphic display of the system derived from the data he had collected thus far. "I'll project it on the view-screen."

Clearly inspired by his subject, Leonidas explained, "Usually a red giant is not dense enough to have much of a gravitational effect, but this one, having such mass, is different. Because of the gravitational pulls, a planet trapped between the two suns would be in a delicate balance, having an elliptical orbit. The balance would pull it off center, nearer the red sun, but still too close to the small one. It would be impossible to live on the side facing the bright sun. I then assume the planet doesn't rotate but, like our moon, puts the same face toward the red sun all of the time. In that case, it would be very cold at the far end of the orbit, when it is farthest from the red giant. It must be unbearably cold. Possibly that accounts for the hair growth and their high metabolism. It would keep them from freezing. Somehow this planet must have survived the explosion of the sun when it went red. It must have been on the very edge of the system then, and cold anyway. The creation of the small hot sun must have created havoc. What's amazing is that any life survived at all! It has to be a very inhospitable place, at best—and the people have to be tenacious.

"I can't tell whether there are any moons—but I would assume, with all that matter having been spewed out, there could be one or more, which would also be trapped in peculiar orbits. It's a really fascinating system, Captain. I know of no other remotely like it. It's a once-in-a-lifetime opportunity for an astronomer."

With the word *fascinating*, Kirk's heart lurched. Spock would have said that.

"In order to leave the planet they had to have the ability to plot the fields and avoid the pulls. We're dealing with an advanced technology, Captain. I still don't understand why they use that archaic launch technique."

"We'll soon find out, Leonidas," Kirk said, stretching his legs straight out, studying the chart.

"Keptin, there's an object, dead ahead." He put his probe on visual, bringing the picture to the view-screen. "Look, Keptin, dat's it, the planet."

Kirk grinned with satisfaction. "I see it, Chekov. Keep it steady, approach slowly, and put us in a high orbit."

"Aye, sir." Chekov began adjusting their course.

"No, Captain," Leonidas interrupted, "we can't establish a standard orbit. The far side of the planet is too close to the hot sun. Put us in a pace orbit, Chekov."

Chekov looked to Kirk for approval.

"Do as he ordered, Chekov. He's the expert."

Martin continued monitoring the sensors as they established orbit. "There seems to be a high population density in a relatively small area, Captain."

"That would make sense," Leonidas observed. "It would be too hot to live on the far side of the planet, and most of the habitable side would be too cold. I estimate only a very small area at the equator to be habitable at all, and that area will be very cold for our comfort."

"Prepare a landing party, Chekov. We're beaming down."

Chapter IV

The Pet

1

IIsa was beginning the evening task of bathing her interesting diversion: Spock. His passive resistance to her ministrations amused her; she found him a challenge. She'd never taken such an intent interest in a captive before, but Spock's pride and strength, before he was incapacitated by his injury, were admirable.

Spock understood his position well; he was essentially her pet, an amusement for her. Knowing his admiration for the art objects in her household, IIsa took pains to bring him things to study and enjoy. The area of the room in which he was kept was cluttered with the collection. Each article was in itself beautiful, but the entire collection amassed in a small area was offensive to the Spartan Spock.

Spock looked up as IIsa entered the room. Her smile revealed her delight in tending to him. Bringing a basin of warm water from the hearth, she came toward him for the daily ritual.

Knowing he had no choice, Spock allowed her to bathe him. He said nothing, trying to withdraw from his humiliation. He found it difficult to remain passive, but logic dictated that the situation called for acquiescence.

"You are very quiet this evening, Spock."

He was silent.

"When I speak to you, you will respond," she scolded, cuffing him.

His lack of reaction infuriated her; although Spock knew she found enjoyment in pleasing him, he knew she derived amusement in inflicting pain. He couldn't risk angering her.

"The days are shorter," he commented, "and much colder."

"We are approaching our coldest season."

Always calculating the passage of time, Spock estimated that he'd been in Ilsa's keeping for a little over a month. She finished her task, combed his hair, and stood back to admire her handiwork. He withdrew further into himself for his continued sanity.

Whenever he was permitted privacy, he unwrapped the tiny crystal sliver Scott had given him and studied its interesting properties. It generated an energy which disturbed normal biological function, and it could interfere with other transmitted energy. He yearned for a laboratory where he could fully analyze the properties of the substance.

With the bathing finished and his dignity somewhat restored, he lay flat as he had been placed, between the rich layers of warm fur. Ilsa was combing her hair, relaxed and pleased. Spock startled her by initiating a conversation. He had not done that before.

"Begum, would you grant me a request?"

She walked over to her captive and stroked his shiny black hair. "If the request is reasonable, I will consider it."

"I miss my companion—Scott. Could I see him, even for a short time?" He hated to beg, but knew her well enough to know she would derive satisfaction from it. "Please, Begum, it is a small thing I ask."

"I will think about it, Spock. Now I have something for you to enjoy." She walked out of sight into the alcove, and returned with a vase. "This is our warmest season. All of the plant life on Tomarii now puts forth flowers and fruit. We don't have a great variety of plant life on our planet, but this is the most beautiful."

Extending out of the vase was a milk-white graceful stem with small heart-shaped leaves attached by slim stems, which fluttered with her movement toward him. A silvery-white seedpod was attached to a lower stem. Another pod, partially open, clung to an upper stem; it contained a number of delicate mauve beans with a splattering of bright red dots. The Begum held the vase in front of Spock for his inspection. He raised up on an elbow to get a better view.

"It is beautiful, Spock, but deadly. The seedpod and beans are poisonous. It is sad that such a lovely thing should be so lethal. Even a few of the beans can kill. But we can admire its beauty, can't we? Here, I will put it near you so you may enjoy it." She placed the vase containing the plant on a shelf near his pallet.

The next morning Spock awoke to see the very welcome face of Scott beaming down at him.

"Ye're a sight," the Scotsman chuckled, "long hair, beard, and if ye got any skinnier we could thread a needle wi' ye."

"Have you seen yourself lately, Mister Scott?"

"Aye, I could pass for a Tomariian if ye dinna look too close."

Turning to a more somber subject, Spock addressed the engineer in a low, intense tone.

"Mister Scott, I don't know how long IIsa will permit you to stay. It is imperative we have a serious talk. Help me to sit, please."

"How are ye doing, Spock? Any improvement at all?"

"No. All sensation is gone. I am unable to move. It is proving awkward and embarrassing, but I have been able to tolerate the inconvenience so far. But my physical well-being is not what I wanted to discuss with you. A sufficient time has passed for us to assume that Placus and the Klingons are not returning for us. I am convinced the Romulan would have returned for Julina if he was able to. It then follows that the escape attempt was unsuccessful or he was killed, which leaves us no hope of rescue. The Klingons cared little for our survival. If it hadn't suited their purpose, they wouldn't have helped us at all. That leaves the matter of escape from this planet to you.

"It is imperative for you to get back to the Federation. The crystal you gave me to study is a find of significant value. Without complete laboratory analysis I am unable to determine the full range of potential of the crystal, but I am convinced it is of great worth, even with the limited analysis I have been able to perform here.

"I believe it to be a trilithium crystal, containing one more lithium atom than our dilithium crystals. That in itself should indicate its value—it is a power source beyond anything we have ever possessed. It interferes with biological function, as you experienced when it was embedded in your shoulder, and it also has the ability to neutralize other power sources. As a start, I think you will find it effective in counteracting the effect of the Tomariians' restraining force. If you could obtain a larger sample, it would be of great value to the Federation."

"Aye, just think of the power we could harness for a starship!"

"Yes. A crystal the size of your finger could power the *Enterprise*. I see you realize the import of your discovery, but there is more. I have gotten a great deal of information from IIsa—there are times when she is most garrulous. This planet is the Tomariians' place of origin, but it is dying. They have retained their government here out of a sheer determination to preserve a vestige of their heritage. We are seeing only the central core of government; the bulk of the population is elsewhere. The Tomariians are numerous and present a formidable force when united. As you know, they consider individual lives expendable, rendering them relentless warriors. Their sphere of influence is considerable, and growing. They have concentrated on this sector, but are now looking to a broader region for conquest. They possess numbers, strength, and resources from many different worlds in staggering abundance. We would be hard pressed to defend ourselves against them. You must get back to the Federation to inform them immediately—our Romulan and Klingon allies realized the threat."

"That all may be true, Mister Spock, but I canna just take off an' leave ye here."

"That's very unrealistic. You are not able to actually protect me. I am helpless. You must accept the fact that I am expendable and find a way of getting back to the Federation. You have established a good relationship with IIob. It should be relatively easy for you to take advantage of that friendship and escape."

"No, Spock. Not wi'out ye. The captain would expect me ta get ye out o' here."

"I am ordering you to leave, Mister Scott. I am your superior officer."

"And I refuse to obey that order on grounds ye are medically unfit ta command."

"You aren't a medical officer, Mister Scott. You haven't the authority or the ability to make a medical judgment."

"Then it's a standoff, Spock. Ye canna force me ta take an order. We're not exactly on the *Enterprise,* ye know!"

As the debate intensified, their voices rose, bringing Ilsa back into the room to find Scott red–faced with anger and Spock tense with exasperation.

"Leave!" she ordered. Scott stalked angrily out of the room.

"Your friend's visit was not what you had hoped. I am sorry. I hoped it would please you. I will see that he does not disturb you again."

Spock replied softly, "That won't be necessary."

Alone again, Spock contemplated the alternatives. He had to compel Scott to leave Tomarii. *While I live, Scott will not leave. I must make another attempt to remove the deterring factor—myself,* he thought coolly. *Scott and Ilsa both assumed it was Julina who had attempted to take my life. I have permitted that assumption. I must find another way and succeed this time.*

Surveying the clutter of artifacts around him, his eyes rested on the vase Ilsa had presented to him on the previous evening. In it, the beautiful and deadly plant shimmered with a silver-white delicacy. He reached for the vase, stretching to cover the distance which would put it into his grasp. It took all of his effort to span the last inch, throwing him off balance and onto the cold stone floor. He lay still, waiting to see if anyone had heard him fall. No one had heard.

Now the vase was within reach. Emptying the opened seedpod, he cupped five small red-spotted beans in his hand. Spock put the beans into his mouth and swallowed deliberately.

With an almost academic interest in the sensations he should soon feel, the Vulcan lay back on the cold floor waiting for the poison to work. At first there was a flush, a tingling of warmth that caused a light sweat. *The poison is acting rapidly—excellent,* he thought. Finding it progressively more dificult to breathe, he tried to give in to the respiratory slowdown, but his body's reflex system would not permit it. The autonomic functions took over, forcing him to gasp for breath; he was thrashing with his body's effort to fight the poison. The sound reached the outer hall, and IIsa and a guard ran into the room to find him convulsed on the floor. She took him in her arms, trying to soothe the convulsions. His breath rattled and slowed, and he lapsed into unconsciousness.

She then saw the toppled vase and the empty seedpod. Realizing what Spock had done, she called for Scott—he was her only hope to save the Vulcan. *He will know what to do,* she hoped. She lowered Spock from her lap, covered him with the furs, and waited.

She was feeling compassion; she had learned to care, to want survival for those close to her. It was disturbing and bewildering, yet somehow comforting. She had been introduced to a new way of feeling which had so impressed her it had become a part of her own behavior.

Studying Spock's still form, IIsa admitted to herself that she was reliant in some way on his continued existence. *I will miss him.* She felt an unaccustomed chill. *He must live!*

2

"Captain, I've located a Vulcan reading," Martin announced, still peering into his sensors. "It's harder to detect a human one down there, but I think I've pinpointed Scott as well."

"Give the transporter chief the coordinates, Martin. Sulu, Leonidas, McCoy, prepare to beam down." He saw McCoy's over-large medical kit, and nodded grim approval.

Scott hadn't gotten all the way out of the compound before he was detained by a guard and rushed back to IIsa's apartment. He immediately sensed the urgency of the situation when Ilsa frantically ran toward him and he saw the unconscious form of Spock on the floor.

"You must help him!" she pleaded in an un-Tomariian way.

The Scotsman felt for a pulse. He noted the gray of Spock's lips and the lack of respiration. "What happened?" he asked, confused by the sudden relapse.

"Poison, he took poison!"

"Spock? Try ta kill himself? That dinna make sense!"

"Help him," she demanded desperately.

With no time to think about the situation, Scott kneeled beside Spock, placing his mouth over the Vulcan's. With no medicine available, the only recourse he had was the old method of mouth-to-mouth resuscitation to keep Spock breathing. Time seemed to halt as he labored over the Vulcan. Scott was becoming faint with the effort of breathing for two and he realized he would have to stop soon, yet there was no one to replace him. He took one last deep breath, concentrating on the rhythm of breathing, trying to ignore the hopelessness of his endeavor.

The familiar hum of the transporter effect filled the room, amplified by the echoes against the rock walls. Solidifying before him was the entirely unexpected but very welcome form of Captain James T. Kirk. There was nothing closer than this moment to a miracle in Scott's experience, for behind the captain was Doctor Leonard McCoy.

Startled, Ilsa froze for a short moment. Then she realized she was seeing intruders appear from the very air. Four burly Tomariians came running with weapons drawn, in response to her cry.

Kirk, Chekov, and Martin, with phasers ready, turned to shoot.

"No!" Scott shouted. "Not now For God's sake, we don't want them down on us in force.

"Begum," Scott shouted excitedly. "It's McCoy—the doctor! A physician! Damn it!" He pointed to McCoy. "He can help Spock!"

McCoy rushed to Spock, extending his medical tricorder. The Tomariian guards poised to strike, but Ilsa held them back.

McCoy directed the efforts to save Spock with lightning

efficiency. "Scotty, you continue the resuscitation. I'll stimulate his heart."

McCoy leaned forward as he applied rhythmic pressure to the Vulcan's failing organ. He then quickly applied a shot of tri-ox to help Spock's breathing, and readjusted the hypo for a large dose of the very unpredictable drug cordrazine, which would stimulate heart action.

"Nothing," McCoy whispered. "Have to try more cordrazine, no matter how risky. . . ." He injected another dose of the stimulant into the Vulcan.

"That's enough to make the dead walk, and he's not responding. Another shot could really finish him."

"And if you don't?" Kirk asked.

"He'll die."

After one glance from Kirk, McCoy pumped another dose of the dangerous drug into Spock. Everyone was frozen in a tableau of tense waiting, straining to hear any evidence that Spock was breathing. After what seemed hours, a ragged intake of air could be heard in the silence.

"That did it, he's breathing again. Heart action is slow. I'll need some oxygen, fast!"

Diverting his focus from Spock for the first time since beam-down, McCoy spoke into his communicator. "Nurse Chapel, beam down a stomach pump and some oxygen."

"You've found Spock? Is he all right?"

"Yes and no," McCoy barked, "Hurry!"

The medical supplies sparkled into existence in front of him.

IIsa watched McCoy carefully as he tended to Spock. He ran his medical scanner over the Vulcan's unconscious form, looking alarmed—Spock's hold on life was tenuous at best. Inserting the tube, he began pumping Spock's stomach.

"What are you doing?" the Begum asked, watching the procedure intently. She could imagine no more effective torture than that which the doctor seemed to be inflicting upon Spock, but dared not stop him for the Vulcan's sake.

McCoy examined the beans he had extracted from Spock's stomach. "The only thing that saved him was that he swallowed these things whole. He only bit into one of them. Nasty little things—deadly poison."

He ran the medical analyzer over the beans again. "Ordinarily, under these circumstances, I'd get him on his feet and walk him until he was alert."

"Why don't you do it now?" Kirk asked worriedly.

"Because he's paralyzed, Jim. I knew that sliver would move. It's as bad as I expected it to be."

"Can you remove it?"

"Not yet, Jim. He's not strong enough to handle surgery of any kind. Besides the effect of the poison, he's undernourished and anemic. There's not enough copper in his blood to fill a thimble. It'll take time to build him up for any surgical procedure."

"What is this surgery you speak of?" IIsa asked.

Kirk answered her question. "It is a procedure which will permit him to walk again if it is successful."

"That is possible?" She was amazed.

McCoy, outraged at Spock's condition, lashed out at IIsa. "He's in a terrible condition and it's your fault."

Scott tried to keep McCoy from making any further attacks on the short-tempered Begum, but it was Kirk who held the doctor in check.

"Not now, Bones. You have a patient to take care of."

McCoy yielded, running the medi-scanner over his charge once more and grumbling in anger. IIsa then spoke to Kirk.

"You came a long way to find your people, Captain. I will have to take your persistence into account and consider that trait in our plans."

Kirk steadily returned the Begum's speculative gaze. "The only plan you should have at this point is to permit us to remove our personnel from here—without interference. When we obtain a full report from the two officers you've detained, I suspect those plans of yours may meet with a few setbacks from the Federation." Kirk contacted the ship. "Landing party and recovered officers to beam up."

Somewhat awed by the power of these newcomers, as evidenced by this miraculous appearing and disappearing, IIsa permitted the intruders to take Spock and Scott away with them. But her newfound compassion had another dimension she was now experiencing: the pain of loss.

Back on the *Enterprise,* Kirk was able to relax totally for the first time since his learning of Spock and Scott's disappearance.

"Scotty, you're a beautiful sight!" Kirk smiled and put his hands on the hirsute engineer's shoulders.

"Aye, a regular caveman, Captain. It's good ta see ye well and all in one piece. Last time I saw ye, ye were in bad shape."

"Do you have any idea as to what the explosion on the *Enterprise* was all about?"

"It was a test, Captain . . ."

"What kind of test?" Kirk asked.

"Ta see how we react in battle or whatever," Scott answered. "Spock thinks they are plannin' ta attack the Federation on a large scale. And they're capable of it, Captain. Dinna let their primitive livin' conditions fool ye."

"What about Spock? Did IIsa poison him?"

"I'm afraid Spock did it ta himself, Captain," Scott replied gravely. "An' when I think back on it, this wasn't the first time he tried it."

"What would make him do such a thing?"

"It's my fault, Captain. He ordered me ta try ta escape. I couldna leave wi'out him. I guess he thought he was eliminating the cause for me stayin' there."

"I wouldn't think he'd go that far; suicide is not a logical alternative."

"It must o' seemed the only way ta get me ta go, Captain. When ya think o' it, it was, under the circumstances. But that changed wi' your comin'."

Both men reflected somberly on the narrow margin of time that saved Spock's life; Kirk remembered his agonizing feeling of urgency as they had approached Tomarii, and he was profoundly thankful he had acknowledged it.

3

In sick bay, McCoy examined Spock more thoroughly.

"You're in no condition to undergo surgery at this time. Orders or no orders, I'm going to delay the procedure until I think you can tolerate it. We'll keep building you up and I'll be the one who decides the proper time."

"You are correct, of course, Doctor," Spock agreed, taking the battle-ready McCoy by surprise. "I would assume my recovery period would be extended."

"Longer than most, Spock. Your muscles have begun to atrophy. At least you can't run off on me now."

"The situation is entirely different now, Doctor. I will fully cooperate with your medical regimen."

"Good, Spock. It's about time," McCoy said, grinning. He finally had his way.

4

With the compilation of Spock and Scott's observations on the Tomariian menace and its dispatch to Starfleet, rest finally came.

The familiar environment of the ship lulled Spock into a feeling of security and he fell into a deep, restful sleep.

Entering sick bay to check on the rescued former first officer, Leonidas frowned. "Where's the security guard?" he demanded of the on-duty nurse.

"There isn't any," she answered, completely bewildered. "What do we need with a security guard?"

Leonidas punched the intercom button. "Security, I want two armed guards in sick bay. On the double!"

He had hardly finished summoning the guard when McCoy, called by the nurse, barreled into the room.

"What the hell are you doing, Leonidas?"

"Putting a guard on the prisoner, Doctor."

"What prisoner?"

"Spock."

"Are you crazy? Spock's not going anywhere."

"It is proper security procedure, McCoy."

Awakened by the loud voices, Spock heard the last statement. "Is there something wrong?"

"You are under arrest," Leonidas announced. "I'm surprised the captain didn't make the proper arrangements."

Kirk, coming to visit with Spock, heard Leonidas's statement and reacted with icy calm.

"You've overstepped your authority, Mister. I give the orders on this ship. If I felt it necessary, I would have placed Spock under arrest myself."

"I was going by the book, Captain. Starfleet regulations, sir."

Kirk wanted to srike him, but held his temper. His face reddened in anger, but he realized he could no longer delay the arrest order. The man he considered to be his first officer was back on board—unable to function and under detention. His chief engineer would have to be confined to quarters as well. Their replacements were merely temporary in Kirk's eyes.

He wondered what had happened to the exuberant and personable Leonidas of the rec room. And Douglas, the contentious engineer, was certainly not Scott, who'd flip backwards to serve both Kirk and the ship. The rescue had been a success, but the captain took no satisfaction in its consequences.

5

The surgery on Spock was not complicated, but it had been too long delayed. McCoy took the fragment of metal from Spock's back, careful not to further damage the surrounding tissue. *It was so small,* McCoy pondered as he examined it, *but had been so much a source of agony.*

He repaired the nerve and muscle damage and closed the incision with his fine laser instruments. It was a long procedure and McCoy was exhausted. The doctor had warned Spock of the long period of convalescence that would be necessary after the surgery, but he knew the stubborn Vulcan would resist any advice to rest as soon as he felt recovered enough to function.

With therapy, McCoy estimated that it would be one month before Spock would be back to normal. Yet in three days Spock walked out of sick bay, unsteadily and wearing a back brace, but definitely on his own. The Vulcan managed a short walk down the corridor and a trip to the bridge to surprise the captain.

His entry onto the bridge was greeted by an uninhibited hug from Uhura—which elicited an amusing attempt to recover his lost dignity—cheers from the remainder of the crew, and joyous relief from Kirk. The captain, even with assurances from McCoy, had still worried about Spock.

The warm moment was abruptly shattered by Leonidas.

"Captain, Mister Spock should not be on the bridge. He is under arrest."

"I know that, Leonidas," Kirk snapped. "But it's my decision to make. Please remember that."

Kirk rarely, if ever, disciplined an officer in view of the crew. The celebratory mood was gone.

"Will confinement to quarters suffice, Mister Spock?" Kirk asked routinely.

"Of course, Captain," Spock answered as expected.

"Good!" Kirk glared at Leonidas. "Satisfied, Commander?"

"Yes, sir," the first officer quietly responded, noticing the hostility directed at him from the bridge crew.

6

Spock was permitted to leave his quarters only to fulfill the medical requirements for exercise necessary to his recovery. Yet for the Vulcan, confinement was not punishment; he used the time to meditate, re-evaluate and study his recent experiences. Although the captain chafed to have him cleared, Spock reminded him that his medical condition made it impossible for him to return to duty immediately in any case. That seemed to ease Kirk's mind to an extent.

With his returning strength, Spock realized that it was time to acknowledge the promise he had made to Julina on Tomarii: He felt obliged to inform the Romulans of the Tomariian threat—and the Klingons, because he had allied with them as well.

He agreed with Kirk that confinement to quarters was sufficient, but he had not given his word to remain in them. It was stretching the truth, but technically Spock was not violating his exchange with Kirk regarding his detention.

He waited for the night cycle to be established, when a minimum crew would be on duty. The auxiliary bridge was deserted when he entered.

One by one, Spock carefully activated the communication panel's connections required to transmit the messages he had programmed in his quarters. Before the communications officer on the bridge realized the override had taken place, the two messages had been sent out over subspace channels.

Returning to his quarters, the Vulcan was met by two security officers and a half-dressed angry captain. Kirk glared at Spock, tersely requesting an explanation.

"Jim, I could not compromise your position. It is against Starfleet regulations to contact either the Romulan or Klingon empires, but I vowed that if I survived, I would inform their empires of the Tomariian threat. I kept my word."

"And by leaving your quarters you broke your word to me."

"Technically, no, Captain. I said confinement to my quarters was sufficient. It was—to serve my purpose."

"Spock, you've made it impossible for me to allow you to be merely confined to your quarters. I'm forced to have you detained in the brig—you've given me no choice."

"It is your only choice, Captain. I accept your position."

Spock walked slowly down the corridor, escorted by the two guards, as a deeply saddened Kirk watched his trusted first officer make his way to the brig in quiet dignity.

Chapter V
Court-Martial

1

Sitting in the legal chambers of Starbase 12, Kirk recalled other court procedures, other hearing rooms, and other officers in place of the three who now entered the room. Kirk remembered the decisions made on those other occasions: The last hearing didn't go well, and he didn't understand the decision when he read the record. Before that, they had always been favorable. He tried to convince himself that this time the verdict would be favorable as well.

A door to the side of the judges' platform opened and he watched Spock and Scott enter, accompanied by two Starfleet security officers. They looked stiff and formal in their dress uniforms. The bailiff ordered the court to rise as the presiding officer entered the hearing room. All eyes turned toward the tall, distinguished man who took his seat at the center of the bench.

Kirk had made a point of looking up the records of the officers who would be hearing his officers' cases. Commodore Pierce had a reputation of being fair but stern. To Pierce's left sat Commodore Kingston Clark, a familiar figure to McCoy from the previous hearing. To Pierce's right was Fleet Captain

Iko Tomako, a man who had a reputation for being extremely conservative.

Kirk was not deeply concerned about the outcome of the proceedings. *Not really,* he thought, brushing off a moment of anxiety.

Spock, unruffled as usual, showed no signs of worry; in Kirk's opinion, he seemed almost too confident. Scott sat rigidly beside Spock, drumming his fingers nervously on the arm of his chair.

When the room quieted and all were seated, Pierce addressed the court: "The General Court-martial of Commander Spock and Lieutenant Commander Montgomery Scott is now in session. Is counsel prepared to present its case?"

The attractive woman sitting between the defendants rose and answered, "Counsel is ready, sir. Ellen Janest, counsel for Lieutenant Commander Scott."

All eyes were on Spock as he rose. "I choose to waive counsel, sir."

Pierce frowned. "The record will so indicate."

Kirk whispered to McCoy, "Waive counsel? Why would Spock do that?"

McCoy shook his head. Kirk mumbled disapprovingly. "Why didn't Clark insist he have counsel? He should have expert legal representation."

Pierce continued. "The charges against Lieutenant Commander Scott are desertion and theft of a Starfleet cruiser. How do you plead, Commander Scott?"

Scott stood beside his counsel and addressed the court. "Not guilty."

"The charges against Commander Spock are treason, desertion, and theft of a Starfleet cruiser. How do you plead, Commander?"

The Vulcan rose, faced the judge, and gave his reply in a completely controlled voice.

"Guilty."

It was hard for Kirk to control his frustration. He nudged McCoy and whispered, "First he refused counsel, now he pleads guilty. Bones, do you know what's gotten into Spock? I don't like the way this is going!"

The doctor was studying the Vulcan with a professional eye. He was as confused as Kirk. "I'm trying to figure him out myself. Maybe he's got something up that Vulcan sleeve of his."

"I certainly hope so," Kirk replied.

"The court, in order to be fair, has decided to hear each case separately. We will begin with the case against Lieutenant Commander Scott. Commodore Bragg will conduct the case for the prosecution."

Bragg, a small man with a high-pitched voice, proceeded immediately.

"Lieutenant Commander, on Stardate 5505.6, did you, without proper authorization, take the cruiser U.S.S. *Raven?*"

The proceedings continued in a sedate fashion. As Kirk listened to the testimony, he scored points for Scott. Janest was extremely competent, and Scott's fate seemed to be in excellent hands.

Kirk sat tensely, watching the woman beside Scott rise and approach the bench to begin her summary. She was one of the finest advocates in Starfleet and her simple beauty and composure added to her effectiveness.

"We must consider the motive and result of Lieutenant Commander Scott's actions. When accompanying Commander Spock, he was essentially following orders since Commander Spock was his commanding officer at the time. There were very beneficial consequences of their mission to Tomarii, not the least of which was the discovery of a trilithium crystal, a more powerful and efficient energy source than dilithium. This discovery and the possible treaty with the planet Paxas, where these crystals were discovered, will be useful to both the Federation and to the people of Paxas. These discoveries will strengthen our forces and give us bases closer to the Klingon Empire, assuring us advance warning of possible attack.

"But the most important result was the discovery of the planet Tomarii and of the extensive Tomariian Empire, of which we were not at all aware. Their threat to peaceful planets is enormous and can now be countered. If Lieutenant Commander Scott and Commander Spock had not taken this initiative, we might have been fully unprepared to deal with this new menace."

As Janest concluded her argument, Kirk nodded approval to McCoy and smiled for the first time that day.

"Before we convene for a decision on Lieutenant Commander Scott's case," Pierce continued, "we will proceed with Commander Spock's." He addressed the prosecuting attorney: "Commander Bragg, you may proceed."

Bragg turned to face Spock. He stood directly in front of the Vulcan as he began his interrogation.

"Commander Spock, on Stardate 5505.6, did you—without authorization—board the cruiser *Raven* and leave Starbase 12 for an unknown destination without clearance?"

"Yes, sir. I did."

"Did you break Starfleet Order 8711KR and contact the Romulan and Klingon empires, warning them of the danger of the Tomariians?"

"Yes."

"You were aware that your action constituted an act of treason, were you not?"

"I was cognizant of the order against such contact and of the consequences of my action."

"The prosecution will now call its witnesses, Commander Spock. You have the right to cross-examine them, if you wish."

"I understand the procedure," Spock acknowledged.

"Commander Alexander Leonidas, will you take the stand?"

The computer summarized Leonidas's service record as he took his seat. Commander Bragg proceeded.

"Commander, you are currently serving as first officer on board the *Enterprise,* are you not?"

"Yes, sir."

"In that capacity, did you not advise Captain Kirk of the danger of bringing the *Enterprise* to the planet Tomarii for a rescue attempt?"

"Yes, I did, sir."

"And did he take your advice?"

"No, sir. But it is his prerogative as superior officer to make the final decision."

"Did the captain risk the ship and the entire crew to complete the rescue?"

"Yes, but he succeeded with no loss of personnel or property."

"Just answer the questions, Commander," Pierce directed.

Leonidas nodded.

"In what condition did you find Commander Spock when you reached the planet?"

The first officer glanced at Kirk before he answered. "He was paralyzed, sir."

"In your opinion, Commander Leonidas, could Commander Spock have completed his *so called* mission of informing Starfleet of the Tomariian threat if the *Enterprise* had not interceded?"

"No, sir."

"Then his whole venture would have been fruitless if not for Captain Kirk's rescue?"

"Yes, as far as I could determine. I logged my opinion, sir."

"That will be all, Commander."

Pierce looked to Spock, who indicated that he wished no cross-examination.

It took all of Kirk's restraint to refrain from interrupting the proceedings with heated objections; all he could do was sit and wait.

His testimony finished, Leonidas stepped down from the witness chair and took a seat in the rear of the room. As he passed the captain, he offered an apologetic shrug.

"Captain James T. Kirk, please take the stand."

With a firm stride Kirk stepped forward.

"Captain, did you have to rescue two of your commanders, risking an entire starship in the attempt?"

"I did follow them to Tomarii, sir. And there was a rescue attempt. But it was my decision to search for them. In a personal message to me, Mister Spock specifically requested that I not search for him. The search and rescue were entirely my responsibility. I am not on trial here, gentlemen. My actions have no bearing on Spock's case."

"On the contrary, Captain," Bragg insisted, "his actions precipitated yours. Commander Spock's action did cause you to jeopardize the *Enterprise* for his benefit."

"I wouldn't put it that way. We were retrieving members of our crew from a hostile planet—a routine Starfleet procedure."

"A matter of interpretation then, Captain?"

"If you prefer, Commodore." Kirk did not like the turn things were taking. "Sir," he interjected, turning to the bench, "I would like to make a statement."

"In defense of Commander Spock, Captain?" Pierce asked.

"Yes, sir."

"You will have that opportunity later, Captain, when the defense presents its case. Proceed, Commodore Bragg."

"Captain, did you not order Commander Spock to be confined to his quarters, and did he not subsequently leave them to contact the Romulan and Klingon empires, thereby committing an act of treason?"

"Technically, sir, I asked Spock if confinement to quarters was sufficient, if I remember my exact wording. It can be checked in the log. He agreed it was sufficient. I assumed he meant to stay in his quarters. My wording was not precise."

"Commander Spock knew exactly what you meant and chose to ignore it. Am I correct?"

"It could be interpreted that way," Kirk grudgingly agreed.

"Captain, you personally had Commander Spock placed in the brig after discovering his contact with the enemy empires, did you not?"

"Yes. Spock explained his reason for the contact at the time. He had allied with the Romulan and Klingon representatives who were also prisoners of the Tomariians. He had given his word as an ally that if he survived the others he would warn their respective empires of the danger. He kept his word. A Vulcan is compelled to, no matter what the personal consequences. In my opinion, he did not jeopardize the *Enterprise* by his action."

"By sending a subspace message to the enemy, Commander Spock gave the coordinates of the starship to them. Is that correct, Captain?"

"Yes, sir. But we were not attacked as a result of his breach of security."

"That is irrelevant, Captain. The fact is Commander Spock willfully committed an act of treason fully cognizant of the possible consequences of that act. You recognized that fact when you had him imprisoned on board the *Enterprise* immediately following the incident. Am I correct?"

Forced into the position of having to support his action, Kirk could only reply, "Yes, sir, I did."

"Thank you, Captain," Bragg said triumphantly. "One more thing, Captain Kirk. There was another incident in which Commander Spock took a Starfleet vessel, the U.S.S.

Enterprise, and set a course for Talos IV, a planet forbidden Federation access. You do remember the incident, Captain?"

"Yes, sir. But there were no charges brought against the commander in that case. Spock acted on behalf of his former captain, who had been seriously injured and could be assisted only by the Talosians. Starfleet understood his motives and there was no action taken against him."

"He did, however, take the ship, Captain."

Kirk had to agree. "Yes, sir, he did."

Smugly, Bragg thanked the captain. "That will be all, Captain Kirk. Doctor Leonard McCoy, please take the stand."

Bragg continued his case. "Doctor McCoy, you issued a medical order to Commander Spock which he chose to defy, is that not correct?"

"Yes," McCoy said firmly.

"Did you warn him of the possible consequences of his action?"

"Yes, sir. It's all recorded in my medical log."

"Is it your opinion that Commander Spock took unnecessary risk and had little chance of completing his venture?"

"He had little chance medically, sir."

"When you found Commander Spock, what was his condition?"

"The sliver of metal embedded near his spine as a result of the explosion aboard the *Enterprise* had shifted, paralyzing him. He was also malnourished and anemic as a result of his confinement."

"Unable to act on behalf of Starfleet or himself, Doctor?"

"Yes."

Kirk envisioned a gag on McCoy in his frustration, as the doctor continued to support the case against Spock.

"Then it is your medical opinion that Commander Spock's venture was doomed to failure because of his physical condition?"

"Yes."

"That will be all, Doctor."

"Sir," McCoy directed to Commodore Pierce, "I wish to make a statement."

"You will be given the opportunity later, Doctor, when the defense presents its case. Do you have any further witnesses, Commodore Bragg?"

"No, sir, not at this time."

"We will proceed with the defense. Commander Spock, you may present your case."

Spock rose and approached the bench. "I have no defense, sir. I am technically guilty of the charges against me. I initiated the entire venture. I planned it and I take complete responsibility for my actions. I did what I believed to be in the best interest of Starfleet. It was a logical decision on my part, based on what I considered to be valid evidence. I make no excuses and I will accept your decision without question."

"You have no witnesses for the defense, Commander Spock?"

"That is correct, sir."

Kirk could contain his frustration no longer. He jumped up, addressing the bench. "Sir, I wish to make a statement in Spock's behalf."

"You are out of order, Captain."

McCoy tugged at Kirk's sleeve. "Sit down, Jim. You can't do any good by losing your temper."

"Somebody's got to come to his defense."

"I know," McCoy whispered, "but I don't think there's a damn thing we can do."

Commodore Clark glared at them—it became very quiet in the court.

"Court is adjourned," Pierce declared. "We will resume tomorrow at 0900 hours with a decision in both cases. Court is dismissed."

Spock remained a figure of calm in the center of the frenzied activity surrounding his detention and trial on Starbase 12. Both Kirk and McCoy were furious with him for not defending himself. They both stood in his cell, not knowing what to say.

The Vulcan refused to speak. He felt his point was made and wanted no further discussion. So they all sat silently, waiting for someone to speak, but no one did.

Spock was relieved when they left. His primary concern was for Scott—he strongly hoped the engineer would be vindicated. As for himself, he would accept whatever decision the court made.

* * *

O-nine-hundred hours was approaching too quickly, or maybe it was taking too long in coming, Kirk wasn't sure which. Either way, he didn't face the day with much enthusiasm. He'd been up for hours, pacing the quarters he occupied at the base. He weighed the testimony, rethought the case, and went through it all yet again. If he were sitting on the judges' panel, he would be forced to find Spock guilty. Scott's case wasn't as clear-cut; he might be cleared if the court were lenient.

But what about Spock? Kirk was counting on his own testimony to convince the judges of his officers' characters and abilities sufficiently to warrant light sentences, at least. He was vaguely disturbed by the seeming reticence of Starfleet on the issue of the Tomariian threat itself. After the full report had been presented to Starfleet, Kirk had been expecting orders for a mission to defuse or counter the now-evident menace this remote civilization presented to the Federation. Now the outcome of the hearing took precedence. Kirk put on his dress uniform and joined McCoy on the way to the courtroom.

When they arrived, Spock and Scott, along with Ellen Janest, were already seated. The bench was still unoccupied. The courtroom was full of familiar faces, since every member of the *Enterprise* crew who could be present was there.

The judges entered. Kirk tried to read the decisions on their faces, but long years of practice had taught them to mask their emotions. After they were seated, Commodore Pierce asked Scott to rise and approach the bench. He got directly to the business at hand.

"Lieutenant Commander Montgomery Scott, the court finds you NOT GUILTY of the charges and specifications filed against you. However, we do feel a reprimand is in order since you did take part in the venture. The court orders a one-year flight suspension, during which time you will teach at the Academy facilities on Starbase 3. Further, there is a reduction in rank to lieutenant. You are ordered to report to your new duty assignment immediately. That will be all."

Scott sighed in relief, and smiled at Kirk. The engineer felt that a one-year flight suspension was tolerable—he could keep up with his engineering journals, and teaching might be an interesting change of pace for a while. The lowering of rank didn't bother him at all. He had come up from the ranks once and he was confident he could do it again before retirement.

Scott returned to his seat and shook the hand of his very pleased lawyer. When he looked at Spock, his contentment diminished.

Standing at attention, Spock faced the bench. Commodore Pierce stood to read the verdict. "Commander Spock, the court finds you GUILTY as charged."

Kirk flinched when he heard the words. He watched the muscles in Spock's back contract. It was the only sign Spock gave of his feelings, and that was imperceptible to anyone but Kirk.

Pierce continued, "Your sentence is based upon your own admission of guilt, as well as the evidence presented against you. You will serve five years at the Starfleet Correctional and Rehabilitation Center on Minos. Sentence to begin immediately. After you have served your sentence, you will be barred from participation in all Starfleet actions and access to its facilities."

As he was led out of the room, an expressionless Spock did not look once at his captain.

Kirk asked for permission to speak to Spock before his removal to Minos. It was granted, and he followed the guards into a small detention room.

When he entered, one of the guards was fastening Spock's hands in front of him with handcuffs secured to a belt around his waist. At Kirk's entry Spock stood, still looking much too calm.

"That's not necessary, Lieutenant. Spock won't cause you any trouble," Kirk said approaching the guard.

"Sorry, sir. It's regulation procedure for a prisoner in transit." He snapped the cuffs shut, restraining Spock's arms completely.

Spoke spoke calmly. "It's all right, Jim. I accept the situation."

"Can you leave us alone for a minute, Lieutenant?" Kirk asked.

"No, sir, I'm sorry." But the guard respected their desire to speak alone and moved to the other side of the room, leaving Kirk and Spock in some measure of privacy.

"Spock," Kirk began, "I'll start an appeal motion—the sentence is unreasonable. We can get it modified. Your father can help. Surely a man in his position should be able to get your sentence commuted. You could be back on the *Enterprise* tomorrow!"

Spock's attitude changed abruptly. "Captain, I absolutely forbid you to contact my father. You do not understand Vulcan relationships. I cannot ask Sarek for assistance, and you *must* not. You must promise me that you will not try to contact him in any way."

Seeing how agitated Spock became at the mention of his father, Kirk agreed quietly.

"I promise, Spock. I won't contact Sarek if you feel that strongly about it. But I don't understand your attitude at all!"

"I do not ask you to understand my motives, Jim. But I do ask that you respect my decisions and actions. Accept the entire situation realistically. I did commit the offenses. I will survive the five years. I want no further discussion. Please, Jim." He tried to reassure his friend. "I will be fine."

But Kirk knew Spock. A rehabilitation center would be unendurable for him. Spock knew that too.

"I am trying to understand, Spock. If you ever need anything, contact me: anytime, anyplace. I'll be there to help you. Remember that!"

"I am sorry, sir," the guard interrupted. "I can't allow you any more time."

The things they really wanted to say remained unspoken. Kirk nodded his head and Spock was led out of the room. The Vulcan turned and looked back when he reached the doorway. With an unwavering gaze, he looked deeply into Kirk's pained eyes.

"Live long and prosper, my friend."

The door closed, leaving Kirk alone.

Chapter VI

Minos

1

"Strip down!"

The security officer barked the order when Spock entered the detention unit on Starbase 12. After the removal of his restraints, Spock began to disrobe. He took off his tunic, neatly folding it and putting it on a nearby chair. He then stretched the stirrups on the pants over his boots to facilitate their removal.

"Hurry up!" the guard prodded, enjoying the power he held over the prisoner. "Everything!" he directed when Spock hesitated after having removed his T-shirt. "Boots, too!"

It was with difficulty that Spock removed his boots. The back brace McCoy insisted he wear until his wound entirely healed restricted his movement.

The guard took the neatly folded bundle of clothing and dumped it in a corner. He handed Spock a fluorescent yellow jump suit and a pair of worn sandals. "Put these on!"

Spock took the suit, made purposely distinctive to discourage escape attempts, and slowly slipped it on. He watched the guard remove the small bundle of clothes he had just taken off. Along with the uniform, his control of his own fate was gone.

Throughout the entire process of prisoner identification and the change of clothes, Spock remained expressionless. He remembered times on board the *Enterprise,* on those rare occasions when prisoners were being transferred, how he had looked upon them with pity. Prisoner transfer had been the security section's responsibility and he had taken only a mild interest. The process was acutely distasteful to him—as the object of all the rigid precautions—but no one would have known; his face revealed absolutely nothing.

The security docking bay of Starbase 12 was located on the far side of the space station. It was therefore necessary to take the prisoners along the main corridor through much of the base. Spock was acquainted with the physical layout of the starbase and dreaded the long walk in full view of any passersby. He withdrew further into himself as the time for his transfer approached.

It was even worse than he expected. The station was full of personnel from the *Enterprise,* all doing their last-minute personal provisioning before returning to deep space. The corridor stretched infinitely long.

Actually, it is 132.8 meters, Spock assured himself as he was led out of the detention unit into the long hall. He immediately recognized a lieutenant who was passing.

Concentrating his sight on the end of the hall, Spock did not look to either side.

There was no doubt as to the identity of the prisoner in fetters and accompanied by guards coming toward the three women as they finished their shopping before returning to the *Enterprise.* Christine Chapel saw him first as a bright spot moving toward them. As he came nearer, she broke into tears and started toward him. She was firmly held at arm's length by one of the guards. Uhura and Rand, their own tears of sympathy barely restrained, led Christine away.

Each glance was almost physically painful as he continued down the long hallway with the guards. Spock was walking a gauntlet. He felt very exposed to the hostility of the onlookers at the station. The only sympathy came from crew members of the *Enterprise.* He shielded himself with Vulcan discipline as, one by one, other people turned to stare as he was led past.

The court-martial had been the main topic of conversation in Starfleet for days, so it wasn't surprising to find a group of Starfleet reporters waiting at the door of the docking bay when the guards approached with their prisoner. Expressionless and silent, Spock tolerated the shoving reporters until the guards led him into the waiting ship.

The brig on the cruiser was much like any other and had the distinct advantage of providing a haven from the blatant stares of curiosity seekers. Except for the guard outside his cell and an occasional nosy crewman who stopped to gawk, Spock was finally alone. He moved his arms briskly, bringing back his circulation after the removal of the restraints, and placed himself with his back toward the door, creating as much privacy as possible. He had no idea as to when he would arrive at Minos since the cruiser had other business en route. It was disconcerting not to have control over his own movements. Within the limits of Starfleet orders and the vicissitudes of missions, he had always had his freedom. There was also the challenge, adventure, and the exhilaration of exploration. And there had been the companionship of his captain and friend, James T. Kirk.

Spock had always prided himself on his self-sufficiency. Forced to spend a lonely childhood, he had learned not to depend emotionally upon anyone else. Over the years he had developed a protective barrier which shielded him from the risks of intimacy. But under that barrier he felt pain. It was Jim Kirk who had been able to break through, who had become his close and only real friend. Now he had to face the unknown without him. He believed the entire court-martial and conviction was harder on Jim than on anyone else.

That is all past, he told himself. *I must manage alone.*

2

Minos was a Class-A planet—life possible with artificial atmosphere and off-planet support—and was under a tight security screen. The actual center was completely underground, with the available arable land under an atmosphere dome for farming. The facility was now almost entirely self-supporting. Vegetables and fruits were supplied by the farm, meat by a large herd of hogs, the only livestock found able to adapt to the environment. All of the labor was provided by the inmates.

Spock still wore the yellow jump suit when he was led into the warden's office upon his arrival on Minos. He stood before the desk in the large, sparsely furnished room with his hands once again bound.

"Sir, this is Spock, the Vulcan convicted of treason," the guard announced loudly.

"I am Commander Bryant," the warden said. He indicated a file on his desk. "Your reputation precedes you, Spock. Please leave us, Lieutenant," Bryant ordered the guard.

"But, sir, that's not the usual procedure," he protested.

"He's a most unusual prisoner, Lieutenant. Please, do as I say."

Spock watched the interchange with interest, trying to assess the warden. He seemed to typify Starfleet: He was tall, of medium coloring, well-groomed, self-assured, and appeared competent.

The guard, obviously disturbed at leaving the warden alone with the prisoner, positioned himself outside the door, anticipating trouble.

It was no more than five minutes later when he was called back in to finish the introductory procedures and escort the prisoner to his cell. Before he took Spock away, the warden once again addressed the guard.

"Remove the cuffs, Lieutenant. The prisoner is not dangerous. He's given me his word that he'll be cooperative."

Spock offered his hands and the guard unlocked the cuffs, freeing him. "Thank you, Lieutenant," the Vulcan said calmly. "That is a definite improvement."

The guard was taken aback by Spock's relaxed attitude. It was too polite, and the tone was that of a superior officer. Feeling he had to assert his authority over the prisoner, he roughly spun the Vulcan about while preparing to take him to his cell.

"Lieutenant, I'll not tolerate rough treatment of the prisoners," Bryant warned.

"Sorry, sir."

Bryant gave the guard a menacing look, and turned back to the pile of work on his desk.

With a tight grip on Spock's arm the guard led him to the cell block.

"I don't know what he told you in there, Vulcan, but you'll get no special treatment here," the lieutenant warned.

"I expect none, Lieutenant," Spock replied too calmly.

The guard was unnerved. "We've never had a Vulcan prisoner here before," he snapped. "This is predominantly a human institution. You understand that?"

Spock nodded.

Before he was taken to his cell, Spock was subjected to a body search. After that, he showered and was given a standard olive-green jump suit. The number M621V, in bold red letters, was stitched on the upper-left side and across the back.

"Learn the number," the guard sneered. "That's who you are now, *Commander* Spock."

Spock noticed that Starfleet had not planned its penal system to accommodate the great numbers requiring it. The screening and training processes were so stringent that they felt the need for correctional facilities to be negligible. But even among the Starfleet select there turned out to be offenders and incorrigibles in sufficient quantities to crowd the facilities set aside for them. The fact that it shared this correctional facility with the civil authorities in the sector only increased the load on the prison. Minos was disgracefully overcrowded.

Spock was aware of four such facilities. This one and the one on the planet Galor were designed specifically for human and like species; the other two served for Starfleet prisoners with different environmental needs. Spock knew he was the first Vulcan to have been sentenced to Minos. He acknowledged that it was not a particularly desirable distinction. He was handed a stack of linens and escorted to the cell which was to be his home for the next five years.

He found himself alone. Examining the cell, he saw it accommodated four, although it had originally been designed for two. The two lower berths and one of the uppers were made up; the only unmade bed, obviously his, was the upper left. He put the linens he was carrying down on the lower bunk and proceeded to make up the bed. His back muscles rebelled. Still encumbered by the back brace which McCoy insisted he wear, Spock could see he would have difficulty raising himself onto the bunk, yet it was the only place for him to sit.

Before making the effort to get up onto the bunk, Spock put an extended finger into the energy field on the entrance of the cell. It was activated and sent a very substantial jolt into him. He raised an eyebrow in acknowledgement and struggled onto the bunk, stretching flat. Grateful for the opportunity to gather his thoughts before the onslaught of prison life really began, he lay quietly in contemplation. He had hardly begun to ponder his situation when the cell's other occupants entered.

With a porcine grunt, the large man who entered first threw himself onto the bed below Spock, sending the entire bunk into vibrations. He was a huge hulk of a man who, Spock estimated, must weigh almost 300 pounds. He was built like a bull, and moved like one.

On the lower bed across from "Bull" Tim Macklen, a small weasel of a man was removing his sandals. Harry Needham didn't even glance at the new occupant of the cell. But it was the man who took the bunk across from his who interested Spock most.

Tall and slim, with the distinctive pointed ear of the Vulcan strain, the man gracefully vaulted to his bunk and sat, legs dangling, facing Spock. The two men openly stared, appraising each other.

Spock made an attempt to introduce himself. "Spock."

No acknowledgement followed.

Realizing he was getting nowhere, Spock lay back, acutely

aware of the scrutiny of the man in the next bunk, but saying nothing more.

A warning buzzer sounded and the occupants of cell 621 prepared for lights-out by stripping for bed. Confronted with the choice of sleeping in his jump suit, the only clothing issued him so far, or with nothing on, Spock chose to strip as well.

He got under the blankets as the lights dimmed, but they did not go out entirely. The ceiling was still partly illuminated. Spock's preference for the dark was an idiosyncrasy well known among the crew members of the *Enterprise*. His quarters were always dimly lit, providing a haven, a place where he could meditate. That privacy was now a thing of the past.

Spock covered his eyes with his right arm, blocking the offending light. His sensitive hearing magnified every sound in the cell block: breathing, the rustle of men turning, the flush of a commode, all were intensified. He didn't plan on getting much sleep this first night in his new home.

A full forty-five minutes and five seconds passed. The sound of even breathing indicated to Spock that most of the men in the block were asleep. Even the jolting movements of Bull Macklen below him had quieted. The usual solace of Vulcan meditation eluded him—the more he tried to relax, the less he was able.

Suddenly the bunk convulsed again. Bull Macklen rose, towered above Spock's bunk, and grabbed the unprepared Vulcan by the arm, throwing him roughly off the bunk onto the hard concrete floor. Bull had raised his foot over Spock's head when a quick, strong hand pulled the huge man off his feet. Bull snorted an obscenity, pulled himself up, and lunged for Spock's protector, who moved quickly aside, letting Bull's momentum throw him off balance. He crashed into the side of the bunk. Bull came to his feet again, charging at Spock with fury. Like a matador, Spock slipped to the side, raising his hand to Bull's shoulder. The Vulcan nerve pinch brought Bull crashing senseless to the floor.

"Thank you," Spock said to his protector.

Responding to Spock's overture this time, his bunkmate spoke. "I am Desus."

"Romulan," Spock commented.

He was answered with a smile.

"What is a Romulan doing in this place? I thought we . . ." he considered his statement and then continued, "the Federation exchanges Romulan prisoners."

Desus gave Spock the needed boost up to his bunk. "Ordinarily, yes. But I am not a military prisoner. I was apprehended for piracy."

"A Romulan of military age, a pirate? That seems illogical." Spock lay prone, easing the ache in his back.

"No more so than a Vulcan convicted of treason." Desus' statement echoed in dead silence.

The groggy Macklen got up off the floor and returned to his bunk. By the time the guard checked the disturbance in cell 621, all was quiet.

The next morning Spock reported to the Labor Division office for his work assignment. He had no notion as to how assignments were designated, but logic dictated that a man's skills would be influential in the decision.

He was wrong. It was hard, even for Spock, not to react openly in dismay when he was told what his work would be. He was assigned to the care and feeding of the hogs. He had no objection to physical work, but raising animals for food was against all of his beliefs. For him to be a part of the process was particularly distasteful, but he made no complaint.

Because automation had made most time-consuming labor obsolete, the normal mechanical devices were omitted on Minos. Heavy work was needed to keep the prisoner population busy and in check. When Spock arrived at the livestock area, he was immediately handed a container of slops to carry over to the feeding pens. The bucket was oversized and heavy. With his back still healing, he wanted no extra strain on the area, so he dragged the bucket over to the pens.

As he was lifting the bucket to dump the rancid contents, a well-placed foot was extended, tripping him. Losing his balance in the slippery mire, he fell, splattering the mess from the bucket. Gales of laughter from the other prisoners accompanied his fall.

Covered with slime and sitting in a dirty puddle, Spock brushed himself off. A dirty but welcome hand was provided to help him up. It was Desus. "Thank you again," Spock said, brushing off as much of the refuse as he could.

"It's the least I could offer under the circumstances. Your arrival has switched their attention from me."

"What's this? Playing in the mud?" a guard barked.

The other prisoners snickered.

"I slipped," Spock answered quickly.

"Back to work," the guard ordered. "Help him, Desus."

"Yes, sir," the Romulan answered, following Spock, who went back to get another bucket.

"It seems the guards are not going to be helpful," Spock observed.

"The guards watch and don't permit them to get too much out of hand, but don't expect them to intercede for you. I've heard the prison gossip. Your crime is not a popular one."

"Treason never is," Spock said seriously.

"From my sources in the Romulan Empire, I have heard some of the details. . . ." Desus probed.

Together they hefted a heavy bucket. "I simply kept my word, Desus. I do not wish to discuss it. It is done."

"And you are here."

"That, my friend, is obvious."

"Hurry up, you two, this isn't a picnic," the guard shouted, spurring them on.

Returning to the hog pen with the bucket, Spock and Desus dumped it and were heading back for another when they were confronted by Bull Macklen, his huge body effectively blocking their progress. Trying to avoid a confrontation, they backed off and tried to go around him, but Bull moved quickly for a man of his size and blocked them again. The guards' backs were turned, whether deliberately or not, Spock couldn't tell. Bull gripped Desus' jump suit, twirling the Romulan around like a toy. Seeing that no one was going to restrain the bully, Spock went into action. With a strategically placed blow with the side of his hand, he sent the huge assailant flying.

Bull, brushing off the clinging mud, charged at Spock, knocking the wind out of him. Desus, waiting for his opening, seized Bull's ankles, sending him sprawling face down in the mire. As long as the confrontation provided an amusing distraction, the other prisoners didn't care who came out ahead. They roared with laughter when the huge man righted himself and spit the muck out of his mouth.

Picking up the bucket as if nothing had happened, Spock and Desus continued on their way. "A minor victory," Desus warned, "but he'll be back for more."

The last thing Spock expected so soon was a visitor. Awaiting him in the small room set aside for the infrequent visitors to Minos was James T. Kirk. He smiled when Spock entered the room.

Sitting stiffly upright in the chair provided for him, Spock remained silent.

"Not even a hello, Spock?" Kirk asked.

"You should not have come here, Captain. Association with me can only cause further difficulty."

"We were cruising in this sector, Spock. What kind of friend would I be if I passed up an opportunity to see how you are doing?"

"A wise friend," Spock answered.

"Not funny, Spock." Kirk sadly noted the dirt-encrusted, broken fingernails on the slender, tapering fingers that were used to playing on a computer console. As Spock adjusted his position on the chair, his sleeve moved up, revealing a large greenish-yellow bruise. He quickly let the sleeve drop to cover the injury when he saw Kirk's eyes resting on his forearm.

"Are you all right?" Kirk demanded.

Spock's silence was distressing. Kirk had seen Spock in all of his moods, and he knew the Vulcan would say nothing rather than admit anything was wrong.

"I'm not leaving here without an answer from you, Spock! Now, what's wrong?"

He knew he had to answer Kirk or he'd have no peace.

"Nothing, Jim."

"That bruise is nothing?"

"An accident. I tripped."

"You lie badly, Spock."

"I cannot lie, Captain. It's against my . . ."

"Oh, please, Spock! I've seen some of your better performances. The truth."

"If you insist," Spock replied with resignation. "This place does not represent Starfleet's finest. It was a slight altercation, nothing serious I assure you."

"And I should see the other guy, right?"

"Exactly."

"That's more like it. McCoy wants an update on your back."

"Getting stronger. The forced exercise seems to be helping."

"That's good. . . ."

The guard interrupted. "Time's up, Captain Kirk."

Kirk went to the door with the guard. "Remember, Spock, if you need anything, anytime . . ."

The last look he had of Spock was of the Vulcan standing immobile, silent. The visit did not ease Kirk's mind.

Desus sat next to Spock in the prison cafeteria, aware of the Vulcan's lack of appetite.

"Why don't you eat, Spock? The food is not good, but it is nourishing," the Romulan said with concern.

"I prefer to fast," Spock answered. "Vulcans can go without food for extended periods. . . ."

"So can we Romulans, Spock. Our common ancient ancestors passed on rugged traits, but we Romulans can't go without food indefinitely and still work. And neither can you, for all of your pride."

Spock's silence was the only response.

"All right, I'll say no more about this. However, if I've noticed, others will. I believe you should ask for a less strenuous work assignment. You seem to be having difficulty with your back."

"An old injury," Spock explained. "It's almost entirely healed."

"You must have other qualifications which would be more useful here."

"They don't seem to need the services of a science officer, Desus, and they have their own staff computer experts."

"Understandably," the Romulan observed. "The entire place is computer-controlled. They wouldn't risk having a prisoner near any computer terminal on the planet."

The buzzer indicating the mealtime's end sounded, cutting their exchange short.

Before lights-out, Spock perched on his upper bunk, trying to relax. He thought of Kirk's visit, wishing he'd never come. It was better not to have contact with him at this point. He lay down, shielding his eyes from the offending light with his arm, and stretched his muscles, trying to ease his fatigue. He could hear his cellmates move about, strip, and one by one retire before the lights dimmed. The cell block settled down and became quiet.

Spock was in that vague state between wakefulness and sleep when the bunk shuddered and he heard Bull get up. The large man's paw reached for his arm. Spock turned quickly, reaching for Bull's shoulder, but missed by just an inch as the giant of a man pulled him off the bunk.

"Please," Spock said, "I have no desire to hurt you. I have strength beyond your knowledge. It is unwise to provoke me."

In a surprising move, Bull suddenly backed away. There was hardly any time for Spock to react as Bull swiftly withdrew a knife from beneath his mattress. Desus came up behind the angry giant, preparing to strike him, when Harry Needham reached out and grabbed the Romulan's foot, sending him sprawling.

Bull slashed at Spock, cutting deeply into the flesh of the Vulcan's upper arm and bringing forth a gush of green. Spock, ignoring the injury, hit the large man with all of his might, throwing Bull against the bunk. He came up thrashing the knife in the air. Desus made another grab for him and was slashed in the chest with the point of the blade before he managed to get in a blow. Spock tossed a warning look at Harry, who wisely backed off. With what little strength was left him, Spock reached for Bull's shoulder, forcing his fingers into the precision nerve pinch that rendered the giant unconscious.

When the guards finally arrived, they found Spock standing in a corner with his right arm dangling limply and his left clasped tightly over his bleeding upper arm in an unsuccessful effort to staunch the flow of blood. They looked to Desus; the cut across his chest oozed green.

One guard, phaser in hand, gestured Spock out of the cell, while another prodded Desus. His phaser on heavy stun, one of the guards checked Bull, who was just regaining his senses. They escorted all three to the infirmary for treatment.

Doctor Lucas Freed was not pleased to be awakened for yet another medical emergency. He had been assigned to Minos three months earlier, straight out of Starfleet medical school. The few months he had spent on Minos had been tiresomely monotonous, with moments such as this night's emergency periodically relieving the boredom.

He knew why the service assigned doctors only one-year tours of duty on the prison planet. It was almost a form of punishment, but necessary, so the lower-ranking doctors took turns, loathing the assignment.

This night's emergency, however, proved to be exceptional. The passive bleeding Vulcan standing before him was a surprise, the Romulan another. He knew the aliens had been assigned to Minos, but, being the only doctor in the facility and frightfully overworked, he was behind with his routine physical exams and had not seen either of them until now.

A quick examination of Bull assured the doctor that he was all right. While one of the guards escorted Bull to a high-security cell, Freed quickly assessed the other two patients' wounds, turning first to Spock's more serious injury. It was a very deep slash, almost to the bone. Freed draped a sterile cloth over the wound before beginning his surgical repair. He had never treated a Vulcan before, so he called up the appropriate computer records, hoping for additional information on Vulcan circulatory systems and trauma. The bleeding, disheveled man before him hardly fitted the descriptions he had read of the proud Vulcan race.

The doctor knew the wound had to be painful, but there was no sign of discomfort from Spock as he cleaned, repaired, and dressed his wound. Satisfied that it would heal well, and awed by his patient's tolerance for pain, he administered a series of shots to block the pain and fight infection, and then turned his attention to Desus.

"You two are really a pair," Freed said, swabbing the unfamiliar green blood from Desus' chest. "I never before treated a patient from either of your races, and here I have the two of you, both bleeding green all over my infirmary." Looking up to Spock, he commented, "I thought I read that Vulcans were dedicated to peace and nonviolence."

"We are," Spock assured him. "However, when provoked, we will defend ourselves from harm."

"Not always successfully," Freed observed, continuing to minister to Desus.

Spock preferred not to address himself to that last statement. He was becoming woozy and leaned heavily on the wall for support.

"Shot taking effect?" Freed asked, coming over and offering a hand. "Let's get you to bed."

He led the Vulcan into the ward, helping him onto a bed. A guard took Desus' arm and guided him to the bed next to Spock's. "They'll both be out until well past morning roll call," Freed told the guard. "Account for them on the sick list for the next day or so."

Spock awoke late into the morning, with the throbbing in his arm reminding him of the unpleasant events of the previous night. He had no intention of moving from the bed in the infirmary until he had to. He looked over to the next bed and saw Desus smiling at him.

"You've slept long," the Romulan said. "I was concerned."

"You saved my life last night, Desus."

"I know you would have done no less for me, Spock. We are truly brothers in blood now."

"Yes," Spock agreed. "There does seem to be a bond of sorts between us, forged by shared adversity. . . ."

"You seem disturbed."

"No, not disturbed." Spock lapsed into thought. What he truly was was confused.

The Romulan and he had become friends very quickly, more quickly than he would have believed possible. He had not considered the possibility of new friendships developing during this ordeal at all. Although brought together by a common enemy in Bull, Spock believed that was not the main factor in their friendship. He had never allowed close personal relationships except for his friendship with Kirk. But he realized that he felt entirely comfortable with Desus. Their physiology was much the same; they were, in evolutionary terms, cousins of a sort. He had never felt that he entirely fit in with the mostly human crew on the *Enterprise*, since he favored his father's race in both his physical appearance and in his personal philosophy. With Desus, no explanations or accommodations seemed necessary.

Spock looked over at the Romulan, realizing he had found a balance for his Vulcan side. *Just as Jim Kirk has been for my human half.* He was somehow reassured but also vaguely disturbed. *These are emotions I should not be allowing myself to experience; they could detract from the successful realization of my plans.*

He felt disoriented. *The aftereffects of the drug,* he thought, trying to shake off his light-headedness.

"Dizzy?" Freed's voice broke through the fog.

"Yes. It must be the medication."

Sounding much like McCoy, Freed responded tartly, "If you lie there and behave yourself, the dizziness will pass more quickly." Examining Spock's wound, Freed redressed it and left without another word.

"He is right, you know," Desus said. "I have discovered it's best to cooperate with them."

Spock looked around the room and spotted a receiver. He began to rise when Desus took the initiative.

"Stay there. My wound is less painful." The Romulan left his bed and approached Spock, knowing he wanted to talk privately.

In a low murmur, Spock conferred with his new ally. "I have no intention of staying here much longer, Desus. I have every intention of leaving—and soon."

"Escape? I have given that prospect some thought myself, but I found no way," the Romulan whispered. "And I have looked carefully and have had more time and opportunity than you have had."

"I have an advantage, Desus. I know Starfleet procedures and codes. If I had an opportunity to get access to the computer, there would be no problem."

"What about a ship? They keep none here."

"There is one. The warden's cruiser. He is due to leave for a conference on Starbase 3 tomorrow."

"How do you know that?"

"My rather acute Vulcan auditory sense. I overheard a guard."

"Why are you telling me this?" the Romulan asked suspiciously.

"Because, Desus, there is at least a racial affinity between us, and your assistance would be invaluable. Will you come with me?"

"Of course . . ." Desus stopped in mid-sentence when he saw Freed, carrying a breakfast tray laden with fresh fruit, come into the ward.

"Try this, Spock," the doctor said cheerfully. "I think you'll find the fruit more to your liking than the usual prison fare."

It was a generous gesture and fully appreciated. Studying the fruit on the tray, Spock picked up a banana and started peeling it. Finishing the banana, he left the remainder of the fruit on the tray untouched.

"Is that all you want?" Freed asked. "Don't you want another piece?"

"You are a younger version of another Starfleet physician, Doctor. I do not require a great deal of nourishment. Do not concern yourself with my diet. I will not starve."

"Let me take a look at that cut." Freed gestured Desus back to his bed. He checked the wound, and satisfied it was healing well, he left them alone again.

"It must be tonight," Spock said, continuing their interrupted conversation.

"So soon?"

"The cruiser is here. We have no idea how long it will be available. The security in the infirmary is light. What better opportunity would we have? What would we gain by delaying? The sooner we go, the less time for suspicion to arise. I do not intend to be the target of sadistic misfits again."

"Where do you plan to go?"

"That is the one problem I have not solved. I cannot return to Vulcan or, for that matter, any Federation ally. Possibly you have a suggestion . . ."

"I think I have a solution. I am with you, Spock. I have been here far too long already. Trust me, and you will have a safe haven."

"I do trust you, Desus. My past allegiances are by necessity forfeit."

3

In the underground living environment of Minos it was hard to tell night from day, but, as on the starship, a night cycle was established artificially. Spock waited for the lights to dim before setting his plan into motion.

Freed's office was dark, and the guards expected nothing. He motioned Desus to be quiet and went to the door to check the guards. There were two, laughing over a shared joke. Putting his hands to the door, he focused his thoughts on the guards' minds on the other side of it. The distance and lack of actual physical contact made it difficult to reach them and he concentrated ever harder. *Check the prisoners in the ward*, his projected thoughts suggested. *Check the prisoners!*

Desus watched Spock's every move, and came up close behind the Vulcan.

The Vulcan's fingers gripped the doorjamb so tightly that the Romulan could see a dent in the metal. Again, Spock's mind reached for the guards. *Check the prisoners in the ward. . . .*

The laughing stopped. "Joe, I just got the funniest feeling," one guard said, shaking his buzzing head.

"Me, too. Think they're up to something in there?"

"Let's check them out."

Spock motioned Desus to the other side of the door. The Romulan swiftly took his place, waiting. The guards, with phasers set on heavy stun, opened the door carefully. The first one went through the doorway and looked about, signaling his companion to wait. He took another step into the room; Spock's hand gripped his neck, and he knew nothing more. Desus quickly dispatched the second guard.

Spock hastened into Freed's office, sat down at the computer terminal, and punched into the security system with practiced ease.

"Just as I thought," he told Desus, "customary Starfleet coding." He selected a computer tape from Freed's medical file, inserted it into the computer, and changed its programming. "This will foul up the system for a sufficient time, I think," Spock reported with satisfaction. He activated the tape; the computer beeped and then went dark.

Threading their way down the corridors, the Vulcan and the Romulan narrowly missed bumping into a patrolling guard. When they reached the docking bay, there were two more guards to confront. Desus aimed the phaser he had taken from one of the guards in the infirmary.

"On heavy stun," Spock ordered, seeing that the phaser was set to kill. "I want no blood on my conscience."

"There are essential differences in our philosophy, Spock," Desus commented, changing the phaser setting as he spoke. He adjusted the phaser for wide dispersal and fired, stunning the guards instantly.

"Don't touch the door," Spock warned. "There's a backup alarm." He pushed open a panel and deactivated it. "Now!"

They rushed into the docking bay, surprising the guard at the cruiser's door. Desus fired; the guard went down, and the alarm sounded.

"He hit the alarm button before I could fire," Desus shouted.

"Too late to worry about it," Spock called, entering the ship. "Let's get out of here—fast!"

A phaser blast ripped into the portal, tearing into the sheathing. Spock reeled back. The door closed, Desus put the cruiser on highest thrust, and they sped away, barely squeezing through the alarm-activated docking bay portals into the planet's atmosphere.

"Are you all right?" Desus called.

"Yes," Spock replied, catching his breath. "There will be a pursuit effort immediately. They can follow our ion trail."

"Not if we're immobile," Desus said, veering the ship from its straight course. "This is familiar territory," he explained. "The main shipping routes are concentrated in this sector. Naturally, a pirate . . ."

Spock completed Desus' statement. ". . . would know the area well."

"Very well." Desus pointed to a dot on the view-screen. "There is where we're headed. We'll drop to the other side of that small planet and wait. They'll be expecting us to make a complete run for it, not to stop here."

"I suspect you have done this before," Spock commented.

"Many times, and it always works," Desus said confidently. "You have a lot to learn about being devious, Spock."

"I have apparently found a master to teach me."

Putting his hand to Spock's shoulder and smiling wryly, Desus replied, "And I can tell that you and I are going to make a superlative team."

Chapter VII

Corsair

1

With the ease obtained from long experience, Desus dodged the pursuing Starfleet vessels and brought the warden's cruiser to a hidden planet in a remote sector.

"Welcome to Corsair, Spock," the pirate beamed.

"I find the similarity of this star system to another disquieting, Desus. It also had a planet located between a red giant and a white dwarf. This planet of yours seems to be in a more favorable orbit than the one I am referring to, but the similarities far outweigh the differences. Are you aware of the planet Tomarii?"

"Yes, inhabitants of that planet have intruded upon our ventures occasionally."

They set down on a well-maintained landing pad. Shielding his eyes, Spock looked up to the huge red sun. *The Tomariians again,* Spock thought. *I may be able to accomplish more than I thought.*

Given the freedom of the planet with Desus' endorsement, Spock set about exploring his new environment. Each pirate compound remained essentially an armed independent unit. His arrival was noticed, but most of the inhabitants of the pirates' lair avoided contact with him at first—trust was not easily won on Corsair.

Life on the planet was very pleasant. Its climate was moderate, but Corsair's fortunate position relative to its sun was not its only grace.

The Romulan community to which Desus introduced him made him feel at home. The inhabitants were so much like him, it was disconcerting after his long experience as the only Vulcan in an all-Terran crew. Spock felt completely healed for the first time since the explosion on the *Enterprise*.

His frequent solitary walks provided him with opportunities to study the pirates' mode of operation. He observed and stored the information in his tremendous memory. Arriving home from his afternoon walk shortly after his arrival, Spock found a note on the table in his quarters. In a careless scrawl the invitation read: Come, join me at dinner. Sunset. Captain Astro.

Taking the note, Spock found Desus. "Who is Captain Astro?"

"My rival on Corsair. He is a very nasty fellow, a true renegade. Why do you ask?"

"I found this note in my quarters."

Desus read it and handed it back to Spock, frowning.

"It's best not to get involved with him, Spock. Treachery is his primary mode of dealing with others. He'd as soon kill you as befriend you. He does nothing without cause; he will probably try to use you against me."

"I will not allow that, Desus. But you have piqued my curiosity about the man. I will accept his invitation."

The crimson glow in the sky had deepened, ushering in the long Corsair evening, when Spock, garbed in borrowed navy-blue suit and boots, prepared to leave for Astro's residence.

The Romulan's eyes were unreadable as he watched Spock's silhouette pass through the compound gate heading for Astro's encampment.

The small, very fair man who greeted him at the banquet table was wearing one of the most outlandish outfits Spock had ever seen. His red metallic jacket topped a pair of bright silver pants, reflecting the sun's last purple glow. A flowing cape of the same fabric flapped in the breeze, throwing glints of light from his costume's metallic surface. He made a rather showy bow to Spock, smiling broadly.

"Captain Astro, at your pleasure."

The pirate gestured around him. "My house is most impressive, is it not?"

"Very much so," Spock answered as he looked about. The collection of treasure scattered carelessly in opulent display was staggering. Spock had thought of the Tomariians as indiscriminate collectors, but the pirate Astro surpassed them by far. There wasn't a space visible which wasn't covered by a profusion of objects; the house was a monument to effusive and untutored taste.

"You see what riches you can obtain from taking up our profession," Astro said proudly. "I am by far the wealthiest man in the galaxy."

"You might very well be," Spock agreed.

Spock found the variety of people at Astro's table fascinating. Astro, seemingly of Terran strain, had surrounded himself with the riffraff of a dozen planets. Sitting to Spock's right was Gurt, a giant of a woman from Vega who shoveled whatever came her way into her mouth with noisy gusto. A rather worse–for–wear Andorian with one sadly drooping antenna clasped his blue hands over a wine glass of Tribidian crystal and looked smugly down the table at the Vulcan. A Histite slithered his moist tentacle around Spock, hissing what he could only assume to be cordial niceties. Astro, obviously enjoying his party, raised his glass in a toast.

"To new associates!"

After a low mumbling, glasses were raised and drained. Taking his black cigar from his mouth, Astro focused upon the Andorian to his left, whose glass, he noticed, remained untouched. "A toast to our new friend," he repeated pointedly.

"No!" the Andorian pirate retorted. "I don't trust him. And you shouldn't, either!"

"He is *my* guest," Astro muttered between clenched teeth.

Spock was very much aware of the sudden quiet which fell upon the occupants of the room. He followed everyone's look to the Andorian's untouched glass. Then he looked to his host. Astro tossed his long blond hair, and his watery-blue eyes became glacial as he coolly studied his recalcitrant guest.

There was a flurry of movement beneath Astro's cape as he withdrew and fired a weapon in one fluid motion.

Gazing dispassionately at the now-dead Andorian, the pirate motioned peremptorily and two servants quickly removed the body.

"Discipline must be maintained," he stated in a business-like manner. He placed his phaser on the table and laughed, bringing a forced response of gaiety from all of his crew.

Spock rose. "I must leave," he said calmly, not displaying or voicing his disapproval of the barbarism he had just witnessed.

"Nonsense," Astro said equally calmly. "We still must talk." He got up from his seat gesturing for Spock to follow him.

The room they entered was smaller than any Spock had previously seen and evidently served as Astro's on-planet office. The display of riches was more selective here, giving Spock the feeling that the pirate was more calculating and selective than he had previously believed.

"Spock, we are, of course, aware of why you are on Corsair, and of your reputation with Starfleet before your court-martial. Your knowledge of shipping patterns in our sphere of influence would be most useful. I understand that you are familiar with our Tomariian neighbors—that would be another valuable asset to us. I want you to join me. The power and wealth we would control together would be unending."

Spock cupped his hands thoughtfully as he listened to the pirate captain, who was now half-obscured by a cloud of dense smoke from his pungent cigar. "I am flattered, Astro. But I had not intended to become an outlaw. I don't know yet what I shall do. I haven't had much of an opportunity to consider my options."

"You haven't got many choices, Vulcan. Join me and be free and rich. You can't go back to Vulcan. It's a Federation planet and would extradite you before you even had a chance to land."

"I am quite aware of that," Spock acknowledged. "I intend to take some time off and enjoy Desus' hospitality before I make any decision."

"You intend to join the Romulan, then?"

Spock opened the office door, preparing to leave. "I came

to your home as a dinner guest, Astro, not to entertain the prospect of becoming a pirate. I thank you for the dinner and a most enlightening evening. But it is late, and I must return to the Romulan compound before the gates are locked for the night."

Picking his way through the scattered drunken bodies sprawled on the floor, Spock let himself out.

Smiling knowingly, Desus joined Spock at breakfast.

"Well, Spock, what did you think of Captain Astro?"

"He is a most fascinating specimen of sociopathic behavior," Spock answered.

"He must have picked up the Starfleet alert about our escape, and then my message on the way in. You are quite a prize, Spock. With your knowledge of Starfleet shipping routes, we could make our ventures safer and considerably more profitable. And that's what we must talk about now. There is a place in my fleet for you, as my second in command, if you will have it."

"I may have been accused of many things, Desus, but my conviction was a technical one. My intent was not treason, but simply the keeping of my word. Piracy would only compound my problems."

"If you don't join us, it will be assumed you are against us. No one remains alive on Corsair who is not one of the brotherhood."

"I am aware of that, Desus, and, frankly, I'm at a loss as to how to resolve this situation."

"You have no choice, Spock. It is a covenant we all keep strictly here. You either join us or die."

Logic, as well as a healthy attitude toward his survival, determined Spock's response. "In that case, I will accept your offer."

"As your first task, I want to make use of your knowledge of computers. You can inventory our rather extensive yield from many successful runs. There is complete chaos here, mostly caused by conflicting claims on contraband. Murders are all-too-frequent solutions, and the most powerful always take the prize. If you could devise a system to keep track of the property, we would have a much more efficient system of distribution. And no one would question your objectivity, at least for a while."

Spock was pleased by the request. "I would be honored to take on the task." The Romulan's trust was greater than he had expected.

Two days later, while working on the inventory, Spock came across an intriguing item. In between the boxes of electronic parts, the cases of exotic liqueurs and drugs, and a cask of Denite glow-gems, he came across a bolt of an extraordinary fabric.

Its properties were unlike any he had previously encountered. Taking it into the light so that he might examine it more closely, Spock found it had the amazing property of being able to absorb light. The fabric seemed to be a shimmering void except for its edges which fluoresced, outlining its contours with either black or red depending upon the direction of the light source on the warp. Scooping up the bolt of fabric, Spock brought it to Desus.

"This has most unusual properties," the Vulcan reported. "It wasn't woven in any conventional manner, but seems to be fused mineral matter." As he unfolded the cloth to examine it further, a pouch made of the same fabric dropped onto the floor. Spock carefully opened the pouch and examined its contents. "Interesting," he commented, as he emptied a number of small black stones into his hand. "They gleam with a dark inner fire like the fabric. Do you know where this came from?"

Desus handled the fabric, watching the black light shimmer. "No. I had no idea it was even here. Check around; maybe one of the crew knows who brought it here."

Casually, Spock inquired as to who had acquired the unusual fabric, but no one seemed to know. It had lain unclaimed for years. Finding no interest in his discovery Spock, in true pirate fashion, claimed the fabric and the seemingly worthless gems for himself. With his scientific curiosity piqued, he was looking forward to being able to analyze his find. Furthermore, the fabric was of more pragmatic than academic interest.

Since his escape from Minos, he had been wearing borrowed clothing, and although Desus' clothes fit him as if they were made for him, they were, nevertheless, not his. He thought his might trade some of the fabric he found for a suit of clothing, but no one was particularly interested. Finally, he approached one of the women in Desus' home to make him two outfits from the unusual cloth.

When the outfits were finished, he made a very striking appearance. The fabric, with its light-absorbing qualities, totally obscured the form within it—except for the edges, which rippled with a scintillating black luminescence, as if the edges were afire. The entire image was made even more dramatic by the addition of a cape which shimmered around the obscured figure within.

Spock did not object to the name the pirates had tagged him with: "Black Fire" was appropriate to the Vulcan, who seemed himself to burn with an inner intensity. Spock set aside his extraordinary outfits for a more suitable occasion, preferring to don a less flamboyant outfit for daily wear.

While he inventoried the pirates' treasures, he had the opportunity to quietly observe the intricacies of the pirates' operations; within days, he was cognizant of Corsair's most well-kept secrets.

While Spock was absorbed in cataloging the compound's treasures, Desus—who had negotiated an uneasy truce with Astro—took off with him on a joint raid. But with their return, the feud burst into a major confrontation.

Loud voices brought Spock into the room. "It's mine," Astro demanded. "You already have a ship of that class. Your flagship, the *Talon*, is a remodeled Federation ship."

"What do you need with a ship, Astro? Your fleet is already more than you can handle. Take the other things. I have no need of jewels or liquor."

They were both shouting now. Spock could see the situation was becoming explosive. He tried to mediate between the two.

"It is impossible to divide a ship, gentlemen. You each must agree as to what is of more value to you."

Desus solved the problem with action. Taking his phaser, set on kill, he pointed it at Astro's head. "Relinquish the ship to me or . . ."

Astro paled. "You win this time, Romulan. The ship is yours."

2

Spock was relieved at Desus' safe return, but his attitude toward the Romulan confused him. Never one to enter into intimacy of any kind easily, he found himself becoming closer to the Romulan than he would have believed possible. This was a man he could respect, in spite of his outlaw profession. If he had had a brother, Spock imagined he would be much like Desus.

Although he could intellectually analyze his feeling of warmth toward the Romulan, Spock could not explain his instinctive trust. This relationship was growing as strong as that with Kirk, which he hadn't thought possible. Jim had been his *only* real friend, until now. Yet there was already an ease in his friendship with Desus which had taken him months to establish with Kirk.

Desus' ready smile greeted Spock when he entered the house. They grasped hands tightly and then Desus spoke.

"It's good to be back."

"Did your business go well?"

"Very well. But that's a personal matter. Let us discuss something of common interest. Do you still have those two outfits you had made from that extraordinary fabric?"

Curious, Spock nodded. "Yes, but of what import is that?"

"I have an idea which will make use of those outfits and, if I might boast a bit, a good one. Ever since we met, I have tried to find a place for you in my operation. It took my getting away for a short time to come to a conclusion. I think you'll find my idea an intriguing one." Desus looked to Spock for a reaction, and seeing none, went on.

"We now have two identical ships—the *Talon* and the Starfleet cruiser we captured in our last raid, the *Sackett*. I have ordered them both painted black, with identical markings. Both will be renamed *Black Fire*, which will be emblazoned boldly in red on each hull. They will appear the same in every way. If you accept my proposition, one will be yours."

Leaning forward, Spock showed more interest. As Desus
had predicted, he was intrigued. Desus had a fine mind, and
any plan he devised was sure to be worthy of serious
consideration.

Enjoying his own presentation, Desus had an idea. "Wait
here, I'll be right back," he said excitedly.

In minutes Desus returned, wearing one of Spock's exotic
outfits. He carried the other over his arm. "Now, Spock, put
this on."

Spock complied, beginning to understand what the Romulan had in mind. When he had donned the outfit, Desus
laughed approvingly.

"Now, put the cowl of the hood over your face to hide it
and I'll do the same. Good. Now, the test." He went to the
door and called for his lieutenant, Relos. "If anyone knows
me best, it's Relos," Desus said while they waited.

It was a very confused Relos who encountered two men
standing side by side looking like a matched set. His hand
went automatically to his chest, but he wasn't sure to which of
the men he should extend his hand in completion of the
salute. "Captain Desus, sir," he said stiffly, hoping one of
them would speak and solve his problem.

Laughing, Desus took down the cowl. Spock did the same,
much to the relief of the confused Romulan pirate. "A good
joke," Relos agreed, laughing along with Desus. "Not even I
could tell you apart."

"That is my point, Spock. You are aware of our physical
similarities, I'm sure. They can work for us." He gestured for
Relos to leave.

"This is my plan. There will be two 'Black Fires.' Two
men, two ships. I have already selected our first two targets.
There is a cargo from the mining colony of Lithos II: their
cargo—dilithium crystals. The other ship is carrying a collection of art treasures from Altos. We will attack the miners'
ship and the other—not at the same time, but at an interval to
make it seem that the same ship attacked both. If our timing is
perfect, it will make it seem as if the *Black Fire* has a warp
potential far beyond any known in the galaxy, approximately
warp 15. Let them figure that out!"

"A clever plan, Desus," Spock acknowledged.

"You will join me then?"

"Agreed."

"We must name the ships for our own communication. The *Talon* will remain my flagship. And yours?"

"The *Equus.*"

The plan was simple and assured success by its very audacity. The crews of both *Black Fires* were hand-picked. A standing order was issued that "Captain Black Fire" was the only name to be used in addressing the leader of each ship. Spock and Desus planned to keep a low profile, appearing strategically in their usual costumes, then staying out of sight as much as possible to add to the mystique of "Black Fire."

The new pirate, Captain Black Fire, struck, quickly and efficiently, taking his prizes easily and without bloodshed. In each case a small gem glowing with the mysterious negative luminosity was left behind as a concrete reminder of the daring buccaneer. A legend was born.

3

Morale in the Romulan pirates' compound ran high when the first missions of the *Black Fires* were such a resounding success. Intercepted messages from Starfleet channels corroborated their triumph: A sudden distinct interest in Black Fire's activities was evident.

Although he had participated in the venture, Spock did not take a very active part. The missions were choreographed by Desus and the crew, loyal to the Romulan, carried through with Spock as more of a figurehead than their true captain. But Desus was delighted. He had, until this time, been surrounded by subordinates, and being a leader of men he knew full well the emotional distance a captain must keep. In Spock he had found an equal and a confidant.

All on Corsair were not elated with the *Black Fires'* successes. Astro, having lost some of his prestige after the exploits of the new team, stewed in frustration and resentment.

Trying to regain some of his former prominence, he was

eager to make a real impact with his next venture. Cruising near the Federation outposts, Astro saw his chance with the spotting of a private cruiser leaving a luxurious space-resort. Its markings indicated it was the property of a wealthy Terran who resided on a station of his own in the Alpha Centauri system. It had to be a rich prize, and Astro attacked.

The private ship had no real defenses and was easily captured. Among the treasures on board Astro found two lovely women: Galicia, the dark and lovely daughter of the ship's owner, and her cousin and companion, Linia. The first thought in Astro's mind when he saw the women was *ransom!* His greed took precedence over prudence and he broke the law of Corsair by bringing the women to the pirate stronghold.

Desus was infuriated. Spock, although he would never admit to such a sentiment as gallantry, was outraged. The women's presence threatened the long-kept pirate secret, and Spock knew the women were in great danger. He took it upon himself to resolve the dilemma by going to Astro to ask him to return the women.

The pirate laughed at the naive Vulcan. "Give up a rich prize?" he blustered. "Utterly absurd!"

"I will pay the ransom myself," Spock offered. "My share of *Black Fire*'s yield is a handsome one. It is yours in exchange for the women."

"I thought Vulcans had no interest in such matters," Astro insinuated with a foxlike grin. "But I accept your offer. They are a nuisance and I am well rid of them."

"Send them to me at Desus' compound," Spock directed tersely, preferring not to spend any more time with Astro than was absolutely necessary.

"So, Black Fire becomes a savior of damsels in distress!" Desus said with amusement. "This, my friend, is entirely your affair. I want no part of it. Don't even tell me how you intend to return those women to their rightful home. Or do you?"

Spock frowned. "Of course I do. And you're finding all of this very entertaining, aren't you?"

"Immensely. On your behalf I have invited the two lovely ladies to join Black Fire at dinner. I hope you enjoy the evening."

"Evening?" Spock asked, looking startled. "Dinner. . . ?"

"They're all yours," Desus said, bowing out. His laughter could be heard from way down the hallway.

A lavish board was spread and the ladies were asked to join Black Fire at table. The feast was elegant, but Galicia's eyes fixed intently on her host. At the head of the table, the shimmering form of Black Fire sat silent and unmoving.

"Sir, I owe you my life. How may I repay you?"

She waited for an answer, watching the dashing black figure with expectant eyes. One of the Romulans at the table, trying in vain not to laugh, choked on his wine.

"Surely, you will reveal yourself to me. You are everything a girl wishes for, a knight come to her rescue."

Spock had no appetite. He drank a glass of water and Galicia watched his every motion, hoping the cowl would drop back to reveal the face of her savior; it remained hidden in the recesses of his hood.

She was not shy about examining him closely. His slim form scintillated and danced as the fabric picked up the candlelight and gave off its mysterious black fire. A glint of the same black fire on his earlobe attracted her attention. "I have never seen such an earring before. What is the stone?" She hoped he would answer her.

The earring of Black Fire, one of the strange black-fire gems, set in the ear Ilsa had pierced, glowed the only answer.

Finally, Galicia heard his voice. She thrilled to its rich tenor, but the words were not the ones she had anticipated.

"Take her and guard her well," he instructed one of the Romulan women. The mysterious pirate left the meal before the last course was served.

By dawn Spock had found a solution to returning the women to their home. He assigned a crew to one of the smaller of the pirate fleet's ships and sent them off to an isolated retreat station where the ship and captives both were left to be recovered. The *Black Fire* orbited above and beamed the pirate crew quickly off the planet, taking off at warp speed to inhibit pursuit.

With the women's return, the legend of Black Fire grew.

Now he became a romantic figure, the tall, elegant, unknown rescuer of damsels in distress. The tale of the pirate's dinner party spread rapidly through the galaxy, and more than one woman dreamt of capture by the mysterious man. Galicia wrote a series of poems based on her adventure which became best-sellers throughout the Federation planets.

It made Spock acutely uncomfortable to realize that there was a romantic legend growing about him. Desus enjoyed every minute of it, reveling in his friend's discomfort. Women of many species throughout the galaxy would have liked to boast a night spent with the infamous pirate, who, as the Romulan and Vulcan well knew, was incapable of returning any of their affections. The last thing either of them needed or wanted was a romance.

The many successful raids by the elusive Black Fire, with his ability to travel at incredible speeds, precipitated Federation action. It had to stop; a huge reward was offered for the capture of Captain Black Fire. Starfleet Command was convinced that the pirate would be betrayed by one of his greedy own.

Now fully accepted by the pirate band, Spock found the guard around him somewhat relaxed. Wealth had never interested him, and he was particularly popular with his men since he distributed most of his spoils amongst them immediately upon their return. However, he still did not have free access to a ship, or to the communications stations on Corsair.

He seemed to take no great pleasure in his success, but instead grew increasingly restive. Desus came up with an immediate remedy. The spirited Romulan could not tolerate his friend's pensiveness and decided to do something about it. He had obtained a copy of Galicia's book of poetry and one night at dinner he surprised Spock with a reading. All but the Vulcan laughed heartily at his dramatic rendering of the sentimental and romantic female fantasies put to verse.

In mock seriousness, Desus arose from his place and began his recitation:

His dark shape flamed through the room,
causing a skipped heartbeat, as he bargained
*   for possession of the women.*

Shrouded in a garment made of lightning,
he took the ladies as his own,
bringing delight clouded in mystery.

To see his face through the veil of dark
flame.
To touch his hand, strong and warm.
To belong to this man of fire, if only for a
moment.
Time too short for love complete.
He is a shadow of mystery.
My flaming love.

"More! More!" The hysterical assembly at Black Fire's table demanded further verses. As the merriment grew, Spock became even more uncomfortable and excused himself, eliciting another wave of merriment.

Desus, enjoying the joke, continued his reading with long dramatic pauses accenting the more lurid portions. Although it was an embarrassment for Spock, even he saw the humor in the situation and later in the evening, rejoined the frolicking household.

It was an evening to remember in the Romulan compound on Corsair.

4

The subtle balance of power on Corsair changed abruptly with Black Fire's successes. Suddenly it was Spock and Desus who were the center of attention and not the cocky Astro. From his point of view, Spock's ransoming of the women backfired badly, making the Vulcan a hero and completely negating his own role in the affair.

While in one of his more self-aggrandizing moods, Astro worked up his anger to a blustering courage and confronted Spock.

"Vulcan!" He drew a knife, threatening Spock.

"Put that away, Astro," Spock countered. "I want no fight with you."

"Afraid, Vulcan? My exploits are well known. You just don't want to risk defeat—coward!"

"Astro," Spock warned, "I am quite capable of tearing you in two. It is unwise to attack me."

But Astro, now having to save face, plunged toward the Vulcan in a sudden move. The blade grazed Spock's shoulder, cutting through the black fabric and staining it with a spot of green. Spock drew his arm back, and with one swift blow sent Astro flying across the compound. The humiliated pirate's eyes slitted in rage as he picked himself up.

"You haven't seen the last of me, Spock. Your mistake was not joining me. It was a mistake you will regret."

The incensed Astro took action to rid Corsair of Spock forever. Astro's spies in the Romulan compound informed him of Black Fire's next planned raid and, breaking all oaths, Astro secretly informed Starfleet of Spock's plans. He gave only information on the course of the *Black Fire/Equus;* having no immediate quarrel with Desus, he did not betray the Romulan.

Unaware of Astro's betrayal, Spock set out on his next raid. As his ship approached its intended prey, it was easily outflanked by the starship lying in wait. Spock knew there was no way the cruiser could defeat the larger, more versatile ship and surrendered immediately, much to his crew's disappointment.

"Prepare to be boarded," announced a familiar voice from the starship, as Captain James T. Kirk and his boarding party entered the transporter. Behind his hood Spock hid his relief. *The Enterprise! What luck!*

With phasers ready, the security team accompanying Chekov and Kirk beamed aboard. Before them stood the lean figure of fire which had become so much sought by the Federation. He was draped in his now-famous cape, his face entirely hidden by the hood.

Kirk approached Captain Black Fire, intending to lower the cowl to reveal his face, but one of the pirate crew suddenly brandished a hidden phaser, set to kill. Spock, seeing the danger, grabbed the pirate's hand, setting the blast off toward the ceiling.

It all happened so quickly, and was so confused, that Kirk

didn't have time to prevent the security guards from firing at the pirate. Kirk grabbed for the pirate's legs, pulling him off balance and sending him hard to the deck. In the scuffle Black Fire's hood slipped back, revealing his face to Kirk.

"Spock!" Kirk shouted in surprise.

"Indeed," Spock responded. "There is something I . . ."

He never finished the sentence. Interpreting Black Fire's gesture as hostile, an over-eager security guard fired his phaser. Spock crumpled; but before Kirk could reach his sagging body, the Vulcan's form shimmered and was gone—transported away!

"Captain." Leonidas's voice sounded unsteady. "A ship identifying itself as the *Sackett,* Captain Melchior commanding, surprised us, sir."

"Surprised . . . ? Explain!"

"Well, Captain, the ship *Sackett* is in our registry with Captain Melchior commanding. Everything seemed to check out . . ."

"Go on, Mister Leonidas, I'm waiting," Kirk said impatiently.

"Well, Captain—it was the—*Black Fire!*"

Kirk readjusted the sound level on his communicator. "I didn't get that, Leonidas. Repeat your last transmission."

"Sir, it was the *Black Fire!*"

"Have you lost your mind, Leonidas? I'm standing on the bridge of the *Black Fire* now."

"I know, Captain. But that's what their last signal indicated after they beamed the pirate captain aboard. We permitted her to approach, thinking it was a backup vessel Starfleet had sent. Her conformation is that of one of ours, sir. When she was close enough for us to see her actual markings, she suddenly warped out and was gone! Captain, I can swear the ship was identical to the one you are on right now—and, sir, as she warped out we received another message . . ."

"Relay it, Commander."

Uhura's voice came in on Kirk's channel. "Captain, I am relaying the message from the *Black Fire* now. It was an unfamiliar male voice; all it said was, 'The fire is quenched.'"

Chapter VIII

Romulus

1

The *Black Fire/Talon* headed directly for the Romulan neutral zone with the *Enterprise* in pursuit. The smaller ship was slower, but it had a substantial lead, having totally surprised the Starfleet vessel in making its escape. Even so, the ship barely reached the neutral zone, and safety, as the *Enterprise* bore down on her.

Starfleet orders were explicitly clear: Under no condition was intrusion into the neutral zone permitted. Spock was safe for the moment, which gave Kirk cause for relief; but this relief was countered by a grave concern for the circumstances which led his friend and former first officer to escape a Starfleet correctional facility, practice piracy, and then seek refuge with the Romulan Empire.

Groggy from the phaser's heavy stun, Spock awoke feeling completely disoriented. Desus' voice penetrated his phaser–stun–induced fog.

"You're on board the *Talon*, Spock. That was a very close call. We just barely beamed you out in time."

"Captain," Relos called, "our escort is approaching now."

Dizzily, Spock got to his feet, supporting himself by leaning on the transporter platform. He looked at the view-screen and saw four Romulan ships of the line approaching the *Talon*.

"Signal our acknowledgement, Sub-Commander," Desus ordered. "We will head directly for Romulus. Come, Spock," he said, offering his arm to his unsteady friend. "You were hit hard by that phaser blast. I'll accompany you to your quarters."

Spock was left alone to recover. Obviously, Desus had contacted his people and informed them that they would be approaching in a stolen Starfleet cruiser. Spock was at a loss to explain the escort. His head pounded and it was difficult to think. He fell into a much-needed deep sleep.

A knock on his cabin door awoke the Vulcan. "Enter," he acknowledged automatically.

It was Desus. "Fully recovered?" the Romulan asked with concern.

"A residual headache," Spock answered. "Nothing of consequence."

"Good. At first I thought I might have lost a friend. I thought you'd want to know that we are on our way to Romulus."

"Really?" Spock asked. "I would have thought we'd not be welcome there."

"Pirates that we are? But Romulans have different values. You will see. You have proven yourself to me, Spock. Both as a friend and as a colleague. How would you like to serve the Romulan Empire?"

"Do I have a choice?" Spock asked realistically.

"Certainly. But there is time. I am sure you must have many questions. They will all be answered when we arrive. Until then, rest. We will be home soon."

2

When Desus and Spock emerged from the transporter chamber on Romulus, they were met by a well-armed security team. "Take him!" the sub-commander in charge ordered. Two guards gripped Spock tightly.

"Wait," Desus commanded. "He's with me—a friend. What is the difficulty? I notified headquarters of his coming."

"Commander Spock, of the U.S.S. *Enterprise?*" the Romulan security chief asked mechanically, anticipating the answer.

"Correct," the Vulcan confirmed with dignity and resignation.

Desus took the security chief aside, not at all pleased with their reception. "Explain!"

"With all respect, sir, I'd advise you not to interfere. It would be best for your career with the Empire if you permit us to perform our duty without interference. Central Command has ordered his arrest."

Aware of the problem, Spock cautioned his Romulan friend. "Do not jeopardize your future with your own people on my account, Desus. I knew the risk I took in permitting myself to be brought here."

"Why didn't you tell me you were known to the Romulan Supreme Command?"

"I didn't have much choice as to my destination. It seemed logical to await the Romulan response rather than anticipate difficulty."

"Sir, this Vulcan is under detention for sabotage to an Empire vessel in an incident of espionage in which our cloaking device was lost. He is under sentence of death."

Spock was brought before the board of inquiry the next day. He observed with an uneasy sense of déjà vu that the demeanor of the three Romulan officers on the panel greatly resembled that of their Starfleet counterparts at his court-martial.

"Commander Spock," the Imperator in the center spoke. "Do you offer any rebuttal to your own testimony at your trial for sabotage and theft of a Romulan military development?"

A young officer switched on a console unit in front of him. Spock watched his own image on the screen and listened to his voice fill the room.

"My crime is sabotage. I freely admit my guilt . . ."

The proceedings were interrupted by Desus, who entered the room excitedly, dressed in the uniform of a supreme commander.

"This hearing must be terminated," he announced. "Our vessel, *Space Hawk,* has been destroyed. I have mobilized the fleet, and this man is to serve on my ship. I will accept full responsibility for his conduct—in my short association with him, I have come to trust him as a friend. He will serve us well.

"Spock, you will join me?" Desus turned to the Vulcan.

"I will accept the commission you have offered me in your service. If you will check your records, you will find that I have already been of assistance to the Romulan Empire. It was I who informed you of the Tomariian threat. That act was responsible for my subsequent court-martial, and set into motion the circumstances which brought me here."

After a brief conference with the other officers, Imperator Melek addressed Spock. "Commander Spock, you will explain more fully the circumstances under which that message was sent."

"While a prisoner on Tomarii, I promised Commander Julina of the Romulan fleet that should I survive her, I would warn your Empire of the Tomariian threat. Since I was the survivor, I kept my word to her. By doing so, I was accused of treason. I was tried and sentenced accordingly."

"Supreme Commander," Melek said, saluting Desus, "the prisoner is yours."

"It will be an honor to serve with the Supreme Commander." Spock studied Desus as he spoke. Surely, the Romulan did not just acquire his rank and authority. It was clear that Desus, the buccaneer, had been operating as a Romulan officer and not the free agent he seemed to be when he was picked up by Starfleet.

The court became quiet. Imperator Melek addressed Spock. "The oath of service is to be taken immediately. Repeat after me: 'My life for Romulus; my death for the Empire. I swear.'"

Spock repeated the words.

"You are now in the service of the Romulan Empire. Serve your commander well and you will be rewarded accordingly. Prove false, and you will die! Salute your commander, Sub-Commander Spock."

Spock raised his hand to his chest and then extended it to Desus.

3

Desus and Spock strolled through the garden in the pleasant Romulan evening, relaxing as best they could in these few hours before they shipped out. The sun had just begun to set, casting deep viridian shadows on the hills beside Desus' palatial home. Lush grasses covered the hills; some slopes were covered with fields of deep red blossoms.

It was a sharp contrast to the stark Vulcan landscape of Spock's youth; Romulus seemed so lush, so fertile. Spock wondered whether the differences between their two closely related races was a direct result of their very different environments: the Romulans emotional, aggressive, and opulent in their tastes; the Vulcans so completely controlled and Spartan.

It was comfortable on the planet Romulus, and Spock already felt an affinity to the people, which gave rise to some uneasy self-examination. Knowing he had no choice in his coming to the planet or in his accepting the commission didn't seem to relieve his doubts. He realized that his loyalties could easily become confused; it was an unexpected turn of events and he was somewhat unprepared for the conflicts within him.

This night Desus had planned a farewell party, which provided an opportunity to introduce Spock, his new crew member, to the remainder of his officers before they were to depart on their mission. The Supreme Commander had not only invited his crew, but also others whom he felt Spock would benefit from meeting, including his sister Clea. Desus had often spoken of his remarkable sibling and the Vulcan was looking forward to their introduction. She had just returned to Romulus the day before and would be shipping out immediately after the festivities.

The first cluster of guests arrived, beginning the festivities of the evening. Romulans knew how to enjoy themselves; the music was lively, if a bit martial in tone; the guests were exuberant with the prospect of battle before them.

Clea arrived just before dinner was served. Desus bowed formally when he introduced her to Spock, who politely acknowledged the introduction. But his primary attention was drawn by her companion.

"My commanding officer," Clea responded to Spock's apparent curiosity.

A shock of recognition followed by an icy detachment revealed the woman's emotional turmoil when she recognized Supreme Commander Desus' new officer.

"Commander Spock," she said stiffly.

"Sub-commander," he corrected her. He took her arm, feeling her go rigid as he led her to a quiet corner.

"I was not aware that you had decided to accept the offer I extended to you to join us. I suppose the death sentence has been commuted. I have been out of touch—on a remote survey assignment."

She was wearing a patterned gown with swirls of purple and red, which brought to Spock's mind the black-and-white gown she had worn at their last encounter on her flagship.

"May I call you by name?" he requested formally.

"I would prefer you to forget I exist," she replied bitterly.

"We did share a rare moment together, whatever its unfortunate consequences, due to our conflicting loyalties at the time."

"Your actions cost me my rank—and my command. Just leave me now."

"As you wish."

She had already turned away from him. Spock stood alone amid the festivities, feeling a loss he had not anticipated. He rejoined the others for the meal, wishing the evening would come to a quick end.

4

Spock's duties were not very challenging. Since he was still suspect after the hastily concluded hearing, he was excluded from any decision-making or access to any information which was considered sensitive. He was assigned the largely mechanical tasks necessary to maintain the data integrator on board the supreme commander's flagship, the *Moonhawk*.

The ship was, by any standards, a beautiful and fully functional craft. Together with her sister ship, the *Sun Falcon*, they were the most advanced ships in the Romulan fleet. This opportunity to study the design of the craft was utilized as Spock spent many hours poring over the information he obtained from the computer. He was officially barred from certain data, but his expertise allowed him considerably greater access than he was permitted.

The few free hours he had on board the *Moonhawk;* he spent mostly alone. It was clear his Romulan shipmates did not fully trust him, and he understood their reticence. Desus was busy with his command. Spock, never lacking projects to occupy his mind, found other diversions: The Romulans did not suspect that the coded messages coming through the *Moonhawk*'s integrator were being deciphered by the expert cryptographer. The cautious Vulcan had not revealed all of his talents, not even to Desus.

Knowing he was constantly under observation, Spock followed the ship's routine without question. If he were to gain the trust of his new shipmates, he had to perform his duties automatically and efficiently. Returning to his quarters after one of his watches, Spock was detained by one of the security officers.

"Sub-Commander Spock, you are to report to Supreme Commander Desus' quarters."

"I shall," Spock responded, continuing on to his quarters.

"I will accompany you *now,*" the officer insisted. "It is a command!"

"Then I shall obey it," Spock said, following closely behind the guard.

When they arrived at Desus' quarters, Spock was ushered in; the guard placed himself outside the door.

"Sit down, Spock," the Romulan said pleasantly. "We haven't had any time to talk since we came on board."

"Is something wrong?" Spock asked, indicating the guard at the door.

"Of course not. I am always under guard when I am on the ship. Is that not Starfleet procedure as well?"

"No, sir. A Starfleet captain needs no guard."

"Foolish, one never knows . . ." Changing the subject, his tone warmed. "Well, Sub-Commander Spock, my friend, what do you think of service in the Romulan fleet?"

"I have not had a chance to really serve yet. While I am still suspect, my duties are simply routine."

"You would prefer more of a challenge, Spock?"

"Yes."

"Then you must prove your allegiance to us. I trust you, but the others—well . . . It is quite some distance to our destination; the site of the destruction of the *Space Hawk* has been pinpointed in a rather remote sector. Meanwhile, I hear there is an interesting game played in Federation territories. Chess, I believe it's called. Can you teach me to play?"

"I would be pleased to. It is one of my preferred diversions." Spock began drawing a board onto a writing surface. "With your military experience, Supreme Commander, you should find chess an absorbing challenge. The pieces move . . ."

The lesson was soon over; Desus had learned quickly and proved a worthy opponent for Spock's skill.

How many times have I played chess with Kirk to pass time on the Enterprise?" Spock recalled sadly as they finished a second game. Two captains, two friends, who if they met were destined to destroy each other. And Spock, now torn between them, knew no peace.

Chapter IX

My Friend, My Foe

1

There couldn't have been a more uneventful and routine tour of duty. The border they were patrolling along the Romulan Neutral Zone was as peaceful as the treaty promised. There were no emergencies, no hostile activity—nothing!

One would have thought that Kirk would be pleased with the respite, but he needed vigorous activity and challenge, anything to keep his mind off Spock. His disposition reflected his inner turmoil, and the crew was put through one drill after another for their perfectionist captain. Nothing satisfied him.

"Captain." Uhura's voice snapped him to attention. "A message coming in."

"Put it on visual, Lieutenant." He looked to the screen and the stern face of a Starfleet commodore appeared.

"Kirk, you are to proceed to Starbase 12 to pick up a change of personnel. We've assigned another engineer to replace Douglas, as you requested."

"Fine," Kirk said tersely. "It's about time Command took one of my requests seriously. Kirk out."

"At last," Kirk said under his breath. "Maybe we'll get someone more cheerful."

* * *

Making his way down the corridor to the transporter room, Kirk wondered who the replacement would be. The taciturn Douglas had beamed down as soon as they had reached the starbase. *Anyone will be better,* Kirk thought, getting impatient with the delay.

"What's taking so long?"

"I'm just getting a signal now, Captain," the transporter chief answered docilely. "It seems the new engineer has too much gear. His message says it's too delicate to beam up. He's taking a shuttle."

"What can be too delicate to beam aboard?" Kirk steamed. "All I need is another fuddy-duddy engineer! Why me? What have I done to deserve this?"

Kirk was too preoccupied to look at his officer; the transporter chief was highly amused by her captain's petulance and was doing all she could to keep from chuckling. Kirk was still muttering when he took the turbolift to the shuttle deck.

"Shuttle deck pressurized, Captain."

"Good. It's about time," Kirk barked, striding through the door. He was prepared to raise hell with the new engineer.

But it was a stunned, speechless Kirk who faced the engineer; finally he recovered his voice.

"Scotty! What are you doing here?"

With a broad grin, Scott shrugged. "I dinna know meself, Captain. I reported ta the Academy as ordered, an' the next thing I knew, I was told the charges were dropped. An' here I am, Captain. I dinna press me luck by askin' too many questions. It's good ta be back."

Kirk continued to ask questions as they walked to Scott's quarters. "They gave you no explanation?"

"Nae, sir. I was told ta report ta Starbase 12 for transfer ta the *Enterprise.* I even got my stripes back." He pointed to his sleeve proudly. "Is something wrong, Captain?"

After a slight hesitation Kirk responded, "Oh, no, Scotty. I was just thinking . . ."

Something was disturbing him. *This is all very peculiar,* Kirk thought.

"I'm delighted to have you back on board, Mister Scott. You were sorely missed. By the way, what was so delicate that you couldn't beam it aboard?"

"It's a small model engine, Captain. Usin' that tiny sliver o' crystal that I got on Paxas. Wait till ye see what it can do. I dinna trust the energy cell to the transporter effects."

"I can't wait to see it," Kirk said enthusiastically. "Have you shown it to anyone in Starfleet yet?"

"Oh, nae, sir. Not yet. It's still experimental."

A summons from the intercom interrupted them. Uhura's excited voice reported promptly at Kirk's response.

"Captain, the *Hood* has been destroyed. All hands lost. We are ordered to proceed directly to the area to investigate. Coordinates follow. . . ."

"Martin, put the coordinates on visual. I want to see where we're going."

"Yes, sir." The science officer flipped a lever and the chart appeared on the view-screen in Scott's quarters.

"I know that sector," Kirk exclaimed. "Tomarii! Starfleet's been dragging their feet on this issue ever since Spock's presentation of evidence after the explosion. Now we'll see what their reaction is."

2

The *Moonhawk* proceeded to the sector under investigation as a result of the *Space Hawk's* destruction. The new Vulcan sub-commander was proving to be a competent officer. He found certain aspects of life on the Romulan ship not unlike those on the *Enterprise*. There was more formality, more consciousness of rank—less interplay between subordinates and superiors—which was to be expected in a more militaristic society. Unlike the *Enterprise*, the *Moonhawk* was a warship and there was no pretense as to any other function.

Spock's attentions were primarily focused on the coded messages he was deciphering without anyone's knowledge. He was beginning to piece together a Romulan plot to capture a Federation ship, but was still unable to determine the target or time element.

* * *

The *Moonhawk*'s routine was interrupted by an urgent message, breaking off all other communication, including the coded messages.

"This is the *Sun Falcon*. We are under attack. Unable to identify enemy. Please respond—coordinates being transmitted. Repeat—this is the *Sun Falcon* . . ." The transmission cut off abruptly.

Desus was grim when he met with his officers after altering the *Moonhawk*'s course to the *Sun Falcon*'s last coordinates. He was all business, but that he was in turmoil was evident to all.

"You all heard the message. It must be assumed that our sister ship, the *Sun Falcon*, is lost. This is the third ship we have lost in this sector. The integrator reports of another Romulan ship aside from the *Sun Falcon* that has ventured there: She and her entire crew were lost." He paused, clearing his husky voice before continuing.

"We know little of the region except that only one person known to us has been in the immediate area and survived." Looking directly at Spock, he studied him for his reaction.

"Sub-Commander Spock, it was you who warned the Empire of the Tomariian threat. It is in that precise area where the *Sun Falcon* has disappeared."

The memories of Tomarii were still fresh and painful; Spock remained silent.

"Sub-Commander Spock," Desus repeated. "I am waiting for a report."

There was no way of avoiding the order.

"If the *Sun Falcon* disappeared in that sector, it would be logical to assume that the Tomariians are responsible." Spock hesitated.

"Yes," Desus probed, "continue . . ."

"Of course you understand that without the complete facts my statement is simply conjecture. We cannot be certain until we have further data."

"Tell us more of the Tomariians, Spock. Your message from the *Enterprise* gave only the coordinates and the source of the danger, and nothing else."

"Under the circumstances, it was the only information I had time to transmit. The Tomariians are irrational. I cannot explain the processes responsible for their erratic development. I can only describe what I have seen and the conclusions I derived from my observations."

"Go on," Desus prodded.

"Tomarii is located in a tri-solar system. If the pirates of Corsair had been explorers and had ventured behind the red sun of Corsair, I believe they will have found a duplicate of their small hot sun on the other side of the red giant."

Desus reacted as if slapped, but said nothing. The fact that he had failed to ascertain this himself rankled.

"The Tomariian red sun is cooling, and the other, smaller sun is in such close proximity as to make that side of the planet uninhabitable. If the planet, by some unexplained circumstance, survived the nova which formed the red giant and the smaller suns, the inhabitants were obviously greatly affected. The cataclysmic events should have destroyed all sapient life on the planet, as it must have on Corsair. Those species who did miraculously survive must have been extremely hardy and adaptable.

"My conclusion is that the Tomariians adapted by evolving new physical characteristics. I believe drastic changes must have occurred in their mental processes as well. As we all know, the selective process takes many generations. However, these creatures possess a very rapid and prolific breeding cycle, and their ability to reproduce so efficiently accelerated their adaptive processes.

"There must have been a fairly high technological development on Tomarii at the time the sun went red, some of which was retained. They did, for instance, keep the knowledge of spaceflight—in its early stages of development, but it enabled them to leave the planet. As their dominion spread, they borrowed new technology.

"Their survival instincts combined with their tenaciousness gave them the characteristics I observed. It is that same determination which keeps the seat of government on Tomarii. They are ruled by conditions which are untenable and which are contributing to their hostile behavior.

"The same breeding cycle which enabled them to survive has forced them into seemingly suicidal aggression. There are other examples of this type of behavior, such as the manuils of Rigel One, who become aggressive and hence murderous, killing each other when population pressures build."

The Romulan officers listened to the Vulcan, not commenting, but reserving their judgment until he had completed his briefing.

"While a prisoner on Tomarii, I discovered that their rationale is the reverse of ours. If they can find a worthy opponent who will reduce their population while affording them sport, they will provoke a war. Since survival of the individual is not paramount to them, they are a daunting and relentless foe."

"And your solution, Spock?" Desus asked.

"At this point I see no easy solution to the problem. They have the resources of many planets and a population, albeit dispersed, far surpassing any other species I have seen in my many years in the space service."

The Supreme Commander rubbed his hand against his chin as he listened to Spock. "You have not come up with a plan—not even for the Federation?"

A raised eyebrow was his response.

"Come, Sub-Commander Spock." Desus stressed the rank. "You cannot permit us to believe that you have not thought of a solution to the problem."

"I did not say that I had not considered a possible solution, sir, just that I had no workable solution as yet. I was injured at the time. I was not at the peak of my efficiency either in strength or mental function. When I had recovered sufficiently, I was court-martialed and imprisoned; I escaped, went with you to Corsair, and then was brought to Romulus. I did not have sufficient time to apply myself to the problem."

"I understand," Desus acknowledged. "I assign you now to work with the other officers on board the *Moonhawk* on an attack procedure which will assure us success."

"Sir," Spock said respectfully, "there are many hazards in space. The *Sun Falcon* may have been destroyed by some as-yet-unknown, different cause."

"What are the odds of that being the case, Spock?"

"Five point three percent."

The Romulan was not accustomed to receiving such a precise answer. He carefully studied his surprising friend, thought about his most interesting traits, and then left the briefing room without further comment.

Spock followed him out. "Desus, something more is disturbing you. May I be of assistance?"

"Find a way to destroy Tomarii, Spock. That is the best service you can do for me. My sister Clea was on board the *Sun Falcon*." He turned away from Spock to conceal his deep sense of loss.

How many times had Jim Kirk done the same, attempting to mask emotion he felt would make Spock uncomfortable? The parallel struck Spock hard. He hadn't been able to help Jim, either—not often enough. At a loss as to how to assist his friend, and hiding his own inner conflict, Spock turned his attention to the problem at hand: Tomarii.

3

"Captain, my sensors are picking up an alien ship. Too far away to identify. It's coming up now—I don't recognize the configuration. It's large—bigger than the *Enterprise!*"

"Larger than the *Enterprise?*" Kirk repeated. "The Tomariians had nothing that big. Keep that ship on your sensors. Sulu, keep us out of phaser range."

"Yes, sir," the helmsman acknowledged, keeping his eye on the view-screen and the ever-expanding object in its farthest visual depth.

"Well, will ye look at that!" Scott exclaimed in surprise. "Those markin's are a wee bit familiar!"

"They certainly are, Mister Scott," Kirk agreed. "Romulans! With their characteristic bird-wing designs."

"And look at the size o' her, Captain. That's nae copy of a Klingon design. It's entirely different. And look at her lines! She's beautiful!"

"This certainly changes the picture," Kirk observed. "Sound red alert, Chekov. We may not be after Tomariians after all."

The klaxon sounded the red alert. There was an immediate deluge of information coming at Kirk.

"Shields up, sir," Scott reported.

"Veapons are battle ready, Keptin," Chekov announced.

"All decks report ready, Captain," Uhura's voice resonated.

"The engines are go, Captain," Scott said.

"The Romulan's shields have gone up, sir. She's seen us!" Martin reported with excitement.

"Let's see what they want," Kirk said calmly. "Open a channel, Lieutenant. Let's see if they'll talk."

The *Enterprise* was jolted by a blast to the hull.

"A hit on number four shield, sir. Engineering section. Shield holding, but weakened. That phaser hit us from a great distance! They must have improved their weaponry range." Martin bent over his instruments, relaying the information to Kirk as soon as he had interpreted it.

"Keptin, phasers are charged and ready."

"No, Chekov, not yet. Uhura, clear that channel for me. I want to know why they're attacking. If they have superior weapons, they may very well have destroyed the *Hood* and we won't have a chance."

"Channel open, sir. They are not acknowledging."

"This is Captain James T. Kirk, of the U.S.S. *Enterprise*."

"Captain, it's obvious that they are the ones who destroyed the *Hood*," Leonidas interjected. "We should attack!"

"I give the orders here, Leonidas. I want to make damn sure it was them and not someone else before we start anything we may not be able to finish."

"Desus!" Spock called as he entered the *Moonhawk*'s bridge. "Stop the attack! It could not have been the *Enterprise*. The *Sun Falcon* was not attacked by a Federation ship."

"Get off the bridge, Spock. You are still too close to your affiliation with Starfleet. I will see justice done!"

"Desus, listen to me. It is not logical to assume the *Enterprise* was the instrument of Clea's death. This is not a sector in which Starfleet usually cruises. There must be a specific purpose for the *Enterprise* to be here—at this time."

"Is it that you do not want to see your Captain Kirk killed, Spock?"

Desus' words stung. "Yes," Spock answered honestly. "But I know him well. He would not attack without provocation. You can see he has held off from returning fire now. Give him a chance to explain the *Enterprise*'s presence here before you attack again."

Desus looked past his Vulcan sub-commander to his weapons chief. "Have the fusion weapons prepared. This will be an excellent opportunity to test their real capability."

Spock stood by helplessly, knowing the new weapon was more powerful than any the *Enterprise* had.

"Desus, listen to reason," he pleaded. "I know Kirk well, as well as any man I have ever known. I am—was—his First Officer—his friend. Listen to what he has to say." The Vulcan's voice was calm, but insistent.

"Put through the *Enterprise*'s transmission," Desus grudgingly ordered. "We will hear what Sub-Commander Spock's former captain has to say."

Spock stiffened in anticipation of hearing Jim Kirk's voice. He knew—very well—Jim's facility for talking himself out of tight situations. *It's up to you, Jim. I've done all I can,* Spock said silently.

Kirk's face appeared on the screen. "This is Captain James T. Kirk of the U.S.S. *Enterprise*. We have no hostile intentions."

Spock watched Desus' reaction, knowing that the Romulan did not believe Kirk. In minutes the fusion device would be triggered. The *Enterprise* would be destroyed—totally destroyed. He had to act—now—before it was too late.

"Desus, permit me to speak," Spock boldly interrupted.

"For what purpose, Sub-Commander Spock?"

"I know Captain Kirk. He will talk to me. Permit me to bridge the differences. Open hostility could precipitate a war with the Federation. We do not want to be responsible for starting a conflagration."

The Supreme Commander sat back, listening to the Vulcan, considering his request. "No, we don't want a war. Not yet!"

Not yet! So the transmissions I have been deciphering are very crucial. War is imminent. The Romulan Empire is planning to breach the treaty. But when? Spock wondered.

"I will speak first." Desus' eyes narrowed as he continued. "You will be given the opportunity to talk to Kirk. Remember, you are still under scrutiny. Choose your words carefully, Spock."

"Yes, sir. I shall not disappoint you. I will do my duty, Desus."

* * *

"Captain Kirk." Desus' image appeared on the viewscreen. "I am Supreme Commander Desus and I speak for the Romulan Empire. You were attacked by the *Moonhawk* as a result of your attack on our command vessel, the *Sun Falcon,* which disappeared in this sector."

"Supreme Commander Desus, I assure you that we had nothing to do with the disappearance of your ship. We, too, are investigating an attack upon one of our ships."

"It seems too much of a coincidence, Captain Kirk, that the *Enterprise* should be present when we have trouble in this sector."

"The same could be said of your presence here, Commander. May I remind you, sir, that this area is not under the jurisdiction of either the Romulan Empire or the Federation. It is free space and any ship may cruise here. Our presence does not automatically imply hostility."

Kirk could see the Romulan turn his attention somewhere offscreen. Then the voice and the image suddenly cut out. "Are our screens still up?" he asked apprehensively.

"Aye, Captain. Four is still weak, but holding."

"Good, we may need them. I don't seem to be getting through to them."

The screen was engaged again and the familiar face and resonant voice of Spock stunned the bridge crew.

"Captain Kirk, this is Sub-Commander Spock. Supreme Commander Desus has given me permission to speak. Please acknowledge."

Kirk stared at the image now on the screen, trying to reconcile the image of a Romulan officer and *Spock!* "I don't believe what I am seeing!"

"Nevertheless, Captain, I am here, and I do represent the Romulan Empire's interests at this time. It is apparent that both the Romulan fleet and Starfleet have lost ships in this area recently. . . ."

Scott and McCoy stood beside Kirk, staring at the viewscreen in open-mouthed shock. Sulu and Chekov were muttering their reactions to the image on the screen. Uhura got up from her console and stood beside the captain. All watched and listened to the familiar voice, trying to absorb the concept of Spock in Romulan uniform—presenting the Romulan position.

The Vulcan's deep voice continued. "That which drew you here is responsible for our presence as well. It is not an unfamiliar situation. It was very much the same circumstances which led Scott and myself to Quest and subsequently to Tomarii.

"I believe I have a plan which will effectively end the Tomariian raids. It will take both of our ships to implement successfully."

Desus looked at Spock in surprise. The Vulcan had not discussed a possible plan with him or any of his officers. He was not pleased.

"I formulated a plan when I realized the *Enterprise* was also in this sector. I have not had time to discuss it with my superiors. They, too, will be hearing it for the first time."

"Go on, Spock," Kirk replied tensely.

"We must establish a working relationship, Captain Kirk. We must trust one another if we are to function as a team."

"Let's hear it first, Spock."

Spock could see Kirk's formal bearing—his rigid back. Then he looked to Desus who looked no more trusting than did Kirk.

"May I continue, Supreme Commander?" He emphasized his next sentence, brought his hand to his chest, and extended it in the Romulan salute. "It is *you* I serve!"

Kirk flinched in reaction to Spock's display of loyalty to the Romulan commander.

Both McCoy and Scott were struggling to conceal their dismay. The doctor knew it was orders of magnitude harder for Kirk, but except for a tightening of his lip the captain displayed no outward sign of his feelings.

You deserve a medal, Jim, old boy! McCoy thought.

Desus acknowledged Spock's obeisance. "I will consider your proposal, Sub-Commander. Speak!" Then, in a lower tone which couldn't be heard in the transmission to the *Enterprise,* he added, "You had better be convincing, Spock. Your conduct is suspect."

Spock was very much aware of the guard who came up behind him as he spoke. "Very well, then," Spock continued.

His voice, confident and calm as usual, struck Kirk as being the right voice coming from the wrong place. He sat back in his command position trying to reconcile the image on the screen with the Spock he knew.

"All right, Sub-Commander Spock, I'm listening," stated Kirk.

Those on the bridge with Kirk were silent. The sounds of the ship and the voice coming in over the transmission were magnified by the unusual quiet. All could see the figure of Spock, his hands clasped behind him, standing at attention on board the Romulan flagship, the magnificent *Moonhawk*.

"In my evaluation of the Tomariian system, I have come to some conclusions which, although unproven, seem to be logical extrapolation of available information. I have briefed the officers of the *Moonhawk* as to my observations, and the information has been entered into our integrator. If you will permit me to tie the *Enterprise*'s computer into our integrator, I will feed you the complete data.

"I believe we can effectively stop the Tomariian threat, possibly permanently. Captain Kirk, you have taken the *Enterprise* through the corridor and are familiar with the passage which protects Tomarii from outsiders. That corridor is the key to my plan."

"Yes, I see." Kirk picked up on Spock's plan instantly. "I see where you're leading. Working together we can block the Tomariians from either leaving or returning to the planet. You're proposing a blockade . . ."

"Precisely, Captain. We can turn the chief means of their defense into the means of their defeat. When we have the planet cut off from the major part of its population, I believe it will be possible to impose restraints upon their aggressive behavior. I repeat, in order to implement the plan we must be able to work together. My agreement with Commander Julina was based upon such an alliance. It proved effective during our imprisonment on Tomarii. You have been to the planet, Captain Kirk, and you know the Begum IIsa. . . ." Spock paused, reluctant to go into detail about his personal ordeal on the planet.

Kirk understood. He spoke before Spock was forced to continue.

"I believe you have the seed of a good idea there, Sub-Commander Spock." Spock's Romulan rank sounded horribly wrong. "If Supreme Commander Desus wishes to discuss the plan more fully, I am amenable. You are welcome to beam aboard the *Enterprise* for that purpose."

Desus watched the byplay between Kirk and Spock with

great interest. The special understanding between the two
men was obvious. Many of Spock's words seemed superfluous
as Kirk perceived the overall concept, anticipating the Vulcan's plan.

"Captain." Spock had not moved from his rigid stance; his
voice was taut. "Both Supreme Commander Desus and
myself are fugitives from a Federation correctional institution. Will we be given safe conduct?"

"Yes." Kirk answered too loudly. Forcing control of his
voice, he continued, "For the duration of this emergency."

"We must have time to discuss your invitation, Captain.
You will be contacted when we have decided our best course
of action. Supreme Commander Desus, out!"

The screen darkened. The bridge remained too quiet. All
eyes were on Captain Kirk. He looked around at the staring
faces and asked crisply, "Don't any of you have work to do?"

Everyone jumped back to business, but it was still much to
subdued on the bridge of the *Enterprise*.

4

Spock had little success in convincing the Romulans that
there would be no Federation treachery. Supreme Commander Desus and his officers beamed aboard the *Enterprise* with
an armed escort. Desus, while wanting to trust Spock, was in
an awkward position; he could take no chances no matter
how close his friendship with Spock had become. The *Moonhawk*'s weaponry was poised to destroy the Starfleet ship,
even at the sacrifice of their own lives.

When they beamed aboard, phasers were very much in
evidence, wielded by the security team in the *Enterprise*
transporter room. It was not the best of circumstances in
which to begin a working alliance.

At Kirk's order, McCoy had stationed himself in the
doorway of the briefing room, waiting for the Romulan
delegation to arrive. His diagnostic scanner hummed as he

pointed it at Spock, when the Vulcan entered the room. Spock was fully aware of the doctor's medical probe and glanced back at McCoy, raising an eyebrow in acknowledgement and amusement. He took his place beside Desus.

The medical scan showed a completely healthy, normally functioning Spock. *So much for a medical excuse for his behavior,* McCoy thought sadly. He shook his head negatively, indicating his results to Kirk.

The physical similarities between Spock and Desus were obvious and startling when they sat side by side and Kirk had a chance to compare the two. *They could be brothers,* Kirk acknowledged. *Maybe that's why Spock joined them. He certainly must be more comfortable with them.*

This was the moment Kirk had been dreading, the moment when he and Spock would meet, face-to-face, representing opposing powers. He covered his discomfort with action.

"Gentlemen, it would be best to remove all arms from this room. We cannot discuss cooperation while we face each other over charged phasers." He gestured to the security men, the door swished open, and they left.

Desus followed Kirk's lead. The two armed Romulans also took positions outside the briefing-room door.

"Thank you, gentlemen," Kirk said. "Now I will introduce my officers. My first officer," he paused to glance at Spock and continued, "Lieutenant Commander Leonidas; my weapons officer, Lieutenant Chekov; and my chief medical officer, Doctor Leonard McCoy."

"Commander Relos, my second in command." Desus indicated the man to his left; then looking right, he introduced his other officer. "Sub-Commander Spock."

An uncomfortable silence followed.

Breaking it, Spock began outlining the plan. He sat, hands peaked in front of him, as he had so many times before in this same room. He was calm and confident; his voice was well modulated, in complete control.

"With Captain Kirk's permission, I have fed the information we will need into the *Enterprise*'s computer. If you will engage the screen, we can begin planning our strategy."

They all watched the view-screen on the table. A chart of the sector appeared on the screen. Spock adjusted the computer visuals and a more detailed section came onto the screen. Martin, resenting the Vulcan's intrusion, glowered at him.

"If you will observe, I have marked the Tomariian corridor clearly. Their escape trajectory puts them into position A or B, depending upon which end of the corridor they wish to approach. Due to the magnetic fields within the passage, they must take an exact route to place them in such precise positions. If the *Enterprise* is placed at point A and the *Moonhawk* at point B, we have formed a blockade."

"What do you propose doing with the ships that are returning or leaving the planet?" Kirk asked.

"Destroy them, of course," Desus said without hesitation.

"Our aim is to stop the Tomariians, to attempt to get them to capitulate, not to destroy them," Kirk said strongly.

"Your aim, Captain—not ours," Desus emphasized.

"Our mutual aim is to stop Tomariian aggression," Spock added, attempting to save the situation. "Whatever we decide must be agreed upon mutually. There is strength in our alliance. Our hostilities toward each other will only stress our weaknesses and make us all the more vulnerable to the Tomariian menace."

McCoy watched Spock carefully as he talked. Any other man in his position would show some signs of stress, but not Spock. *Damn it, Spock! Show some reaction. Can't you see Jim's nearly torn apart?* The doctor looked to Kirk, whose exterior calm hid tensions imperceptible to anyone but himself—and Spock.

The captain was purposely keeping his eyes averted from the Vulcan, looking directly in front of him at Desus. Only an occasional glance in Spock's direction revealed his turmoil.

Doesn't Spock see the hurt? Or is he so callous he doesn't care? McCoy fumed.

"I believe we can force the Tomariians to cease their hostilities by inhibiting their ability to provide basic necessities to Tomarii, and by cutting their government's ability to rule their off-planet peoples," Spock continued.

"No," Desus interrupted. "A bargaining position would not benefit the Empire. An enemy must always be destroyed."

Spock took a dangerous position, knowing he was threatening his credibility. "Supreme Commander Desus, a personal motive does not prompt rational decision. You have suffered a loss. It has dulled your analytical ability. Permit Commander Relos to speak for Romulus. He is not personally involved."

Relos, who had had no trust in Spock, now saw the Vulcan in a new light. He saluted Desus before he spoke.

"Supreme Commander, sir, I would be pleased to accept the responsibility. We all know of your loss and understand your grief."

Desus was cornered. If he insisted upon imposing his views, he would appear to be following personal interests. Spock had maneuvered him into an untenable position. He sat back reflecting upon how he would handle the Vulcan—later.

With their joint tactics planned, the Romulans returned to their ship. Kirk remained alone in the briefing room. *How awkward it must be for Spock,* he mused. *He certainly isn't trusted. What are his motives? Now there is no coming back to the Enterprise. He's allied himself with them and he has to live with that decision. It's got to be difficult for him. Is it better than imprisonment? Or is it imprisonment of a different kind? Spock, why?*

There were no answers: only more questions. And there *was* Spock, standing as he had so many times before in that same briefing room, contributing his skills in preparing for another mission.

But it was not at all as Kirk would have wished.

5

The *Enterprise* was in position; Kirk transmitted his coordinates to the *Moonhawk* and was answered with a confirmation of the Romulan's position. The trap was ready to be sprung.

The first Tomariian ship that approached the opening of the corridor was completely unaware of the starship blocking its exit. The small transport ship was no match for the *Enter-*

prise. A warning shot was all that was needed to send it ducking back into the corridor.

The *Moonhawk* encountered a Tomariian ship returning home and, with as much efficiency as the *Enterprise*, sent the Tomariian ship back into space without a fight. It was as Spock predicted it would be: The Tomariian's means of defense was now becoming the means of their defeat. Kirk sent a subspace message to Starfleet informing them of his position and tactics. It would take considerable time for the message to reach Starfleet, but it was standard procedure and he followed it. He did not mention Spock.

Communications between the Romulan and Starfleet ships were kept open at all times to facilitate prompt response. In the lulls between action, Kirk could hear Spock's voice coming from the Romulan ship.

He belongs here, beside me—on the Enterprise. One thought hounded him, repeating, incessantly: *Spock, why?*

It was the coldest season on Tomarii, the time when most of the inhabitants were forced into their underground lairs or off the planet on their forays. Kirk remembered the conditions well. The traffic in the corridor was heaviest at this time. It wasn't long before the *Enterprise* had four departing ships bottled in the corridor and three held at bay outside. The small ships they encountered were not equipped to tackle a starship; their primary purpose was for the transportation of the Tomariian attack forces.

Like buzzing mosquitoes, the small craft darted and dodged, trying to pass the larger ship. The *Enterprise*'s fire was directed not to hit any of the Tomariian craft, only to discourage their approach to the corridor. The view-screen showed a split-screen view of the ships trapped in the corridor and those trying to gain entry. A bright flash whitened the screen. The first casualty of the blockade was credited to Starfleet, as a desperate Tomariian ship hurtled directly into a line of fire.

The Romulan ship was holding a group of five ships in their approach area, and three within the corridor. Their extended firepower made their effectiveness greater than that of the *Enterprise*.

"Captain!" Scott exclaimed while he studied the performance of the *Moonhawk*. "I do wish I could get more information about that ship. If I could just get a wee look at her specifications or a look inside o' her . . ."

"I don't think they are going to invite us in for an inspection, Mister Scott." Kirk frowned and turned toward his security chief. "Chekov, try to keep that fire further away from the Tomariians. I don't want another destroyed."

"Yes, Keptin. But they flew into our fire, sir. Ve cannot control dere movements."

"Do the best you can, Lieutenant."

"Yes, Keptin."

"Captain," Uhura reported, "the *Moonhawk* reports two Tomariian ships damaged, one destroyed. The Tomariians tried to attack in force. The Romulans are holding the remainder as before."

"I don't want to keep score, Lieutenant. Let's just hope we don't have to keep up this siege too long." He turned to Chekov again. "How are our phasers holding up?"

"Ve vill haf to recharge dem again, soon. Ve are not capable of keeping dis up indefinitely."

"Get a power-level report from the *Moonhawk*, Lieutenant."

"They report full power, sir. Mister—I mean Sub-Commander—Spock reports all is going as planned." When she finished her report Uhura wanted to retract her words. The effect of her verbal slip was evident in Kirk's stiff back; she turned away. Chekov buried his face in his sensor and Sulu fidgeted with his controls. When Kirk looked to Scott, he found the engineer busily checking the readings on his monitor. Leonidas stood beside Kirk unaffected by it all. Once again, the bridge became very still.

Kirk's fingers beat a tattoo on the edge of his command chair.

"Captain Kirk."

Spock's voice stopped the captain's nervous motion.

"Sub-Commander Spock here. We have reached the point where we must wait for the Tomariian response to our blockade. It may take some time. Do you need assistance?"

"No, we have things under control here."

"The *Moonhawk* has far greater weapons potential, Captain. Our screens are of superior design. We possess a greater ability to hold our present status. Please advise us if you are unable to continue at full power. We are only as strong as our weaker ship."

"We don't need your help, Sub-Commander," Kirk replied angrily. "Kirk out!"

Scott waited for the captain to cool before he spoke.

"Captain, did ya realize what Spock just told us? He did give us a detail or two about the Romulan ship."

"Yes, he did, didn't he?" Kirk turned to face Scott. "Now, why do you think he did that?"

"I don't know, Captain. But we do know a wee bit more than we did before. That's for sure . . ."

Peculiar, Kirk thought, *Spock's not one to make such a slip. That had to be intentional. What is he up to?* Kirk perked up.

"Martin, feed that last message from Spock through the computer. See if there's any hidden message there."

"Sir?"

"Just do as I say, Martin. I don't have time to explain my reasons now."

The science officer asked the computer to analyze the last message from the *Moonhawk*. Kirk left his seat and stepped up to the science station to hear the computer analysis himself.

"Working—analysis of last recorded message—*Moonhawk*. No concealed information. . . ."

Kirk hissed in frustration as he returned to his seat.

"The Tomariians are massing for an attack, sir. They are approaching from both sides. Six ships from the corridor and three from the outside!"

"More power to the shields, Mister Scott."

"Aye, sir. Those small ships can't do much damage, individually, Captain."

"Let's not take any chances. Remember the *Hood*."

"They're coming at us now, Captain." Martin grabbed the console in front of him as the ship rocked.

"They have pretty good stingers," Kirk said, righting himself. "Are you sure they can't damage us?"

"Well, Captain, a hit in the right place can damage any ship," Scott reported ruefully.

"Inform the *Moonhawk* we are under attack, Lieutenant."

"Information already relayed, sir. I get no response."

"With allies like that, we don't need enemies." Kirk

grabbed the arm of his chair to keep his balance as the ship careened with another blast.

"A hit, Captain. In the port pylon."

"Bad?"

"Bad enough. We're listing to port. The power from the reactor in that section had been cut off. I've a repair crew on its way, Captain, but it'll take time ta evaluate and correct, if we can."

"Use your magic, Mister Scott. We need it now."

"Aye, Captain, we're doin' our best."

"Captain, the Tomariians are being driven off!" Martin reported excitedly.

Kirk looked to the view-screen. Four ships—shuttle-sized —were engaging the Tomariians. "Fighters from the *Moon-hawk!*"

"A message from Supreme Commander Desus, Captain." Kirk listened as he watched the battle. " 'Captain Kirk, our birds of prey will destroy the game.' "

"Will you look at that, Captain!" Scott pointed at the view-screen. The fighters, fully painted like birds of colorful plumage, gracefully darted around the Tomariian attack ships, rounding up the less capable ships with speed and precision.

"The Romulans haf the Tomariians completely under control, Keptin. Ve are all clear now."

Kirk spoke ship-to-ship. "Supreme Commander, we are in your debt. A most impressive display. Thank you."

"You are most welcome, Captain Kirk. Our ships are most impressive, are they not?"

"Indeed they are, sir. What other surprises do you have on board that ship of yours?"

Kirk's query was answered by laughter.

The captain relaxed in his seat. "I wouldn't tell you anything, either," he observed philosophically.

"Captain Kirk." Spock's voice and image interrupted this exchange. "Do you need assistance with repairs? I believe the Tomariians have sustained extensive damage and will not attack again soon. Is the *Enterprise* fully functional?"

"No. We have a damaged pylon; power on the port engines has been cut off. Repairs are in progress." He called out to Engineering. "Scotty, how are you coming along?"

"We'll have full power soon, Captain. But that pylon is

verra weak. We can put a temporary brace through the damaged area, but I dinna recommend any fancy maneuvers until we get her back for a complete structural refitting o' that area."

"Did you hear that, Spock?"

"Yes, Captain. Do you have full sailing function?"

"As far as we know."

"Good. Then the *Enterprise* can safely navigate the corridor. It will be your responsibility to bring our combined delegations to the planet when the time comes. Mister Sulu, do you still have the course stored in your navigational computer?"

"Yes, Mister—ah, Sub-Commander . . ."

Spock did not react to Sulu's slip. "You are agreeable to transporting our representatives to Tomarii, Captain?"

"Yes."

"Now we wait for the Begum IIsa to make the next move." The screen darkened. Spock's image and voice were gone.

Siege warfare was not a routine Starfleet procedure. The studies of ancient wars was required but not stressed in the Academy. Spock, with his superb memory, was qualified to plan such a tactic, but Kirk felt inadequate without him on board. Taking advantage of the lull now in progress, Kirk took time to familiarize himself with the history and tactics of the siege.

There were no walls to breach, no moats to cross, no arrows raining down, but the parallels were there. The *Enterprise* and *Moonhawk* had successfully cut off any contact Tomarii had with their supply routes and their people. The planet, unable to provide the most basic necessities, would soon become intolerable. Like the cities of old, there would be famine—and death—if IIsa proved stubborn. It wasn't clear how long the Tomariians could hold out. Both Kirk and Desus had called for backup and other ships would be arriving to assist them.

Spock knows how long they can hold out, Kirk thought. *Or he has a very good approximation of the time it will take. It can't be too long. It isn't practical or safe to remain in one position too long.*

These were not the days of horse and knight; the Tomariians could mass and attack again at any time. *And the*

Enterprise *is damaged. Not good.* He looked at the view-screen. Two of the Romulan fighters had remained as support for the *Enterprise.*

I don't like being dependent upon the Romulans. Not at all. He shook his head and concentrated on the library console in his quarters.

The Romulan contingent beamed aboard in preparation for the parley with IIsa and her council. The strategy meeting held in the briefing room on deck eight was attended by only a privileged few. Spock and Relos sat flanking Desus. Kirk, with Leonidas, Martin, Chekov, and McCoy faced the Romulans.

"We've corked the bottle, Spock. Now, how do you propose we convince IIsa to behave?" Kirk asked seriously. "She didn't strike me as exactly the rational type."

"Indeed, Captain, she is far from rational. The Tomariians are individually suicidal but not genocidal. They are an intelligent race caught in a grave imbalance. We must offer them viable alternatives."

"Birth control?" McCoy suggested. "From what I saw on that planet, it wouldn't be readily accepted."

"If presented properly, it may be one solution, Doctor."

"And who is presenting our combined demands?" Kirk asked.

"Why, you and I, Captain," Desus answered.

Kirk's reaction wasn't at all expected. "No way. IIsa wouldn't have a thing to do with either of us. But she might listen to Spock." He could see Spock's discomfort.

"Captain," Spock hedged, "I haven't the authority . . ."

"IIsa's got a crush on you, Spock. I think that in her own way she loves you. That's why she kept you alive, remember?" He could see by Spock's expression that he most definitely did.

"The role of ladies' man has customarily been yours, Captain," Spock replied icily.

That's one for Spock! McCoy scored.

"Not this time, Spock. It's your turn. We can use her attraction to you to convince her to negotiate. Don't you agree, Supreme Commander?"

"A point well taken, Captain Kirk." He looked to Spock. "We must use all of our resources."

6

The planet Tomarii was cold, bleak, and inhospitable, just as Spock remembered it. He shivered imperceptibly, not from the cold but with revived memories that were best forgotten but still persistent.

Facing them, when they materialized on the surface of the planet, was Ilsa and her council. She looked different. Her hair, now more fully grown, made her seem more akin to her race than she had appeared before. Spock could see her eyes, resting intently on him. The Vulcan drew his warm cape closer about him instinctively, as if to shield himself from her piercing gaze. This was not going to be easy for him, he realized. So did Kirk and Desus, who were watching his every move.

They had passed twenty trapped Tomariian ships along the passage as they came through it. The bottle was still corked, now with the summoned backup ships which had taken the place of the *Enterprise* and *Moonhawk* at the corridor's entrances.

Spock stepped forward.

Ilsa was quick to notice his change of uniform, but she dismissed the observation as irrelevant.

In the great hall, the large council table was extended to accommodate the meeting of the Tomariian governing body and their adversaries. The chairs, designed for the comfort of the smaller Tomariians, were not suited to those of the other races. Even the shortest of the Starfleet contingent were forced to sit knees up, while the taller Romulans and Spock were quite cramped.

Despite her lack of stature, Ilsa looked every inch a queen. Her rich fur robes glistened in the firelight; the jeweled dagger on her arm band shone brightly, sharply reminding Spock of his suicide attempt, and Julina's death. Even with the fire blazing close by, the room was frigid. Kirk and his officers were snug in their protective arctic issue. The Romulans brought their capes tighter about them to keep out the penetrating cold. Even the hardy Tomariians had fur capes draped lightly about their shoulders.

Spock, reluctant spokesman for both the Romulan Empire and the Federation, stood to begin. He towered over the low table. He stood silently for a long moment before he spoke. His voice, like the cold, seemed brittle. His breath showed in the chill; each word was punctuated by an abrupt white fog.

"Begum IIsa, I speak for both the Romulan Empire and the Federation. You have been completely cut off from your Empire and must listen to our demands."

She was staring at him, causing the usually imperturbable Vulcan to stop. He pulled his cape tighter to shelter him before he resumed. In a subliminal way, Kirk was enjoying Spock's discomfort. And McCoy was actively savoring the Vulcan's predicament. Clearing his throat, Spock continued.

"The raids upon our combined shipping will stop. You will no longer be permitted to attack anyone, or to perpetrate any further hostile action. Neither do we intend to declare war as you would like. Your designs to spread your domain are now limited, if not completely stopped. With our combined strength we have the ability to destroy this planet."

Kirk almost protested the harshness of this threat, but controlled his urge to interrupt. Desus seemed satisfied with Spock's comments so far.

"You will be relocated to another planet in this same system. It is located on the other side of your red sun and is far more hospitable than Tomarii. At this moment the planet Corsair is being evacuated by a Romulan force. . . ."

The Vulcan's revelation was a complete surprise to Kirk, who found himself on his feet facing Spock. "We were not informed of that action. . . ."

"No, Captain Kirk, you were not," Desus answered smugly. "There was no need to inform you. Our familiarity with the planet has made the task routine. Go on, Sub-Commander," he ordered.

Spock deferred. "Captain Kirk will explain what the Federation can offer." Kirk stood to face IIsa.

"The Federation will be pleased to assist you with the relocation process. Our science and medical personnel can teach you many methods of controlling your population. You may choose the one best suited to your people. We will beam down the personnel who will assist you in preparing your people for the move. As agreed, a Romulan delegation will remain here as well so that the Empire will be assured we have all kept our bargain."

"You have no choice," Desus boomed. "Captain Kirk has more gentle solutions than I would have preferred. Noncompliance will bring instant military action from the Empire."

It was no idle threat, and the extremely intelligent IIsa considered the alternatives. "This has always been our home; we cannot leave Tomarii."

"You must," Kirk interjected. "This place is dying. Your people need your leadership in finding a better way of life. We can help you. There is no need to send your children off to wars to be killed. You are a proud and hardy race and can become an asset to the Federation. Let us help you."

"The Federation, Captain?" Desus asked. "And what of the Romulan Empire?"

"Tomarii belongs to no one," IIsa proclaimed. "What is your recommendation, Spock?"

This was the moment Spock could not avoid; it was the time when he had to take a position. He stood between his two friends, looking from one to the other, knowing that whatever he said would favor one and deny the other. There was no satisfying both.

He saluted his Romulan superior before speaking. "I am in your service, Supreme Commander, and it is you to whom I have sworn my oath." Desus smiled in acknowledgement. It was good to have Spock show his fealty to the Empire in front of Kirk. Spock's pledge cut Kirk deeply.

"But Captain Kirk's peaceful solution is the one I favor. I have no wish to see the Tomariian people destroyed, no matter their treatment of me."

"You would help us, even after all that has occurred to you at our hands?" IIsa asked in amazement.

"Yes, Begum, I would. You couldn't help yourselves, and my wish is for the survival of your people."

Addressing her council, IIsa made a proclamation. "I can compromise no less than Spock. We must change in order to survive. We will try this move. Spock, you will assist?"

"No, Begum, I cannot. But you may trust Kirk and Desus both."

"They do not even trust each other," she observed wisely.

"They have agreed to a joint effort here, IIsa, and both are honorable men."

"We do this only for you, Spock."

"You will find, Begum, that peace is better than war, and your people will survive. For that, I am grateful."

Kirk and Leonidas met with Desus and Spock after IIsa had agreed to their terms.

"Captain, will you need assistance with logistics?" Spock asked, ignoring the angered Desus. "I am sure I can obtain permission to help . . ."

"No, Sub-Commander. Mister Martin is quite capable of assigning the personnel needed here." He was finding it difficult to be polite. "Without you, we wouldn't have been able to accomplish this, Spock. I thank you for that."

"You are most welcome, Captain Kirk. Given the Begum's incomprehensible affinity for me, I was in a unique position to be of service in this particular situation."

"I'll say you were," Kirk said under his breath.

Spock caught the hushed words and raised his eyebrow.

Kirk called Martin and McCoy over. "Assemble the teams who are to remain on Tomarii. Get Leonidas to help you with the gear and provisions. Bones, assign what medical personnel might be needed." He spoke into his communicator. "Mister Scott, I will need one of your minor miracles. Can you arrange for some transportation to serve our personnel down here?"

"Aye, Captain, I can adjust one of their ships with launch capability."

"Get to it, engineer. I want our personnel to have a reliable mode of transport." When Kirk had concluded his orders, he turned to Desus.

"Well, Supreme Commander, it seems our joint mission was a success."

Desus did not look entirely pleased. Spock, the object of his attention, was talking to IIsa at the far end of the hall.

"A strange pair, are they not, Commander?" Kirk commented.

"Most decidedly, Captain."

"I meant what I said before. We may not have gotten the Tomariians to agree peacefully without Spock."

The Romulan continued watching the Vulcan.

"Our loss is your gain, Supreme Commander. He is a fine officer."

"Your service didn't seem to think so, Captain."

"He did all of the wrong things for the right reasons," Kirk observed sadly. "You must know why he was court-martialed."

"Of course, Captain."

The polite conversation was wearing thin. Desus excused himself and went over to talk to Commander Relos. Kirk overheard the two Romulans planning which of their personnel would remain behind. He was thoroughly chilled and moved to the warmth of the fireplace.

Seeing Kirk alone, Spock came over to join him. "Captain." The Vulcan's voice was strained. "I have a favor to ask of you."

"A favor, Spock? Is it the ex-first officer or the Romulan sub-commander asking?"

"That remark was unfair, Captain. My options were quite limited. Is it surprising to you that I would choose freedom to imprisonment, and service to the Romulan Empire rather than disgrace?"

"I guess not, Spock. But at this point I'm not sure of anything concerning you."

"You consider my behavior atypical?"

"Yes."

"Interesting, but not relevant to the favor I would ask of you. When you have finished here, would you consider bringing the *Enterprise* into the area adjacent to the Neutral Zone and remaining there for a short time?"

"For what purpose?"

"We have set a precedent, Captain. The Romulan Empire and the Federation have, in a fully cooperative venture, countered a major galactic threat. We have proven it is possible for us to work together for our common welfare. I see it as a very promising first step to a possible end to the enmity between us."

"How easily you identify with the Romulans, Spock," Kirk said bitterly. "Why, you're speaking as if you've served them all of your life."

"Forget me for a moment, Jim." Spock's voice softened. "This is a matter of great significance. It goes beyond our personal concerns. . . ."

Kirk's reproach was lessened by Spock's use of his name. "I know that, Spock. It's just that . . . I know I must consider the Federation's interest in peace above all else. But the *Enterprise* is damaged. She needs major repair. It's not a good time . . ."

"Captain, there will be no strain on the ship if you simply cruise in the vicinity of the Zone. This is the one chance we may have of facilitating a peace agreement. You cannot lose such an opportunity."

Spock seemed almost desperate, which was unlike him. Kirk was puzzled. He turned his back to the fire while mulling over the Vulcan's request. Knowing better than to press Kirk, Spock waited silently for him to make up his mind.

"I'll check with Scotty. If he thinks we can delay the repairs, I'll take you up on your invitation."

Spock seemed relieved. "Thank you, Captain. You won't regret this."

Odd, Kirk thought as he watched the Vulcan return to his commander's side. *He is acting strangely*. Stretching in the warmth of the embers, he reassured himself, *I'm just on edge*.

Desus had overheard most of Spock's conversation with Kirk. "That was a most interesting exchange, Sub-Commander. What was your purpose in inviting Kirk to bring the *Enterprise* to the Neutral Zone?"

"Peace, as I told the Captain."

The Supreme Commander was holding up an integrator decoding device. "Come on Spock, give me credit for more intelligence than that!"

Spock looked at the decoder in Desus' hand. "You are aware of my cryptographic exercises, then, Supreme Commander."

"Very little happens on my ship that I don't know of, Spock." He turned the device in his hand. "You are fully aware of our plans to acquire a Starfleet Constitution Class Cruiser. And yet you have just arranged to put the *Enterprise* and your friend, Captain Kirk, in the best position to be captured. You *do* know that!''

"Yes, Desus. I am fully aware of the consequences of my actions.''

"Why did you do it?''

"My conduct is still suspect. What better proof do you need of my loyalty? I have successfully delivered a starship, disabled and easily defeated, into a position where we can capture her.''

"You have done that, Spock. Why, then, do *I* have the feeling of being betrayed?''

Spock did not answer.

Chapter X

The Neutral Zone

1

He was alone.

Command had always set a captain apart. Centuries of sailing ships, from the magnificence of the clippers to the elegance of the *Enterprise*, had not changed the captain's solitary position. Surrounded by over three hundred crew members, Kirk was isolated. There had been other times he had felt the weight of his command, but he had had one special friend—and now he was gone.

They had been cruising in the area of the Neutral Zone for three days. Kirk had revised his original plan, deciding to spend two more days there in order to give Spock a chance to accomplish his peace plans and contact them. The second extra day was almost over, and there had been no signal from Spock. Even the subspace chatter seemed to diminish as the day ended.

And so Kirk sat, disappointed. He hadn't quite gotten over the shock of seeing Spock functioning as a Romulan officer. Each time Spock had saluted his Romulan superiors, Kirk felt it acutely. Had anyone but McCoy noticed?

The chief medical officer stared at Kirk's untouched brandy. "Try a sip; it'll relax you, Jim. You're more jittery than a roomful of anticipating virgins."

"Thanks, Bones, but I don't want it. Spock knew I couldn't ignore a chance to achieve peace with the Romulans, but we can't stay here indefinitely. It isn't safe. I'm going to have to give the order to leave soon." He tried to ease McCoy's mind. "I'm all right. Leave me alone, will you? You're worse than a mother hen!"

McCoy rose and headed out the door. "Okay, have it your way. All I can do is try."

"Three more hours, Spock. It's now or never." Kirk checked his chronometer. "Two hours and fifty-seven minutes." He stood up to pace, needing movement to calm him. The intercom signaled and he responded immediately.

"Captain, I'm getting a signal—in a Romulan code . . ."

"On my way, Lieutenant." He made it to the bridge in record time.

"Sir, I'm decoding now. We broke this code about a month ago, Captain."

Kirk was leaning over Uhura, mentally pushing her to hurry. "Well?"

"It doesn't make sense, Captain: 'Permission to come aboard'—it repeats it over and over. We may have picked up a Romulan simply requesting clearance to come aboard one of their ships, Captain."

"Damn!" Kirk went to his command chair and sat down heavily. His disappointment was apparent to all.

Martin suddenly hovered over his sensor console. "Captain, there's an object coming at us at great speed!"

"Can you identify it?"

"Not yet, Captain. It's small, and moving at warp speed."

"Prepare for evasive maneuvers, Mister Sulu. Red alert!" Kirk ordered.

Scott's voice came in over the intercom. "Captain, that pylon won't take any stress. . . ."

"I know, Mister Scott," Kirk acknowledged. "It's unavoidable." He watched the object coming out of the Neutral Zone, getting larger on the view-screen in front of him. It was still a pin point, even at the greatest magnification possible. "Any details yet, Martin?"

"It's coming into sensor range now. It's a small ship, Captain. One life form—Romulan!"

"Are you sure?"

"Yes, Captain. One life form only."

Uhura broke in, "Captain, the signal's getting stronger. Still the same: 'Permission to come aboard . . .' "

"Open a hailing frequency, Lieutenant."

"Channel open, sir."

"This is Captain Kirk of the U.S.S. *Enterprise,* please acknowledge."

He looked to Uhura.

"Nothing, sir."

"This is Captain James T. Kirk . . ."

"Still no response, Captain."

"It's too small to attack us," Kirk thought aloud.

Martin continued reporting. "It's approaching fast, sir, and compensating for our evasive action."

"Uhura?"

" 'Permission to come aboard,' Captain. That's all he's sending!"

"Get a security team to the shuttle deck, Leonidas." Kirk rose and headed off the bridge. "If he wants to come on board, we'll invite him. Check to see that it's not a booby trap. Then signal the Romulan to enter the shuttle deck."

Kirk was already gone when the ship's sole passenger replied, again in code, "Message received, please relay coordinates."

Leonidas had taken the central position on the bridge. He nodded approval and the coordinates were transmitted. It was at Kirk's insistence, over his objections, that they had remained in this position as Spock had requested. *Spock,* Leonidas thought resentfully. *He's in my way even when he's not on board.*

The captain was waiting impatiently for the shuttle deck to pressurize. Six security men, accompanied by Chekov, were waiting with him.

"Six men, Chekov? Isn't that overkill? There's only one Romulan on board that ship."

"Ve can't be too careful, Keptin."

Scott had joined Kirk outside the shuttle-deck door. He couldn't wait to get a chance to see the Romulan ship. The light finally flashed, indicating it was clear to enter, and the door opened. The fighter was secured in the center of the shuttle deck. It was a sleek ship, like those they had seen come from the *Moonhawk*.

"She's a beauty!" Scott exclaimed. He started to approach the Romulan ship but was held back by Chekov.

"Ve don't know vhat to expect, Mister Scott," Chekov warned, as he stepped forward with phaser drawn.

The hatch opened without a sound. The occupant of the fighter stood up and handed his weapon to Chekov before he stepped out and down onto the deck. He was wearing a protective helmet, but Kirk didn't have to see his face to know who he was.

"Spock!"

Martin had come up behind Kirk. "Romulan, Mister Martin? You'd better brush up on your characteristic readings of life forms."

"Vulcans and Romulans are very much alike, Captain. It was a Romulan ship . . ."

Kirk didn't hear a word of Martin's explanation. His attention was focused on Spock, who now stood in front of him.

"Captain," Spock said urgently, "we have no time to lose! Get the *Enterprise* out of here, immediately!"

Kirk pointed to Spock and turned to Chekov. "Get him to the brig—top security—now!"

Chekov had stopped dead, phaser still drawn but not aimed. This was Spock, whom he admired, not a Romulan. It was difficult to think of him as an enemy, but duty came first. He forced himself to give the order to his men to surround Spock and move him out. Some of the guard had served with Spock; their reluctance showed, but they did as they were ordered.

"Jim, please. You must listen," Spock insisted. "A Romulan attack is imminent. I have come to warn you. I expect the attack to commence in thirteen point two minutes."

"Wait a minute, Chekov." Kirk paused. "You don't expect me to believe you, do you, Spock? It could be a ploy to get the *Enterprise* out of the way. You stressed your loyalty to Desus and the Romulan Empire very convincingly. I can't believe you'd switch loyalties again."

"Captain, you don't have to believe me. It will do you no harm to move the ship and warn Starfleet. They plan on capturing the *Enterprise*. If there is no attack, nothing would be lost. If there is, you have everything to gain. But you must move quickly. I barely made it ahead of the attack unit. I had hoped my use of the Romulan code would delay their pursuit, but I had underestimated Desus' shrewdness.

"As for my loyalty to the Empire, for the moment let's just say it was necessary. There is no time to explain further."

Kirk was not satisfied. He indicated he was finished with Spock, and as the security team took over, he headed for the nearest intercom. "Leonidas, set a course for Starbase 12, immediately. Warp three."

Spock heard Kirk's order and turned back toward him. "Captain, you must move faster than that."

"We canna, Mister Spock," Scott explained. "The damaged pylon will not hold up ta further stress."

It was the engineer who felt most deeply for Spock at this moment. They had shared the ordeal on Tomarii, and Scott was aware of the penalty Spock faced with his return. Had Spock offered his life to save them? It was entirely possible. The Scotsman kicked the deck in frustration. There was nothing he could do for Spock. His excitement over the acquisition of a new Romulan ship was gone. He returned to his station in engineering thinking thoughts only a dour Celt would appreciate.

Chekov's security men prodded Spock to move on. Before they left the area, Kirk called to the security chief. "Chekov, have McCoy check him out. I want to know if he's acting on his own or if he's being controlled by them in any way."

"Captain, I am functioning normally, I assure you. . . ."

Kirk and Martin had already stepped into the turbolift and were on their way to the bridge. Spock, seeing that he would get no further, went along with the armed escort without further resistance.

2

Entering the bridge, Kirk took action before he got to his seat. "Lieutenant, send a subspace message to Starfleet immediately. 'Suspect Romulan attack imminent.' Give our coordinates. Warn the outposts along the Neutral Zone. Reinforcements needed immediately. The *Potempkin* and the *Republic* are within range and their assistance is required."

Uhura turned to look at the captain. "I haven't received any messages indicating those ships were in this sector, Captain."

Kirk smiled. "Neither have I." He took his seat, then turned toward the communications officer. "One more thing —'Spock under arrest. Please advise.' Send those messages in code A6238."

"The Romulans broke that code over a month ago, Captain."

"I know that, Uhura. Send it."

"Captain." Leonidas was bending over the long-range sensors. "Sensors are picking up a number of ships moving toward us, coming from the Neutral Zone!"

"Can you give us more speed, Mister Scott?"

"It'd be risky, Captain, but I can try."

"Ease her to warp five, Mister Sulu."

Sulu bit his lip as he gradually increased their speed. "Warp five, Captain."

They could feel a vibration, a violent shuddering; the ship bucked.

"Captain, we've lost power to port. The pylon has collapsed!"

"Damn! What about those ships out there, Leonidas?"

"They are still in the Neutral Zone, sir. They seem to have slowed. They've stopped!"

"Stopped? Are you sure?"

"Yes, sir. They are staying within the perimeter of the Zone."

"Keep us moving away, Mister Sulu. We don't know what they're up to."

"I can manage warp one, Captain."

"The ride will be rough, Captain," Scott announced, "but we're just managin' warp drive."

"Keep it up, Mister Scott. Get us out of here."

"The Romulans aren't following, Captain," Leonidas reported with relief.

"So far, so good," Kirk said quietly. He peered at the view-screen which showed only an array of stars. There wasn't a ship close enough to be in visual range. The captain stared at the screen for a long while, counting the moments, judging the distance they would need to be clear. Finally, he looked around at his reliable crew and left his seat:

"I'll be in the brig. Leonidas, keep us on a heading away from here."

"Yes, sir," Leonidas acknowledged the command and took the captain's chair.

Martin moved to the sensors. As preoccupied as he was, Kirk noticed the smooth shift of personnel. It was like a well-choreographed ballet, and he always took pride in its beautiful execution.

"Readings are becoming vague, sir. We are getting out of range. . . ." Those were the last words to reach Kirk before the doors closed and he was taken to the lower decks.

The security area of the *Enterprise* was designed for utility and not for comfort. Kirk passed a row of neatly kept, rather sterile cubicles before coming to the top-security unit in which Spock was being held.

The extra guard at the door was noted without comment. *Chekov is certainly doing his job,* he acknowledged. Kirk could not help but grin when he realized the extent of his security chief's respect for their prisoner and the action he took to assure that Spock was kept secure. Spock *did* have a way of escaping from tight-security situations; more than once he had helped Kirk out of one confinement or another. The extra security was justified.

The more he thought of Spock's return, the more agitated he became. His inner sense kept saying, *something is wrong,* as it had been saying so often recently.

All he could think of was Spock's vulnerability. Kirk was

well aware that Spock's return was a sacrifice of his freedom
—and possibly his life. *Sometimes I wish I never attained this
position of authority, of responsibility. This is one of those
times.*

Spock rose when he saw Kirk approaching. He stepped to
the front of the cell, avoiding the energy screen which held
him in confinement. He was sure the screen was at full force;
it had the strength to kill a man at such levels. He had not
tested it.

With a touch of the control unit, Kirk cut the force field. It
immediately reactivated when he entered the cell.

"Now, Spock, tell me what's really going on."

Spock knew Kirk's gruffness covered his genuine concern.
"I did, Captain. By now the *Enterprise* should have been
attacked."

"But it hasn't been, Spock. We picked up a fleet in the
Neutral Zone; they haven't done anything yet."

"You *did* notify Starfleet, Captain?"

"Yes."

"The signal could have been picked up by the Romulan
fleet, could it not?"

"I hope so, Spock. I did everything but call them personally."

Spock was satisfied. "Then it is obvious. With the surprise
element gone, they've called off the attack. The entire plan
was based upon catching the *Enterprise* unawares. When
Central Command realized I had left to warn you, they must
have changed their plans. I suspected they would."

"Spock," Kirk asked gently, "what have you been up to?"
He almost sounded as if he were questioning a recalcitrant
child.

"Up to, Captain?" Spock answered in his most distinguished manner, and with eyebrow raised. He relaxed.
"Jim, what evidence is there that I was up to something?"

"All right, Spock. This entire situation has been peculiar
from the start. Ever since the court-martial, you've been
acting strangely. Your escape, joining the pirates, then the
Romulans. None of it makes sense. Everything that has
happened has been wrong—totally, inexorably *wrong!*" He
finally voiced the thought which had been bothering him all
along.

"What do you think, Doctor?" Spock directed his question to McCoy, who was approaching the cell.

McCoy remained outside. "You're in your right mind, Spock. But I wish you weren't. If you think they were hard on you at the court-martial, just wait till they get their hands on you now!"

"You see, Captain. McCoy knows I'm fully functional."

"Well, would you hear that!" McCoy declared. "He finally acknowledged my medical expertise!"

"Only because it substantiates my sanity, Doctor."

"Can't give in, can you?" McCoy grumbled.

"Enough, both of you," Kirk ordered. "This isn't funny, Bones. Spock, you're in a hell of a mess."

"I appreciate your concern, Captain. But this is not the time to address yourself to my problems. The ship should be your first concern."

"It is, Spock. Scott has everything under control now."

"I don't think so, Captain. The ship feels wrong. Even here, deep within the hull, I sense a vibration, an unusual sound emanation. There is something gravely wrong."

"I don't feel anything unusual," Kirk said, signaling the guard to let him out of the cell. He was sick with anxiety for Spock, and tired of the unsatisfactory answers being offered.

"I am more sensitive than a human to unusual and subtle stresses, Captain. If you will permit me to investigate . . ."

"No, Spock. I'm sorry, but that's impossible. Come on, Bones, let's get out of here."

McCoy walked ahead, leaving the security area before Kirk. The captain looked back once more at Spock before he reached the end of the corridor.

"Captain," Spock called, "there is something wrong. Believe me!"

Spock's insistence was disturbing. Besides himself and Scott, no one knew the ship better than Spock. He began feeling apprehensive. Turning, he almost headed back to the brig. *Maybe I should let him check the ship out? No!* He continued out of the security area.

With every nerve keyed to the ship, Spock paced his cell. He knew the *Enterprise* was in trouble.

3

Kirk was in the turbolift when he heard the distinctive gut-wrenching sound of metal shearing, then a loud snap. He was thrown off his feet and his head hit the control panel. Still dizzy from the fall, he punched the intercom button. The unit was dead. He engaged the manual override and felt the elevator slowly respond, then begin to move upward again.

He entered the frenzied yet disciplined bridge. The damage reports were coming in rapidly.

"Captain," Leonidas reported, "the starboard pylon has buckled. One crewman dead. Sick bay's just reporting in now."

"Buckled how? We were hit on the port side."

"Scott's reporting in now, Captain," Uhura interjected.

"What happened, Mister Scott?"

"The stress on the starboard pylon was too great, Captain. When the port pylon went, it put excess stress on the starboard side. We've lost all warp power and e'en the impulse engines are not fully functional. We're dead in space, Captain."

"Anything else?"

"Aye, Captain. Life support has ta be cut back. We'll need all the power we've got ta get us out o' here."

"Do you need additional help down there?"

"Aye, Captain. A small miracle will do nicely."

"You've got your miracle, Mister Scott. Kirk out." The decision he had just made was logical and practical; he felt relieved. He turned to Uhura. "Have Mister Spock report to Scott, on the double."

"Mister Spock, Captain?"

"You heard me, Lieutenant. That's an order!"

Turning back to her console, Uhura contacted Security. Then she turned back to Kirk. "Captain, Chekov wants a direct order from you."

Kirk spoke into the intercom. "This is an order, Mister Chekov. Please, release Mister Spock and see that he gets to Engineering without delay."

"But, Keptin . . ."

"My responsibility, Lieutenant. Now get to it!"

"Yes, Keptin, right away, sir."

Leonidas started to protest, but one look at Kirk's face silenced him.

"Put me on audio, Lieutenant." Kirk rubbed the painful area on his head, and felt his fingers wet with blood. "This is the captain. Emergency procedure Three A is now in effect. All nonessential systems will be cut off at 0600 hours. All personnel are to vacate all levels below six. Life systems on all decks below six, except for Engineering, will be cut off. This is no drill. I repeat. This is no drill! Please acknowledge."

Kirk could hear Uhura checking as each deck reported in. "Get McCoy up here," he ordered, shaking his head to clear it. He had a splitting headache.

McCoy entered the bridge, took one look at Kirk, and headed straight toward him. Before the captain even knew the doctor was there, he heard the whir of his medical scan.

"It's just a headache, Bones."

"Drippy one, isn't it?" McCoy commented as he continued with his work. Applying a wound sealer with his metabolic protoplaser, he administered a shot of antibiotic, and then stepped back. "I'll bet you have a granddaddy of a headache."

"King-sized," Kirk agreed.

"You have a slight concussion, Jim. I'd recommend bed rest for a day or two."

"Not now, Bones. Just give me something for the pain and get back to sick bay."

"All right, but as soon as things calm down, I want you in sick bay. It's required procedure, Captain," McCoy reminded him.

"All right," Kirk said sharply. "After this emergency is taken care of."

Uhura turned to Kirk, having received the last of the reports from all stations.

"Captain, all decks below six are cleared."

"Thank you, Lieutenant. Martin, have all systems below

six shut down. Then get to Engineering to assist Mister Scott."

"Aye, sir."

"Spock here, Captain." The Vulcan's calm and modulated voice from Engineering was welcome. "We now have things under control. Impulse power is now fully operational. It would facilitate operations and put less strain on the ship if you could request a tow when we are in range of a starbase."

"Done, Mister Spock."

4

With the immediate emergency under control, Kirk—headache throbbing—reported to sick bay. He was confident that Scott and Spock had things well in hand while the *Enterprise* slowly made her way to within range of a starbase.

Once McCoy had the captain in his domain, he kept him there with steely determination. Since there was no active crisis, Kirk chose to remain where he was for a time. But his ship came first and he called a briefing session at his bedside.

Scott and Spock arrived together, with Martin and Leonidas following close behind. Before Kirk had a chance to greet his officers, Leonidas was speaking. He faced the Vulcan, voicing his long-seething resentment.

"Captain, Spock should be under arrest and in the brig. An executive officer's briefing is hardly the place for a man convicted of treason."

Martin's comments surprised the first officer. "I disagree. Since this current emergency, I've been forced to work with him. I've never met anyone who could handle a ship so well. I think he knows things about the *Enterprise* the designer doesn't!"

Kirk could see that Martin had been converted. His two senior officers were glaring at each other like two rams ready to butt heads. His strength of command resolved the question.

"It is my decision and mine alone to make. Spock will remain unconfined. I will take full responsibility for his actions. I don't want to hear another word about this. Now, I want a status report, gentlemen."

Scott reported first. "The ship is sailing wi' surprising stability, Captain. All is under control. It's slow goin', but steady."

Spock looked over his shoulder at the two guards who had been following him as he went about the ship. He was somewhat amused by Chekov's diligence. Turning back to Kirk, he gave his report.

"Captain, the *Enterprise* will need repairing. This is the perfect opportunity to update the ship and incorporate some of the more interesting elements I studied on the *Moonhawk*, as well as our own advances.

"I would assume, since you have not indicated otherwise, that you are still unaware of the data I placed in the computer when I linked the Romulan integrator with the *Enterprise*'s computer."

"We have gone over all of the information you programmed about Tomarii," Martin protested.

"Yes, Commander Martin, that is obvious. However, I coded additional information through the output of the integrator. The *Moonhawk*'s structural details and weapons capability are completely available within the *Enterprise*'s computer, if decoded properly."

Martin was visibly disturbed. "I hadn't noticed any additional coding."

"Nobody knows those computers like Spock does, Martin," Kirk replied, not intending to criticize the science officer's abilities. "I suspected you may have left a message for us somewhere, Spock. I just had Uhura looking in the wrong place."

Spock looked pleased. "Mister Martin, if you run through the Romulan code, you will find that if you rerun the second number, then, in sequence, the fifth, followed by the ninth, and so on, that each of the numbers you retrieve have two orders of meaning. I would be happy to assist you. . . ."

"That won't be necessary, Spock. I can handle it."

"As you wish. If I had not returned, it might have been some time before the information was retrieved."

Martin excused himself and left.

Kirk mulled over the byplay between Spock and Martin without comment.

"Anything to add, Leonidas?" Kirk asked.

"No, Captain, nothing that I haven't covered," the first officer responded, throwing a sharp look at Spock. "I'll be on the bridge should you need me, sir."

"I'll be back to m' bairns, Captain." Scott hurried out, eager to get back to his engines.

Finally alone with Spock, Kirk voiced his concern.

"And what of you, Spock? Your return prevented a war, but Starfleet won't overlook your escape from Minos, and your exploits as Black Fire are well known. I can't even begin to think how they will regard your joining the Romulans, even if you did ultimately return. It will go hard with you."

Spock didn't seem concerned. The captain attributed his attitude to Vulcan control, and not to an absence of anxiety. "You shouldn't be so relaxed about your status, Spock. Once I turn you over to the Starfleet, you'll find yourself in a hell of a mess. I can't keep you on board the *Enterprise* indefinitely."

"I'm not unconcerned, Captain."

"You're certainly giving a good imitation of it, Spock."

"You were the one who said the entire situation seemed wrong. That was your word, if I remember correctly. I suggest you trust your human instincts."

"*Wrong!* That's the word, Spock. Wrong!" He stopped speaking and stared up at Spock, looking long and hard at him.

It was then Kirk knew his gut feelings had been right all along. He nearly jumped out of bed. "You were a plant! By God, Spock, you aren't a traitor after all!"

Hearing the captain's raised voice, McCoy ran into the room. "Calm down, Jim. You've got a concussion, remember? What's all the excitement about anyway?"

"It was all planned, Bones! Everything!" Kirk kept repeating himself; he was beaming in relief and excitement.

"You may know what you're talking about, Jim, but I'm still confused."

"Spock isn't a traitor. It was a set-up. Don't you see?"

"It is simple, Doctor," Spock explained. "When the *Enterprise* was bombed, it was apparent that devious means were the best approach to investigate the attack. It was decided that I be a double agent. From the time I left the starbase with Scott, I have been on special assignment.

"When I was accused of treason, Starfleet had an opportunity to exploit my status as outcast to root out the pirates on Corsair. What better cover could I have than as a convicted traitor, sentenced to prison? It was necessary to learn where the pirates were based; their planet seemed to be in the vicinity of Tomarii, and we wanted any lead to resolve that situation. My escape from Minos was planned. Surely you don't suppose it is that easy to escape from a Starfleet maximum-security facility."

"If it were anyone but you escaping, Spock," Kirk interjected. "But you can get out of anything."

"That made the escape all the more plausible, Captain. Desus is not easily deceived. Of course, conditions at the prison helped. I had not intended to form a friendship with him. Even so, I was not completely trusted and had no real freedom of movement on Corsair, or even as Black Fire. I was waiting for my chance to get back to Starfleet when you captured Black Fire."

"His rescue of you wasn't part of the plan, then?"

"No. What happened subsequently was completely unforeseen. I had no choice when I was brought to Romulus. Either I joined them or I would be put to death. Joining them gave me a chance to observe their operations. Having the choice between death and entry into their service, I chose to become a Romulan officer. It was then that I discovered that Desus was no ordinary pirate. He was a Romulan officer whose mission it was to obtain, in detail, information on Starfleet's movements and strength. When I found out they were planning to capture a starship, there was still a missing factor. They had not indicated a time for their attack. It was imperative that I remain until the entire plan was available so that I could notify Starfleet. The successful conclusion of the Tomariian issue was a corollary benefit, of course."

"So you had me wait at the Neutral Zone on the pretext of a peace agreement."

"Yes. The *Enterprise* served in two ways. My request to place the ship in proximity to the Neutral Zone where it would easily be captured gave the Romulans further reason to trust me. It allowed me access to the last information I needed: when they would attack. And, Captain, it was my only means of escape from the Romulan Empire.

"If you had chosen to repair the ship rather than pursue the possibility of peace, I would have had no means of leaving."

Kirk realized the significance of his decision. "It would have meant your death."

"Yes. I would have relayed the information to you in any case. I remember when a Romulan commander once said one could be friends with one's enemies in a different reality. So it was with Desus and myself. By befriending me, he risked his life. And I, by doing my duty to Starfleet, condemned him. His choice within Romulan custom is limited: either execution or suicide. I am sure he chose to take his own life. It is my one regret. I respected and admired him. We truly were friends. In another reality . . ." Spock turned away.

"I really want to believe all of this, Spock. I mean, I do believe you, but . . ."

"You must check with Starfleet. I know, Jim. The decision to keep my undercover mission from you was a difficult one. You had been seriously injured. It was thought best to keep the entire affair a very closely guarded secret. I hope you understand."

"You could have told us what you were up to, Spock," McCoy scolded. "It would have saved a lot of anguish."

"You were disturbed, Doctor?" Spock raised an eyebrow.

"You know I was, you son of Satan. Those pointy ears really fit, you know. And so does that Romulan uniform."

Kirk leaned back and inspected Spock. "He's right, Spock. That uniform doesn't look half bad."

"I'd rather it be Starfleet issue, Captain."

Kirk grinned. "I think we can arrange that."

"That would be appreciated, Captain."

Uhura appeared at the door. "Captain, a message from Starfleet."

"Why didn't you relay it over the intercom, Lieutenant? It wasn't necessary to hand carry it down here."

"Yes it was, Captain. Doctor McCoy shut off the intercom so you wouldn't be disturbed."

Kirk looked to McCoy, who shrugged and looked sheepish.

"What's the message, Lieutenant?"

"Commander Spock has been cleared of all charges. Explanation to follow. Prepare for towing operation to begin at 0800 hours." She felt like kissing Spock, but she knew it would embarrass him. Instead she greeted him with a warm smile. "Welcome back, Mister Spock. We've missed you."

5

Fully recovered and feeling wonderful, Kirk returned to his command position. He jauntily stepped onto the bridge, enjoying the sounds of his ship. "How is she going, Mister Scott?"

"As well as could be expected, Captain." He looked to McCoy and commented lightly, "Maybe the doctor has a wee bit o' tape ta hold the ship together for a short time. We can use all the help we can get."

"I'm a doctor, not a mechanic!" McCoy said adamantly. He looked to Spock, grinned his most disarming southern smile, and added, "The only machine I treat is Spock. I do make exceptions in your case, you know."

He strode off the bridge looking smug, and returned in a minute carrying a decoratively bound book.

"Ya know, Spock," McCoy drawled, "there's one thing I never did before." He thrust the book at Spock. "You can do me a great favor, Spock. I never asked for a celebrity's autograph before. So, here's to new experiences. Would you sign my book of poems, Black Fire?"

He grinned with fiendish glee. "I always knew you were a pirate at heart, Spock!" Producing a pen from beneath his tunic, he handed it to him. " 'To belong to this man of fire, if only for a moment'—'My flaming love.' I wouldn't have believed you had it in you. Pretty heady stuff, eh, Captain?"

He couldn't keep from laughing and neither could Kirk, who watched Spock lift an eyebrow.

Then, with a flourish worthy of Black Fire, Spock removed his iridescent black earring, placing it in McCoy's hand. "I'll do better than that, Doctor. A gift from Black Fire."

The black jewel gleamed its strange luminescence in McCoy's palm, but it was no match for the gleam in Spock's dark smiling eyes.

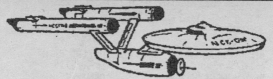

STAR TREK®: THE LOST YEARS
by J.M. Dillard

What exactly became of Captain Kirk, Mr. Spock, and the rest of the *Enterprise* crew after their historic five-year mission? How did that mission end? What did they do before they were reunited for the STAR TREK movies? Even the most casual STAR TREK fan finds him/herself asking these questions from time to time…

Here, at last, is the book that provides the answers to those questions—a book as anticipated, in its own way, as SPOCK'S WORLD, the first STAR TREK hardcover and a major *New York Times* bestseller. In THE LOST YEARS, J.M. Dillard has written her best STAR TREK book to date—and the way she's answered the above questions will excite and delight STAR TREK fans.

POCKET
BOOKS

THE STAR TREK

PHENOMENON

THE

STAR TREK

PHENOMENON

_____ **STAR TREK– THE MOTION PICTURE**
67795/$3.95

_____ **STAR TREK II– THE WRATH OF KHAN**
67426/$3.95

_____ **STAR TREK III–THE SEARCH FOR SPOCK**
67198/$3.95

_____ **STAR TREK IV– THE VOYAGE HOME**
63266/$3.95

_____ **STAR TREK: THE KLINGON DICTIONARY**
66648/$4.95

_____ **STAR TREK COMPENDIUM REVISED**
62726/$9.95

_____ **MR. SCOTT'S GUIDE TO THE ENTERPRISE**
63576/$10.95

_____ **THE STAR TREK INTERVIEW BOOK**
61794/$7.95

POCKET
B O O K S

Simon & Schuster Mail Order Dept. STP
200 Old Tappan Rd., Old Tappan, N.J. 07675

Please send me the books I have checked above. I am enclosing $_____ (please add 75¢ to cover postage and handling for each order. N.Y.S. and N.Y.C. residents please add appropriate sales tax.). Send check or money order—no cash or C.O.D.'s please. Allow up to six weeks for delivery. For purchases over $10.00 you may use VISA: card number, expiration date and customer signature must be included.

Name_____

Address_____

City_____ State/Zip_____

VISA Card No._____ Exp. Date_____

Signature _____ 118-16